PART THE CURTAIN
Theatre Play Collection

By
Richard Mousseau

MOOSE HIDE BOOKS
imprint of
MOOSE ENTERPRISE PUBLISHING
PRINCE TOWNSHIP
ONTARIO, CANADA

cover illustration by Rick Mousseau

Part the Curtain
By
Richard Mousseau
Copyright February 20, 2019

Published June 1, 2019
by

MOOSE HIDE BOOKS
imprint of
MOOSE ENTERPRISE PUBLISHING
684 WALLS ROAD
PRINCE TOWNSHIP
ONTARIO, CANADA
P6A 6K4
web site www.moosehidebooks.com

NO VENTURE UNATTAINABLE

CREATED IN CANADA

Library and Archives Canada Cataloguing in Publication

Title: Part the curtain : theatre play collection / by Richard Mousseau.
Names: Mousseau, Richard, 1953- author.
Description: Three plays. | Includes index.
Identifiers: Canadiana (print) 20190075635 | Canadiana (ebook) 20190075643 | ISBN 9781927393598
  (softcover) | ISBN 9781927393604 (PDF)
Classification: LCC PS8576.O977 P37 2019 | DDC C812/.54—dc23

PART THE CURTAIN
Theatre Play Collection

INDEX:

LIFE RAFT
Copyright May 4, 1996
Richard Mousseau

STAGE:
BLACK OR SKY-BLUE BACKGROUND TO RESEMBLE THE
EMPTINESS OF AN OCEAN. THE FRONT OF STAGE IS A
SIMULATION OF A SEA. FLOOR IS DARK BLUE WITH WHITE TO
RESEMBLE ROUGH SEAS. IN CENTRE OF STAGE A LARGE RAFT.

LIGHTING:
LIGHT AND DARK TO EMPHASIZE THE CHANGING SEA AND THE
CHANGE OF NIGHT AND DAY w1TH A MOON SPOT.

SOUND:
WIND, WAVES, GULLS WITH THE SOUNDS OF A SHIP AND FOG
HORN AND THE SOUND OF A STORM.

ACTING PARTS:
FIRST LEAD:	CAPTAIN CRAB
SECOND LEAD:	WILLY
THIRD LEAD:	LILLY FAMISH
FOURTH LEAD:	WADESWORTH
FIFTH LEAD:	CHARLES LIMBOCK
SIXTH LEAD:	DIVA
SEVENTH LEAD:	FRIDA FELPS
EIGHTH LEAD:	FRED FELPS

CHARACTERS:
CAPTAIN CRAB:
IS AN OLDER SAILOR ABOUT FIFTY YEARS OF AGE OR OLDER, HE
LOOKS LIKE A PIRATE WITH A PATCH OVER AN EYE. HE WEARS
THREE QUARTER LENGTH SAILOR PANTS WITH A LONG SLEEVE
STRIPED NAVAL SHIRT, HAIR IS UNKEPT WITH SOUTH SEAS TYPE
BRAIDS, DOESN'T SAY MUCH BUT GESTURES A LOT.

WILLY:
A YOUNG SAILOR IN HIS TWENTIES, THE BACK BONE OF THE
CREW AND A FRIEND OF THE CAPTAIN, HE KNOWS ABOUT THE
SEA AND SURVIVAL, HE WEARS LONG SAILORS PANTS, BELL-
BOTTOM BLUE WITH STRIPED SAILORS SHIRT AND A CANADIAN
SAILORS CAP, HE SPORTS A SHORT PONY TAIL.

LILLY FAMISH:

A BUBBLY HAPPY PLUMP WOMAN BETWEEN TWENTY-FIVE AND THIRTY-FIVE SEARCHING FOR WHAT SHE FEELS SHE HAS MISSED IN LIFE, SHE WEARS A LONG FLANNEL NIGHT GOWN WITH LONG SLEEVES, NIGHT GOWN LOOKS ANGEL LIKE, INNOCENT.

CHARLES LIMBOCK:
A PLAYBOY IN HIS MID FORTIES BUT ACTS AT TIMES CHILDISH, THINKS OF HIMSELF AS A LADIES MAN, HE WEARS A POLO SHIRT, SHORT PANTS, A SWEATER OVER THIS SHOU LDERS AND CARRIES A TENNIS RACKET.

WADESWORTH:
A BRITISH MAN'S MAN IN HIS EARLY FORTIES, NOT GAY BUT SHOWS SOME MANNERISMS, HE IS AN EXPERT IN ALL ASPECTS OF COOKING, CLEANING, CLOTHES,
HISTORY. HE WEARS TYPICAL ENGLISH BUTLER ATTIRE, VEST, MORNING COAT,
BOWTIE, SUSPENDERS WITH ARM GARTERS, HE IS A DIGNIFIED MAN.

DIVA:
A SKINNY MODEL IN HER MID TWENTIES, SHE IS GULLIBLE AND EASY TO LEAD AND YOUR TYPICAL DUMB BLONDE IMAGE, SHE IS WELL PROPORTIONED AND HER SKIMPY AMOUNT OF CLOTHES HELP SHOW IT, SHORTS AND SHORT STRETCH TOP.

FRIDA FELPS:
A PLUMB WOMAN IN HER LATE FIFTIES, SHE LOVES AND HATES HER HUSBAND, SHE IS TYPICAL TOURIST AND WEARS OLD FOLKS LEISURE WEAR, A BIG SUN HAT, SHE WEARS ALL OF HER JEWELRY, SHE TENDS TO CONTROL HER HUSBANDS LIFE.

FRED FELPS:
AN ANGRY MAN IN HIS LATE FIFTIES WHO HAS PUT UP WITH HIS WIFE'S WAYS, HE IS A PROCRASTINATOR THINKING ABOUT BECOMING A LEADER NOT A FOLLOWER, HE WEARS TYPICAL OLD MAN ON VACATION CLOTHES, HE IS WILLING TO ARGUE WITH HIS WIFE BUT IS THERE TO PROTECT HER.

BASIC STORY LINE:
ALL OF THE CHARACTERS ARE VACATIONING ON A YACHT, WHEN THEY SEE WILLY AND CAPTAIN CRAB TAKING A RAFT TO GO FISHING, THEY MISTAKE IT FOR BEING ABANDONED,

EVERYONE GETS INTO RUBBER RAFT AS YACHT FLOATS AWAY,
LIFE-RAFT IS NOW ADRIFT WITH ALL CHARACTERS DISPLAYING
THEIR ANTICS FOR SURVIVAL ON THE HIGH SEAS.

SET AND PROPS:
LARGE RUBBER RAFT
GANG PLANK
WATER SKIS
ROPE
SWORD FISH
FISHING ROD
DIFFERENT SIZE FISH
BACKGROUND, BLUE SKY AND CLOUDS
FACE OF STAGE TO SHOW ROUGH SEAS
TEA CUPS
PLATES
FAKE BONES TO RESEMBLE A LEG AND ARM
SUIT CASES
VARIOUS SOUVENIRS
TENNIS RACKET
BINOCULARS
YARD STICK
MOP
FAN FOR WIND
RAIN FOR EFFECT

SONG:
The Castaways
Copyright May 4, 1996
by
Richard Mousseau

LIFE-RAFT
PART ONE

THE STAGE IS BLACK, THE SOUND OF THE SEA CAN BE HEARD
ALONG WITH THE SOUND OF A YACHT'S BELL AND A FOG HORN,
THE GENERAL SOUNDS OF A SHIP'S MOVEMENT AND THE WIND
AND SEA AND THE CONSTANT CRY OF GULLS ARE HEARD. THE
LIGHTS SLOWLY COME UP ON A LIFE-RAFT [N THE MIDDLE OF
THE OCEAN. TO ONE END OF THE RAFT CAPTAIN CRAB, HIS EYE
PATCH ON HIS LEFT EYE, IS SITTING ON THE RAFT WITH HIS LEGS
DANGLING IN THE WATER. WITH A FISHING ROD IN HIS HAND HE
IS MOVING IT UP AND DOWN. WILLY IS MOVING ABOUT THE

7

RAFT BAITING ANOTHER FISHING HOOK. EVERYTHING IS TRANQUIL, THE GULLS ARE CALLING, THE SEA IS CHURNING AND SLAPPING THE RAFT. THE SOUNDS OF THE SEA FADE A BIT, ONLY THE SOUND OF THE YACHT AND THE GULLS ARE HEARD. ALL OF A SUDDEN FROM THE WINGS THERE IS A LOUD COMMOTION FROM VARIOUS PEOPLE ON THE YACHT. FROM THE WEST END A GANG PLANK IS LOY/ERED ONTO THE RAFT. CAPTAIN CRAB CONTINUES FISHING BUT SHOWS SIGNS WITH GESTURES OF HANDS, FACE AND FACIAL MANNERISMS SUGGEST HE IS UPSET ABOUT THE NOISE. THE SOUNDS OF THE OCEAN AND THE GULLS FADE BUT CONTINUE THROUGHOUT THE PLAY AND BUILD AS NEEDED. FROM THE EAST END THE SOUNDS OF VARIOUS VOICES OVERLAPPING BEGIN To SPEAK, SOME ARE EXCITED, SOME ARE FRANTIC, SOME CALM AND SOME UNCARING.

LILLY:
Is there room for me in that little rubber boat?

CHARLES:
(faint yell) Abandon ship.

FRIDA:
Hurry up Fred...You're always last.

FRED:
Yes dear.

CHARLES:
(faint yell) Abandon ship.

WADESWORTH:
Four polo shirts, ten angora sweaters...twelve boxes of graham crackers.

DIVA:
OH, I'd just die to be able to eat a graham cracker.

WADESWORTH:
Sorry Miss Diva...this is Master Charles Limbock's preferred cracker for his caviar,

CHARLES:
(moderate yell) Abandon Ship... Wadesworth do you have everything?

LILLY:
Gang way.

WILLY:
Captain Crab... l, think there is something wrong on board the ship!

CRAB:
(wave Willy off and continue to fish)

WILLY:
(drop fishing gear and steady gang plank)

CHARLES:
(loud yell) ABANDON SHIP!

FRIDA:
Fred...grab those bags.

FRED:
Yes, Frida dear.

FRIDA:
My suntan lotion...my big hat...my pillow… my...

FRED:
Yes dear.

LILLY:
Oh, the board is shaking. (start to waddle along the gang plank, board begins to show spring action)

CHARLES:
(Loud yell into Lilly's ear) ABANDON SHIP!

LILLY:
(freeze in place and put hands to ears and yell) AHH...

CHARLES:
(bump into Lilly) This is no place to stop for a rest...hurry up. (take Lilly by the elbows and hurry her toward the raft)

WADESWORTH:
(move along the plank with a suitcase in each hand, Diva is hanging onto his shoulders) Caviar is a much craved for delicacy...world renown.

DIVA:
But what is it Wadesworth?

WADESWORTH:
The best caviar is extracted from the most distinguished fertile ocean sturgeon.

DIVA:
What's a sturgeon?

FRIDA:
Hurry up Fred. (step on gang plank with arms full of souvenirs) You're always last.

FRED:
Yes dear.

FRIDA:
Fred you were late getting on board...I really think you wanted me to leave without you.

FRED:
Yes dear. (with an angry tone begin to place suitcases and Frida's odds and ends on the gang plank)

FRIDA:
You're so slow...you're going to miss getting into the life raft...Would you rather go down with the ship than be saved with

FRED:
Yes dear.

(all slowly move along the gang plank, Fred with only one plastic bag in hand steps over the suitcases and odds and ends, Willy helps Lilly into the raft, Lilly almost smothers Willy in her arms and bosom)

LILLY:
This rubber dingy will hold all of us won't it, Willy? (concerned as you hug Will)

WILLY:
(trying to breath) Yes Miss Famish.

CHARLES:

(with tennis racket in hand begin stretching the webbing) Willy...why are you and Captain Crab abandoning ship?

WILLY:
We're not. (pause then move to help Wadesworth into raft)

CHARLES:
But...it seems like you are.

WADESWORTH:
(hand suitcases to Willy then turn to face Diva to help her down) Miss Diva...a sturgeon in layman's terms is a fish, and caviar is an expensive way of saying...fish eggs.

DIVA:
(make a sour face and lightly slap Wadesworthts chest) UHG. (pause with a childish smile) OH...Wadesworth you're just funning me.

WADESVORTH:
I assure you that is not my intention.

DIVA:
Men fun me all the time...they say they want to know what's in my mind...while they try to take my clothes off.

WADESWORTH:
(turn abruptly, eyes rolling, pull at collar as if sweating) from a man's point of view...l see the connection. (move onto raft)

WILLY:
(place hands on Diva's hips and slowly lower her into raft, her body slowly sliding against yourself, your mouth is wide open) A mind should never be wasted.

FRIDA:
Her mind was wasted long before she developed a skinny body like that...right Fred...(pause)...Fred... (pause)... (raised voice) FRED.

FRED:
(obviously watching Willy and Diva, when you hear the last 'Right Fred' casually look towards audience and the sea with innocence on his face) Yes Frida dear.

(Willy moves about still holding onto Diva, as Frida attempts to get into raft, Wadesworth after neatly storing luggage to sit on, notices Frida and attempts to help.)

FRIDA:
(with outstretched hand try to look down into raft over the souvenirs) Hey sailor...you're wasting your time on her mind. (pause as Wadesworth takes your hand) A real gentleman... (you tumble dropping everything and fall onto Wadesworth to the bottom of the raft)

WADESWORTH:
(with a desperate loss of voice and breath) Please Madame....Please.

(Willy and Diva are still in each other's arms, Charles is trying to worm his way between them, Lilly is looking over the end of the raft where Crab is fishing, trying to see into the ocean, Fred with back to raft is looking over Frida's luggage)

WADESWORTH:
Madame...Please.

FRIDA: Fred...Fred?

FRED:
(not concerned) Yes dear.

FRIDA:
(in desperation yell) FRED!

FRED:
(turn and look around. start to walk down plank as you look over the edge into the water) Yes Dear...where are you?

(all others rush to help Frida get off Wadesworth, Crab continues to fish)

WADESWORTH:
(with a fainting voice) Help... help...help!

FRIDA:
Fred, you, worthless man.

FRED:
Coming dear. (rush to raft, get into it and begin picking up souvenirs as others help Frida up)

12

ALL:
(in various stages of concern and manners of speech) Are you okay...let me help you...oh you poor thing...did you hurt yourself?

CRAB:
(continue to fish as you turn and shake your head)

(Willy, Charles and Lilly help Frida up, Diva helps up Wadesworth. concerned chatter continues, as all settle and take up places in the raft with their backs to the gang plank it slowly moves away from the raft with Frida's luggage still on it)

DIVA:
OH...Wadesworth...I hope that big woman didn't hurt you... (brush Wadesworth's coat with your hands down towards his waist)

WADESWORTH:
(with a cracking voice) Fine...quite fine... (begin to pull at pants and stiffly turn from Diva as she continues to brush your shoulders) ...Thank you... thank you so much.

FRIDA:
(with hands on hips scornfully look at Fred with his hands full of souvenirs) ...Thanks for the help... (grab at the souvenirs)

FRED:
Doing my best dear... (turn towards gang plank and notice it is gone, begin to struggle with yourself as if you should mention the missing gang plank or just watch it float away)

FRIDA:
Lilly Famish... (begin to sit down beside Lilly) ...Men...you can't train them...you just have to put up with them.

LILLY:
It is so hard to find a good one Mrs. Felps, I've thought of becoming a Nun...but they have some vow against having sex.

FRIDA:
Fred took the same vow.

CHARLES:
Wadesworth ... (begin to take sweater off shoulders and look at it) ...this sweater clashes with the weather.

WADESWORTH:
Yes Master Charles...I would say it does...Should we wait until the weather changes to suit you..or shall I retrieve your light blue cardigan?

CHARLES:
The medium blue one Wadesworth... with the little alligator emblem over the heart.

WADESWORTH: very well sir.

(they make the change of sweater, Wadesworth fuses over cleaning and folding sweater into a suitcase, Charles poses for just the right look)

DIVA:
Willy… could you tell me why we have abandoned ship?

WILLY:
(in awe of Diva) Abandoned ship.

DIVA:
We are floating away in a raft...on the ocean.

FRIDA:
Men are not worth the trouble...take Fred...At times I wish someone would take him off my hands...useless...can't get him to do anything around the house. Frida, you need a man like Wadesworth ...Look how he fusses all over that Charles guy.

FRIDA:
He's a man's man ... he took the same sex vow as Fred.

LILLY:
Erectness pro limpness.

FRIDA:
Lilly Dear...You said it all.

CHARLES:
Wadesworth ...do you think this abandoning ship think will take long?

WADESWORTH:
Master Charles, I shan't think so.

CHARLES:

I had fancied a game of bridge before tea.

WADESWORTH:
(thinking) 1 shall consult the Captain. (move towards Captain crab)

DIVA:
The yacht seems to be floating away...1, don't think it is sinking. (still not thinking clearly) Of course it's not sinking, it is a fine ship... Captain Crab and I have been sailing her for five years now.

(Fred begins to make his way towards the Captain at the same time as Wadesworth, the Captain pretends to get a nibble on his fishing line, both men become excited and begin to watch the water)

LILLY:
What about Prince Charles there... good looks, seems to have money.

FRIDA:
That's what he's in love with.

LILLY:
Willy.

FRIDA:
Too young.

LILLY:
Captain Crab.

FRIDA:
Too old.

LILLY:
Mr. Felps?

FRIDA:
Who?

LILLY:
(surprised) Mr. Felps, your husband?

FRIDA:
OH...him...

LILLY:
Doesn't he measure up?

FRIDA:
Anatomy-wise his is . . .,

FRED:
A big one...do you have a big one on the line Captain Crab?

CRAB:
(a come see come saw attitude with gestures)

WADESWORTH:
With the tension of the line and the acute bend of the resin rod I surmise that the creature will exhibit mass proportions.

CRAB:
(extend hand to show length of proposed catch)

FRED:
Big eh.

CRAB:
(nod yes)

WADESWORTH:
Captain Crab...May I inquire ...1 apologize for deviating you from your quest for a trophy catch...but may I ask...how long shall we be on this proposed abandoning ship drill?

CRAB:
(confused look on face)

FRED:
Yes, Captain we are all aboard the raft and the yacht is floating...floating... floating away...

WADESWORTH:
Captain Crab...His Lordship Master Charles was inquiring about tea.

CRAB:
(shaking head and waving hand no, as if to say not for me thanks)

WADESWORTH:

My apologies Captain Crab... Master Charles was inquiring about tea for himself.

DIVA:
Willy the yacht is shrinking...getting smaller and smaller. (begin - to look over his shoulders to where the yacht was)

WILLY:
(with a giggling laugh) The yacht can't shrink.

FRIDA:
If Fred was the catch of the day, I'd throw the small fry away. (toss a souvenir overboard) In my life of loneliness...oh what I would do to have a small fry for my own.

CHARLES:
(put tennis racket to the brim of head, as if to shade the sun and strain to see out to sea) Ship-a-hoe...ship-a-hoe. (all turn to see what Charles is looking at, except the Captain who is busy playing with his fish)

WILLY:
That's ship-a-hoy...(yelling) SHIP-AHOY...That's our ship...what happened to our ship...Captain... Captain Crab?

(all move to east end of raft. Captain Crab stands on end of raft with a hand on Fred's head)

FRED:
It was a little late to mention...but I didn't want to mention to Frida that I left her luggage on the gang plank.

FRIDA:
FRED...FRED...I just know this is your fault.

CRAB:
(move eye patch from left eye to the right eye, handing rod to Fred scurry to the west end of the raft through the panicked crowd, when at the end pause then slowly wave good bye, turn to face the passengers, sit on raft's edge and shrug shoulders, the group backs away bunching together with scared confused look on faces, point at Diva and begin to attempt speech)

DIVA:
I noticed you and Willy in the raft, and I mentioned it to Mr. Charles Limbock.

WADESWORTH:
Master Charles asked me to pack his belongings because he said you were abandoning ship.

LILLY:
I heard Prince Charles yelling to abandon ship...I thought we were sinking.

FRIDA:
I wasn't going to be left behind.

(Crab looks at Charles and stands up with arms folded, begins nodding his head, Willy steps beside the Captain, all others turn and accusingly face Charles)

CHARLES:
1...1 saw you two sneaking into the raft...what was I supposed to think?

CRAB:
(shake finger into Charles' face as others back away)

WILLY:
You thought we were abandoning

CHARLES:
Well...yes...it looked that way.

CRAB:
(gesture to Willy to throw Charles overboard)

WILLY:
No Captain we can't make him swim for the ship...there's sharks in these waters.

CHARLES:
SHARKS! (all step away from the sides of the raft)

CRAB:
(step forward, all move back more, Captain sit back against the raft and gesture with thumb over your shoulder)

WILLY:
Now the yacht is floating away, and we are adrift at sea.

WADESWORTH:

We may set a mast and sail...and sail.

CRAB:
(shake head no)

DIVA:
Get out those flat things with long arms.

LILLY:
Oars or paddles.

WILLY:
No oars, paddles or sail.

FRIDA:
You must have a small outboard motor hidden someplace.

CRAB:
(place hands on head and slide them down face)

WILLY:
No outboard motor...no drinking water and no food.

FRED:
(at east end of raft, the fishing rod is bending drastically in your hands) I got one...I GOT A BIG...ONE.
(all turn moving closer to Fred)

WADE5VORTH:
Even tension Mr. Felps...play him evenly.

LILLY:
Frida...there seems to be a lot of play left in Mr. Felps.

FRIDA:
Now all he has to do is move it to the bedroom.

FRED:
He's big...maybe a hundred-pound salmon.

DIVA:
Just like that pink stuff that comes in a can.

CHARLES:

Play him man...give him some slack then pull back, tire him out.

WILLY:
Don't lose him, we could use a good meal.

CRAB:
(sit at west end of raft and imitate the same moves as Fred)

CHARLES:
Wadesworth, start the tea.

WADESWORTH:
Do you prefer lemon or lime?

LILLY:
Lemon ... and do you have those fancy little cookies to go with the tea?

DIVA:
Don't take out any of that baby eggs...l just couldn't eat any of that stuff.

FRED: I've got him, I've got him.

(all lean forward as Fred dips rod into water, then quickly all lean back holding onto the sides of the raft and each other as if the raft is speeding along the ocean, Captain Crab falls out of the west end of the raft)

WILLY:
(yelling) Captain overboard...Captain overboard (rush to west end looking for the Captain)

LILLY:
Throw him a life jacket or...one of those round life savers.

WILLY:
None on board.

FRIDA:
Don't let go Fred... reel that mother in... pull... crank...pull....

DIVA:
Throw him these water skis...they're made of wood...they'll float.

LILLY:
They'll float...Good thinking.

20

(Diva and Lilly each take a ski and push them into the water)

WILLY:
Grab hold Captain, I'll throw you a line.

CHARLES:
Look at the way that fish is pulling.

WADESWORTH:
By my calculations Master Charles, we should be sailing at three knots.

CHARLES:
At that speed we should hit land by nightfall.

WADESWORTH:
(look around raft and out to sea) I fail in my efforts to distinguish in which direction land should be reached.

CHARLES:
Fred old boy...make sure you steer him in the right direction.

FRED:
I'll do my best.

FRIDA:
Just reel him in Fred...l think we need to eat first.

CHARLES:
Land first.

FRIDA:
FOOD!

CHARLES: LAND!

WADESWORTH:
(breaking up the pair) Madame, Master Charles.

FRED:
HELP, I need help...

WADESWORTH:
(Move to Fred and take out handkerchief and fan Fred's face) There you go Mr. Felps.

CHARLES:
(in lower voice) Land.

FRIDA:
Food.

CHARLES:
LAND!

FRIDA:
FOOD!

WILLY:
(tossing a rope) Grab hold Captain.

DIVA:
He's got it.

LILLY:
Hold tight Captain Crab.

WADESWORTH:
There she blows!

(all lean back to accentuate speed)

CHARLES:
It's a whale, Fred you've hooked Moby Dick.

FRED:
I think I see Captain Ahab...he's waving.

FRIDA:
(begin to rub Fred's shoulders) A hallucination. Fred, concentrate on the fish...there will be plenty to go around.

WILLY:
(start to pull the rope taunt) I've got him...Hang on Captain.

LILLY:
You're almost here,

DIVA:
Look... Look...the Captain's doing tricks.

22

(Lilly, Diva and Willy pull on rope, slowly the Captain comes skiing towards raft waving one hand, gets on board and leaves skis in the water, they float away, just as Captain Crab is in the raft the line on the fishing rod breaks, everyone tumbles into the middle of the raft.)

(pause)

(Fred and Frida are first to get up, Fred eyes the fishing rod then looks out to sea a bit confounded, Frida straightens up her hat and clothes and slugs Fred with her handbag)

FRIDA:
I was looking forward to sinking my teeth into that whale,

FRED:
Yes Dear...(pause) you have the mouth for it. (head to east end of raft)

FRIDA:
What did you say?

LILLY:
(stand up in front of Frida then move to north end of raft) Frida...he did his best...fishing is like falling for a man...if you don't like a man... you throw him back...There are plenty of fish in the sea.

FRIDA:
You can throw them away, but HE keeps coming back.

(Lilly and Frida sit at west end of raft, Diva and Willy get up close in each other's arms)

DIVA:
Thank you for the help.

WILLY:
You are quite welcome... here let me help you sit down. (close together sit down at northwest end of raft)

(Charles and Wadesworth get up close together, Wadesworth has a small broom he uses to dust Charles off with)

WADESWORTH:
Are you quite alright sir... no broken bones I trust?

CHARLES:
(notice how close Wadesworth is and fearing others may see turn and brush Wadesworth away as you sit, Wadesworth continues brushing and follows to northea.st of raft) Quite enough Wadesworth...quite enough.

WADESWORTH:
My pleasure sir...there...there... you are quite presentable.

CRAB: (is last to get up in a dizzy and dishevelled manner, shake the incident off, can't decide which eye the eye patch goes on, decide to put it on the left eye, begin to pace in front of passengers, stop and point as if ready to speak, continue to pace, stop and point again then wave it off, go and sit on the east end of raft, look at the people and the sea, then shake head, pull out harmonica and begin to play tune of theme song "The Castaways")

(Willy begins to hum then is slowly joined by Diva then the others, Charles is first to start to sing first line then others joint in at various times)

IWILL TELL YOU A TALL TALE,
OF A LOUSY, LOUSY, TRIP.
IT STARTED WHEN WE SET SAIL,
ON A CRAMPED AND TINY SHIP.

WILLY IS A LITTLE SAILING MAN.
CAPTAIN CRAB JUST LIKES To FISH.
SIX PASSENGERS HAD A HOLIDAY PLAN,
BUT OUR LITTLE BOAT DID VANISH.

THE WEATHER WAS OH SO GRAND
NO NEED TO ABANDON OUR BOAT.
NOWHERE AROUND US IS THERE LAND.
IN THIS LIFE-RAFT WE JUST FLOAT.

OUR LIFE-RAFT FLOATS ENDLESSLY,
ON A BIG, BIG, TROPICAL SEA.
WITH WILLY AND CAPTAIN CRAB
THERE'S FRED AND FRIDA FELPS.
DIVA, OUR SKINNY, SKINNY, MODEL.
BONNY PRINCE CHARLES AND,
WADESWORTH HIS BUTLER TRUE.
AND LILLY FAMISH LOST AT SEA.
ALL OF US LOST, LOST, AT SEA.

24

(everybody sighs and becomes depressed except Captain Crab who baits hook and begins to fish, then points to Willy)

WILLY:
Right Captain...don't worry folks, Captain Crab will catch a fish...in... no time at all.

WADESWORTH: (stand and straighten self up) I say, a good cup of hot tea for everyone...it shall do everyone a world of good.

(all begin to nod)

LILLY:
Would you happen to have some English crumpets to go with that...tea?

WADESWORTH:
Oh...much better than that... Master Charles insists that when he travels abroad, I am to make sure there is ample supply of Graham crackers and caviar.

CHARLES:
(stand) Wadesworth, not my caviar...not for these... these...

WADESWORTH:
PEASANTS...COMMONERS... ORDINARY PEOPLE...

CHARLES:
NO.., NO, I did not say that.

WADESWORTH:
(face to face to Charles, Charles places tennis racket between both faces) Charles...old... boy...

CHARLES:
Wadesworth, what are you saying..., I am your employer?

WADESWORTH:
Old...boy, sit down... everybody is hungry...and we shall have tea...crackers and caviar...with your compliments. (Charles puts tennis racket to nose and backs away, sitting)

DIVA:
(jump up and grab Wadesworth's arm) Wadesworth you're such a sweet man... I would love some crackers, I'm starving...but no fish eggs.

WADESWORTH:
My extreme pleasure Miss Diva. (begin to make tea as Diva helps)

FRIDA:
(in English accent) Are you as famished as I am Miss Lilly Famish?

LILLY:
(in English accent) Quite famished Mrs. Frida Felps...and extremely parched... Are you parched Mrs. Frida Felps?

FRIDA:
(English accent fades to rural Canadian) Extremely parched...as parched as a fish out of water baking on a hot prairie wheat field.

(both begin to giggle and talk to themselves as Diva hands out quarter size crackers with a dab of jelly on them. Wadesworth passes around dinky little cups of china. Lilly and Frida act typical English mocking Charles as he sips and nibbles on his cracker. Willy places crackers on a hook for Captain. Fred downs his and begins to ask for another. Wadesworth obliges. Diva passes out more. Small unimportant talk should be carried out during this episode. Fred devours last of crackers, Captain catches a small fish, looks at fish then at group, shakes head and casts out again)

LILLY & FRIDA:
(add lib talk about tea with English accent)

FRED & WILLY:
(add lib talk about the ocean and raft)

DIVA & WADESWORTH:
(add lib talk about caviar and butler trade)

CHARLES:
(begin to fan face, dab back of neck, look at hot sun) It is getting bloody hot...I cannot take it any more...We shall die out here...snack food for the gulls...skeletons adrift on the ocean. (become hysterical) I do not deserve this fate...I demand we put ashore...immediately...it is so hot...my tender skin is beginning to blister... (look at sun) ...I, see spots in my eyes....

LILLY:
Don't look directly at the sun.

WADESWORTH:
Miss Diva, Charles fancies himself an actor of the English stage.

CHARLES:
I am becoming delirious...l can see...l can see...dear old dad....my life is flashing before my eyes.

DIVA:
Oh Wadesworth...Charles is good... real good.

WADESWORTH:
Substandard...minor applause (begin a silent hand clapping) for his efforts.

CHARLES:
There is a light...a bright light at the end of a tunnel. It is the after life...l am going...l am almost there... (child like talk) Mom...Dad.,.

LILLY:
(slap Charles' face) Snap out of it... we've only been out here a short time.

CHARLES:
WELL... you did not have to hit me so hard...l bruise quite easily. (hold hand to face, continue to show discomfort of weather and time on raft)

DIVA:
The weather is beautiful. (lean across raft and open up top a bit and extend chest to the sun) We are on vacation...we should enjoy ourselves... Come on Wadesworth, loosen up. (begin to loosen his tie and the buttons of his shirt)

WADESWORTH:
(hesitates then joins in, removes overcoat and rolls up sleeves) Yes, why not? (go to suitcase and get sun tan lotion and apply some to Diva's shoulders)

CRAB:
(reel in a bit bigger fish, you feel it is not big enough, cast it back out)

WILLY:
(begin to scan the sea with binoculars) Captain...we are a little way from the main shipping lanes, should we inform the passenger.

CRAB:
(attempt to give explanation)

WILLY:
(build to excess) I guess you're right...it would only create panic...they may want to blame someone...they could take revenge...on someone in

authority...the organizer of this trip...the owner of the yacht...the Captain...YOU!

CRAB:
(take off Willy's hat and begin hitting Willy over the head)

WILLY:
Sorry Captain...sorry...l wasn't thinking... that guy Charles started it.

CRAB:
(put Willy's cap back on Willy's head and go back to fishing)

WILLY:
(adjust cap to head and eyes to the binoculars) Aye, aye, Captain...l won't let them take it out on you.

FRIDA:
Lilly...we could be out here a long, long, long time.

LILLY:
What are you trying to say Frida?

FRIDA:
It is just...that I don't see anything on board.

LILLY:
Frida...what don't you see on board? Food...water, blankets...what?

FRIDA:
The most necessary of all inventions in the civilized world.

LILLY:
A motor...face make up...a real man...we've got a butler...

FRIDA:
No, no Lilly you don't understand, we are civilized women... they are men.

LILLY:
Yes, l, do know the difference...

FRIDA:
It has been hours since we left the boat...hours...and we had tea...several cups...

28

LILLY:
Hours...and several cups.

FRIDA:
Several.

(Frida and Lilly begin to fidget and cross their legs several times as they hold their stomach)

LILLY:
Did you have to mention the tea?

FRIDA:
There is no curtain... no... no...

LILLY:
No lavatory...no porcelain fixture...no john...no can...

FRIDA:
Lilly shush... l, know what it is...and there is none...what are we going to do? I can't dam up a river forever.

LILLY:
Think of something else...get your mind off a raging waterfall...

FRIDA:
They never tell you about this stuff in the vacation pamphlets...they never explained what to do in case you are adrift in a life raft for days on end...day after day with men and no facilities.

LILLY:
And they never show it in the movies...they show naked people...explicit sex...but never where the washroom is or how to...when in a crisis.

(Lilly and Frida begin to look about the raft)
CRAB:
(stand up on edge of raft facing towards back of stage and show motion of undoing pants fly, when ready put both fists on hips, from off stage the loud sound of water pouring is heard, extend time and loudness)

FRIDA:
(with open mouth gasp, turn fanning face) Men, in broad daylight, and in plain sight.

29

LILLY:
(lean back to peek) Well... he had to go... and he is demonstrating how it is done.

FRIDA:
And are we to follow suit? Lilly don't watch him...should we drop our drawers and dangle our backsides over the side...in plain view?

CRAB:
(water pouring stops, Crab makes motion but then stops, and resumes stance, water pouring continues)

LILLY:
Frida there is no floating gas station coming by for us to make a pit stop.

CRAB:
(water pouring stops, Crab zip up and continue to fish)

LILLY:
Think of...of babies.

FRIDA:
Wet diapers.

LILLY:
A walk in the park.

FRIDA:
Dogs peeing on trees.

LILLY:
March winds.

FRIDA:
April showers.
LILLY:
A desert.

FRIDA:
An oasis...palm trees...a water pool.

(Lilly and Frida rock back and forth holding their stomachs)

CHARLES:

Wadesworth...is there any caviar and crackers left? (begging in distress manner)

WADESWORTH:
I am afraid not...we will have to wait for the Captain to master the art of fishing.

(all look towards the Captain, Crab senses eyes on his back, shrugs feeling off)

WILLY:
In no time at all...we'll have a fish to eat...or a ship will come by to rescue us...or we will land on an island...where there will be all kinds of fruit.

FRED:
Or cannibals...we could be their appetizers of the day.

WADESWORTH:
ABSURD...we are in the Bermuda triangle.

CHARLES:
We may be picked up by aliens... disappear off the face of the earth.

FRIDA:
Are there sharks in these waters?

LILLY:
There are sharks in all waters...more so in warmer waters like this.

FRIDA:
And you intend for us to hang our butts over the edge of the raft when nature calls?

DIVA:
Why is everybody so scared...think of this as a vacation...a big new adventure.
FRIDA:
Sharks. (look over edge of raft)

LILLY:
Small ... (carefully look over edge) and they don't jump out of the water to bite someone's butt.

FRED:
I've heard that cannibals eat women first.

WADESWORTH:
Yes, that is true...but 1 should mention that cannibalism takes place on several small islands several hundred leagues from our present position.

DIVA:
See...nothing to worry about, (hold onto Wadesworth's arm) is there?

CRAB:
(reel in a half-eaten fish, cast it back out, put head on fist in a thinking manner)

WILLY:
Everybody calm down...this raft is safe...the Captain is thinking of all possible opportunities.

(all questionably look at the Captain then go slowly back to their previous activities, Frida and Lilly obsessed with needing to pee, Diva stretches out to sunbathe, Wadesworth takes out a handkerchief and fans Diva's face, Willy scans the sea with binoculars, Fred watches the Captain)

CHARLES:
(fan face with tennis racket) It is so hot, not a cloud in the sky...another couple of hours we will be fried...our flesh shrivelled up... (make way to south of raft)...soon gulls will be over our heads circling like vultures...waiting...waiting for us to die...then they will pick our bones clean, the sun, is blistering hot, can't take it... Wadesworth, Wadesworth, a cool glass of lemon aid...I should end it...I would rather be a shark's meal then to slowly die of hunger...wasting away...or heaven forbid crave to devour a fellow human being, just to sustain my own life...which one, eni-meny-miny-moe, ...the sun...hot...blistering...

(the sounds of the ocean builds, different gull sounds build. The lights slowly dim to black. Sounds continue through sequence. Lights slowly build. Charles is hanging over front of the raft. Wadesworth and Diva are leaning back to back sleeping. Fred and Willy are holding a blanket from front to back using one hand each, with a finger of that hand stuck in one ear, their other hand covers their eyes. Lilly and Frida are behind blanket to the west end of raft, they are sitting on the edge of raft with their butts over the end. Off stage the sound of water pouring into water, Crab reels in a little fish, holds it up, looks sneakily back, takes bite out of fish then casts fish out again.

Lights slowly fade, sounds build, lights slowly build. Crab is fishing, all the other men are at the north end of raft standing on the edge peeing, the off-stage sound of water pouring into water. Crab is fishing at east end. Lilly and Frida are at south end of the raft. Lilly has fingers in her ears, Frida has hands over her eyes. Diva is at north end with a yard stick, she is leaning over the edge her arm and stick extended out over water.

CHARLES:
Beat that distance.

WADESWORTH: Gladly master Charles.

WILLY:
Let wee Willy's Willy show you how it's done.

FRED:
If you need a man size job done call Fred Felps ...no plumbing job is too small.

DIVA:
The winner is...

(pouring water sounds fade, lights fade on Diva's line. Ocean and gull sounds build, lights slowly build. Charles is sitting with knees up to chest, his head on knees, he is sleeping with thumb in mouth at north end. Willy and Wadesworth have their head on Fred's chest at northwest end, Fred is leaning back. Lilly, Frida and Diva are hanging over south of raft. Crab lifts Diva's arm and checks for thickness. Crab moves to Lilly and lifts her arm, examines it and smacks lips, licks his lips, opens mouth to take a bite, stops and reaches for a salt shaker and sprinkles some on her arms, smacks lips, opens mouth wide and chomps down as Lilly moves. The lights fade.

Lights build, all are huddled together at the west end of raft, an interlocking mess of bodies, arms and legs, tangled together. Crab is at east end of raft and has a big fish on his line, he is working it back and forth, at times he motions for others to help. Ocean and gull sounds fade slightly.)

WILLY:
Captain...do you have a big one...a fish...food. (gets untangled and goes to Captain's aid)

FRIDA:
I could eat a whale.

DIVA:
Me too.

WADESWORTH:

I will start the tea...shall I poach...fry...bake or shall we have the fish sushi style?

CHARLES:
Wadesworth, at this point in time who cares...l will eat the fish raw.

(all finally get untangled and head to the east end of the raft to assist Crab)

WILLY:
You've got a good hook into the fish Captain.

DIVA:
What kind of fish is it? I hope it is a pretty one...l, don't think I could eat an ugly one.

FRIDA:
Fred, give the Captain a hand, and don't you dare lose it this time.

FRED:
Yes dear.

LILLY:
Pull Captain...reel...slack...pull... reel...pull...

DIVA:
Do you know how to fish Lilly?

LILLY:
When you are out fishing for a man it is the same thing...when they get close to the boat you club them.

DIVA:
I don't have to do that.

LILLY:
If I had your bait, I wouldn't have to do that either.

FRED:
Frida move your butt, give us a hand.

FRIDA:
Yes dear.

WILLY:

Charles lean over the side and help me grab hold of the gills when the fish gets close to the raft.

DIVA:
(jump for joy) Look... Look... the fish is jumping out of the water.

LILLY:
Reel...pull...slack...reel...pull...

WILLY:
It's a sword fish...look out. (all on last pull fall back into the middle of the raft, except Willy and Charles who are leaning over side of raft)

(instant black out, pause, instant lights, all get up and look out to sea, looking for the fish. Lilly is still down in the middle of the raft)

WILLY:
Where did it go?

CHARLES:
I saw it fly right over the raft...it was flying.

(all look from east to west, from horizon to sky to horizon, Crab lifts hands and shrugs, Diva gives a little wave. After a pause all gather in a semi-circle in the middle of the raft and look down into the middle. Crab shakes head back and forth, Frida and Wadesworth hug together and put their handkerchiefs to their noses, Willy cradles Diva, Fred puts hand to his heart, Charles puts hand to lips as if to throw up)

LILLY:
(get up with a sword fish stuck in belly, stagger a bit) Oh...it kind of tickles. (comic endeavors)
Ou...what a big long nose you have...you must have sharpened it nice and sharp before the Captain hooked you... Look I'm a human shishkabob...a female orderve...ha...ha... this cuts me up. (become sentimental) Frida...you were a good friend....and Fred ain't all that bad. (Fred hold Frida) Wadesworth I hope you cook this fish up real good. (Wadesworth sniffle and nod) Diva...you're too skinny...you eat my share of the fish (Diva nods and holds Lilly's hand) Charles...Charles...Charles... Charles the crackers were good...but...you are a little skimpy with the jelly. (Charles nods with confusion) Captain Crab and Willy...it has been different...but fun...wish I could hang around longer...but hey it's kind of hard to belly dance...with you know what hogging the dance floor...Ta ta everyone...oh one last thing...(yell) get this damn thing out of me.

(Frida, Fred, Wadesworth hold onto Lilly, Diva holds her hand, Willy, Crab and Charles grab fish)

LILLY:
(as they are pulling on the fish make sounds associated with sex)
OH...AH...FASTER... ALMOST
THERE... FASTER...OHH...AHH...

(fish is popped out, Crab and Willy leave Charles holding the fish. Charles discontentedly look at fish, turn east and throw fish back into the sea. Crab leaps onto the edge trying to reach fish. Others drop Lilly to bottom of raft and stare at Charles, Crab snaps fingers at attempted try, then turns to Charles and points finger into his face.

CHARLES:
What...What?

WILLY:
You threw our food away.

WADESWORTH:
(walk up and slap Charles with handkerchief) Moron.

CRAB:
(questioning)

WILLY:
Now what are we going to eat?

(pause)

CRAB:
(turn and slowly look down at Lilly)
FRIDA:
You couldn't, you can't.

FRED:
Why not...if we bury her at sea the fish will eat her.

CHARLES:
It is immoral...disgusting.

FRED:

We should quarter you Charles...and eat you...you're the one that threw the fish away.

CHARLES:
I was not thinking...I was delirious...from the heat and the sun beating down...cooking our brains inside our skulls.

(Frida and Wadesworth slap at Charles with handkerchiefs)

DIVA:
Maybe we could dip her in the water...use her as bait to attract other fish.

FRIDA:
Then we could catch the smaller fish.

CRAB:
(shake head)

WILLY:
She would only attract sharks, after they feed, they might attack the raft.

WADESWORTH:
How shall 1 prepare her... poached...steamed...baked. (pause) RAW.

DIVA:
I am famished...I don't think Lilly Famish would mind if I had a little bite of her...she thought I was too skinny anyway...she would want me to put on a few pounds.

CRAB:
(nodding yes, smack lips)

WILLY:
It is not that it has not happened before.
FRED:
Yeah...and they say...people taste like sweet chicken...she does look like a plump succulent broiler hen.

FRIDA:
Fred how could you...would you eat me if I was down there...dead.

FRED:
Without a doubt...you might be a little tough though...but if seasoned a bit...

FRIDA:
Fred, Felps, you are trying to get rid of me...you don't love me.

FRED:
Not now Frida...we have more important details to deal with.

CHARLES:
Should we not say something dignified over her first...something proper for the occasion before we...

DIVA:
Yes, she would like that.

WADESWORTH:
Please...everyone bow head in reverence...In the name of our heavenly Father, Son and Holy Ghost...the first one to have the guts to go first will eat the most.

(Crab is first to dive in with a grin and smacking lips, Fred washes his hands and jumps in, Willy forces hat on tight and jumps in, Diva puts hands over her eyes and goes in. The sounds of the ocean and gulls build. Wadesworth straightens handkerchief in chest pocket, adjusts collar and descents. Charles and Frida stare at each other as both make hesitant moves, Frida rubs stomach, Charles tugs at his throat, both start to nod yes to each other, they hold their noses and slowly sink down. Sound builds and after a few seconds bring sound down a bit)

WADESWORTH:
(quickly stand, dabbing handkerchief to lips, in loud sombre voice) For this abundance we are truly thankful...AMEN. (drop back down.)

(sound of ocean and gulls build, instant black out)

END OF PART ONE

PART TWO

THE STAGE IS DARK, THE SOUND OF THE OCEAN AND GULLS IS HEARD. THE LIGHTS SLOWLY COME UP. CRAB IS SITTING ON THE EAST END OF THE RAFT BUSILY GNAWING ON A LARGE LEG BONE. WADESWORTH AND DIVA ARE SITTING TOGETHER AT THE NORTH END OF THE RAFT. WADESWORTH IS SHOWING DIVA HOW TO DRINK TEA PROPERLY. WILLY IS DIPPING A MOP INTO THE OCEAN AND MOPPING THE FLOOR OF THE RAFT. FRED IS LEANING ON RAFT EDGE ON THE WEST AND IS SLEEPING WITH

HIS HANDS RESTING ON HIS BELLY. FRIDA IS SLEEPING BESIDE FRED WITH HER HEAD BOBBING FORWARD AND BACKWARDS AS SHE SNORES. CHARLES IN THE NORTHWEST OF THE RAFT IS BUSILY TRYING ON DIFFERENT SNEATERS TO THROW OVER HIS SHOULDERS.

THE SOUND OF GULLS AND THE OCEAN FADE AND CONTINUES AT A LOW VOLUME THROUGHOUT THE PLAY.

WILLY:
Captain Crab you have been chewing on that leg bone for over two weeks now...l think it is time you start fishing again.

CRAB:
(look at rod, then ocean, then slowly look around Willy to the others)

WILLY:
(step toward Captain) No Captain...just because Lilly tasted so good...you just can't pick someone else to eat.

CRAB:
(make a fist to play a game of odds and evens)

WILLY:
You can't pick someone that way either...we can't go about eating each other. (hand Crab a fishing pole) Here, try fishing again. (begin to turn) And not a sword fish...a lot of little fish will be fine. (begin to mop floor)

CHARLES:
Wadesworth ... l can't for the life of me decide which sweater to wear on a day like today... Wadesworth.

WADESWORTH:
Sorry ole boy...you will have to figure that out for yourself...Can you not see I am entertaining this lovely creature bestowed upon me by unmitigated circumstances.

DIVA:
I get all goose bumpy when you talk like that.

CHARLES:
Wadesworth, I will double your salary.

WADESWORTH:

Not interested.

CHARLES:
Double time and a half per hour for every hour we have been on this raft.

WADESWORTH:
Do not bother me old boy...I cannot spend the money... anywhere.

CHARLES:
I cannot take anymore... am at my wits end. I desperately need you, you are the only one that can help me...I am at a total loss without you.

WILLY:
(stand close to Fred and questionably eye Charles) Mr. Felps, I think we have a lovers' quarrel happening.

FRED:
I thought there was something odd about Charles...but to try and bribe someone with money...right in public...and his boyfriend.

WILLY:
Maybe he's been at sea too long.

FRED:
I wouldn't turn my back on him.

WILLY:
(turn back away from Charles, continue to mop floor of raft)

CHARLES:
Please Wadesworth...please do not desert me in my hour of need.

DIVA:
Wadesworth, he, is grovelling.

WADESWORTH:
Charles old boy you are creating a spectacle of yourself...get it together.

CHARLES:
Please...I, beg of you.

WADESWORTH:
Fine...fine...the light grey sweater with a pale blue polo shirt.

DIVA:
Oooo ... you know just the right colours and outfits to pick...what do you think I would look good in? (stand and pose, press out features)

FRED:
Nothing!

FRIDA:
(waking quickly) What did you say Fred?

FRED:
Nothing...l said nothing looks good on me...these awful old folks' clothes.

FRIDA:
What?

FRED:
Wadesworth, was about to give fashion tips...He selected Bonny Prince Charles' daily outfit.

FRIDA:
Maybe not on you...but I dress in style...the latest fashion wear...from Saks of 5th Avenue.

FRED:
And it cost me sacks of money... it wouldn't be so bad if you were Diva's size...l would save money on all that excess material.

FRIDA:
I am a perfect size eight.

FRED:
You sew those size tags on your clothes yourself.
FRIDA:
If you paid more attention to me...take me out at night dancing, maybe I wouldn't pig out on junk food...sitting at home alone watching the love boat.

FRED:
I work until I can't stand anymore...I'm dead on my feet when I get home...All I want to do is relax a little.

FRIDA:
That's not the only part of you that is relaxed.

FRED:
Leave our sex life out of this.

FRIDA:
You left it out in nineteen sixty.

FRED:
(turn back, fold arms, make a grimacing face)

DIVA:
(begin to sit beside Frida) I know exactly how you feel...men just don't know how to love a woman.

FRIDA:
I can't see you having that kind of trouble...men must be all over you.

DIVA:
That's the problem...they're all over me...but they don't love me for me.

FRIDA:
Sometimes I pray that someone would be all over me.

FRED:
(speak to audience) Three near sighted old cronies.

FRIDA:
(with back hand knock Fred to the floor of raft) Men...l can do without this one.

FRED:
(in groggy speech) Frida...Frida...

(Wadesworth and Charles help Fred up, Willy puts broom up toward women, Crab turns around to face the action and picks up leg bone and begins to chew on it)

WADESWORTH:
Madame please...control yourself.

DIVA: He...he, he deserved it.

WADESWORTH:
Diva, not you too.

FRIDA:
Us women must stick together.

DIVA:
You men have ruled the world long enough.

FRIDA:
And we are fed up...you're not going to rule this raft...there's going to be changes.

CHARLES:
I would like to see you run this raft...it takes a good sailing man to handle a raft at sea.

FRIDA:
You can't even decide what colour sweater to wear.

WADESVORTH:
Madame please.

FRED:
You've ruled the roost long enough in our marriage... it's time I put my foot down. (stamp foot)

WADESWORTH:
CHARLES:
WILLY:
HEAR...HEAR.

DIVA:
Fiddle sticks.

FRIDA:
(move forward rolling up sleeves) Fred you're an ungrateful little runt.

WILLY:
(poke mop towards Frida) Stay back Madam...don't make me use this.

DIVA:
Try it peep squeak. L will break you in two.

WADESWORTH:

Diva please...Mrs. Felps, there is no need to get hostile...we need...we must learn to get along with each other... besides...this is a raft...we just cannot leave.

FRIDA:
Why not...I wouldn't mind throwing a couple of you overboard...There's too many of you as is. (peer down on Fred)

CHARLES:
What do you mean by that?

DIVA:
You made us eat Lilly...so maybe it should be one of you men next.

WILLY:
But...she was already dead...the sword fish killed her

(egging the men on, Crab watches as he chews on the leg bone. From the northeast of the raft, a ghost looking Lilly is walking on water. She is testing it as she walks uncertain, wondering if she will sink or not, a very small set of wings are on her back)

FRIDA:
I could roast one of you up...and have you for a snack all by myself.

DIVA:
Me too.

FRIDA:
(look up and down the skinny frame of Diva) You?

DIVA:
As a model we are always on a diet...I figured I got ten years of eating to catch up on.
FRIDA:
It's just the two of us against them...you game?

DIVA:
Let's go for it.

CHARLES:
You would not dare.

WADESWORTH:

I believe she would.

FRED:
Believe me, I know she will.

WILLY:
Back off before I have to use this mop. (poke mop towards women)

(Frida and Diva inch forward, Diva is behind Frida pushing, Frida is swatting at the mop, Charles is behind all the men giving instructions, Fred and Wadesworth are supporting Willy's arms, all are exchanging insults in low volume as Lilly approaches raft)

CHARLES:
Don't let her get too close.

DIVA:
Grab the mop Frida.

CHARLES:
Don't let her get her hands on the mop...it is the only protection we have.

FRIDA:
You little fish of a big fish flopping on dry land.

(leaning on the raft beside Crab on the northeast side Lilly places her chin on her hands)

LILLY:
So, what's going on here?

CRAB:
(continue chewing on bone, do not really notice her, flop hand back and forth in an uncertain manner)
WADESWORTH:
You...you spouting ... beached whale.

FRED:
Hey that's my wife you're talking about.

WADESWORTH:
My most humble apologies sir...I was caught up in the moment.

FRED:

That's okay...but in the future I'll do the mud slinging.

FRIDA:
You and whose army mama's boy?

DIVA:
(girlish laugh) Haaa...haaa. a mama's boy.

FRED:
Me and my mate's motor mouth.

FRIDA:
Why you, little toad.

WILLY:
If I had more room... I'd mop the deck with the both of you...single handed.

LILLY:
How long have they been bickering like this?

CRAB:
(look at sky through an ok sign of the hand, then hold up two fingers)

LILLY:
Two hours...and you haven't put a stop to it... what kind of captain are you?

CRAB:
(shrug shoulder)

LILLY:
Not a very good one, if I was in charge I'd straighten things out...right quick.

(Frida grabs mop from Willy and at same time puts a head lock on him, Diva takes the mop and fends off Wadesworth and Fred)
CHARLES:
What kind of men are you...you gave up our weapon...and our military man?

WADESWORTH:
If we had the assistance of your help instead of your verbal connotations ... maybe, we would have the upper hand.

(Fred and Wadesworth grab Charles and pull him forward as Diva sticks the mop into this stomach)

DIVA:
Take that Bonny Prince Charles.

FRIDA:
Say auntie. (rub knuckles over Willy's head) say it... say auntie.

WILLY:
No way.

DIVA:
We take no prisoners...we capture... devour...and discard...who wants to be next?

FRIDA:
Say auntie, I give ... say it.

FRED:
Frida, let Willy go...you bully.

FRIDA:
You're next dough boy.

(all poke and jab, pull and push each other, mumble to each other, Lilly slowly and awkwardly climbs onto raft and sits by Crab)

LILLY:
Hey...Captain Crab...that looks like my leg bone.

CRAB:
(stop chewing, pause with mouth open)

LILLY:
How does it taste...it must taste good...you nibbled it down to the bone...picked it clean...polished off every tender morsel?
CRAB:
(nod and continue to gnaw on bone)

LILLY:...NOT EVEN THE MINUTEST, ITSY-BITSY, TINY-WINNY NIBBLE TO SATISFY A LINGERING HUNGER.

CRAB:
(look at bone, look away and hand it to Lilly)

LILLY:

No thanks, not a bit hungry... in heaven we are never hungry.

CRAB:
(quickly continue licking the bone)

LILLY:
Heaven...it takes awhile to get used to it...walking on water...wings and all...
(point to wings) small aren't
They. I will get bigger ones after I do a good deed for the mortals I left behind.
(stand and shout) WHY DID YOU ALL EAT ME?

(all freeze in mid motion, very slowly look from one another then slowly turn
heads only and stare at Lilly, after a long pause everyone except Crab yell.
'AHHHH....' Willy hugs Frida like a frightened baby, Fred and Diva huddle
behind the mop, Wadesworth and Charles hug each other, all freeze in last
stance with eyes wide and mouths a-gap. Crab grabs two bones and makes a
sign of a cross to ward off evil)

LILLY:(grand standing) OOPS...you all can see me? (all nod yes)
OOPS...(look skyward) Sorry Saint Peter...I messed up a few of your
rules...(look at crew) See what you made me do...now it's going to take me
longer to get my full wings...(point skyward) Saint Peter says 'I'm suppose to
forgive you for eating me...okay... I forgive you for eating me...okay...I
forgive you...(look up)...satisfied...Oh yeah..I'm suppose to help you help
yourselves and protect you from (angry pause, forceful voice)...from eating
each other... (pause) Okay...close your mouths...you're creating a draft...just
pretend I'm...I'm...

DIVA:
Dead.

LILLY:
No, no, just think of me as one of the gang, a fellow castaway.

CRAB:
(give ok sign and continue chewing on bone)

FRIDA:
I don't believe in ghosts..., l, don't, l don't.

FRED:
You believe in the tooth fairy Frida.

DIVA:

48

I do.

WADESWORTH:
There is no such thing as a ghost or a tooth fairy.

CRAB:
(wave hand gayly at Wadesworth and Charles)

WILLY:
You two should talk about fairies.

(Wadesworth and Charles break away from hugging each other, Charles wipes his hands over his chest and upper legs as if washing away Wadesworth who at the same time tidies himself up gentlemanly like)

CHARLES:
Who said we were like fairies?

WADESWORTH:
Willy button your lips... mommy's boy.

FRIDA:
(drop Willy to bottom of raft) You should talk Fred...a grown man... who still sucks his thumb.

FRED:
I do not. (look at thumb then stick it under arm pit)

WILLY:
I'm not a mommy's boy. I've been at sea all my life...you...

LILLY:
(grab everyone's attention) Quiet, I've been sent back as a nurse maid to a ship of fools.
CRAB:
(shake head and point to raft)

LILLY:
I know it's a raft...l was using a metaphor...a ship...a boat... a raft...but you're all still fools.

DIVA:
Lilly...did you bring us any fooood?

LILLY:
Speaking of fools...what do I look like... a Domino's delivery person?
You did say you were here to help us.

LILLY:
With divine and mystic guidance.

DIVA:
No food uh?

CHARLES:
Can you push our raft to safety?

LILLY:
No.

FRED:
Can you direct a rescue boat towards?

LILLY:
No

WADESWORTH:
Is using your wings to carry a message...out of the question?

LILLY:I'm afraid so.

DIVA:
No food uh.

FRIDA:
Yeah...rm getting hungry too...you can't conjure up a meal out of thin air...can
you?

LILLY:
Nope.

WILLY:
You did say you were here to help us.

WADESWORTH:
To us it is mystic...and only the divine knows what guidance you possess.

DIVA:

So you're saying we are still stuck in the middle of the ocean...in a rubber raft...with no fresh water...doomed to the elements...doomed to the misery and the madness of endless days...weeks...years ...without rescue from a male dominated naval ship... to be weakened to death, to have gulls pick our bones...to wander the ocean currents until eternity...to be sun burnt...to be deprived of sunblock p.f. 109...our clothes to disintegrate and leave our bodies naked . . .

(Frida covers herself, all others glare at Diva)

DIVA:
...to suffer with pain...the lingering agony as life is sucked from our bodies...our minds ever longing... longing... craving...

LILLY:
Get to the point.

DIVA:
No food uh.

(Lilly, exasperated, places hand to forehead slowly shaking it from side to side)

WILLY:
A lot of help you are Lilly.

LILLY:
I didn't ask for this job...if you would have thrown me overboard when that sword fish stabbed me...I wouldn't be here ... noooo ... you had to eat me... trapping my soul on earth...Now 1 have to help you in order to retrieve my soul and enter the pearly gates of an everlasting spa for angels.

DIVA:
Lilly I'm so sorry.
FRIDA:
So am I.

FRED:
My apologies.

WADESWORTH:
My most humble regrets dear lady.

CHARLES:

I am so ashamed.

WILLY:
We have disgraced ourselves.

DIVA:
We are so...so sorry Lilly.

FRIDA:
(point towards Crab) He...he made us do it.

CRAB:
(innocent in manners, attempt to hide leg bone)

LILLY:
Oh...alright, I forgive you. l would have done the same thing. (get down from raft edge and enter centre of raft hold out arms) I missed you guys.

(all gather for a group hug, all saying I miss you, I'm sorry then separate and sniffle dabbing wet eyes. Crab is left kissing Lilly's hand then opens mouth to bite her arm. Lilly pulls away as Crab chomps on air)

FRED:
So, what do we do now?

(Lilly leans on north end of raft, Frida on northwest. Diva on northeast, Fred on west end, Crab on east end, Willy on south end, Wadesworth on south west, Charles on southeast.)

WILLY:
Just sit here and wait...unless someone has a brighter idea.

CRAB:
(shrug shoulders and begin to fish)
CHARLES:
Anyone fancy a game of bridge... (look about) ... hearts, crazy eights... fish?

DIVA:
So, what's it like to be dead, Lilly?

FRIDA:
That's not a polite question to ask...a dead person.

(all three begin to giggle)

52

FRED:
If we all hang over the end of the raft and kick...we could head in one direction.

WILLY:
Sharks.

WADESWORTH:
In what direction do we head ... and where in bloody hell, are we now?

CHARLES:
There are several word games we could play.

FRED:
Sharks huh...too bad. A big sea turtle didn't come along...we could use it to tow us.

WILLY:
We may be going in the wrong direction.

FRIDA:
So, Lilly...up in heaven...did you meet anybody famous?

DIVA:
Elvis...was Elvis there?

LILLY: I asked around...and everybody I asked said Elvis spends most of his time here on earth.

DIVA:
You mean it's true, those stories?

FRIDA:
Then it really was him I saw at K-Mart.

DIVA:
Anybody else up there?

WADESMORTH:
If we had a sail...we would be able to harness the wind.

FRED:
We could tie all of our clothes together to make a sail.

CHARLES:
Not my angora sweaters.

WILLY:
Without clothes we'd get sun burnt.

LILLY:
I did meet James Dean?

FRIDA:
DIVA:
Ohhh

DIVA:
(self realization) Who's James Dean?

LILLY:
James Dean...Giant...Rebel Without a Cause...East of Eden.

FRIDA:
If you knew him...you'd think of him as a hunk.

DIVA:
A hunk of what?

FRIDA:
A real man to die for...oh sorry Lilly...l wasn't thinking.

LILLY:
That's okay...there are all those fine men up there...but they don't allow any hanky panky.

FRIDA:
No sex, what kind of place is that to look forward to?

(a faint sound of a motor boat going by)

CRAB:
(as boat goes by calmly wave)

CHARLES:
Wadesworth, please play a game with me...any kind of game...please.

WADESWORTH:

Anything to keep you quiet for a spell.

CHARLES:
Great... your choice... what would you like to play.

WADESWORTH:
Anything that you care to play.

CHARLES:
You may select first.

WADESWORTH:
By all means, you may go first.

CHARLES:
No, you first.

WADESWORTH:
Please be my guest...you first.

CHARLES:
You first.

WADESWORTH:
You first.

CHARLES:
You.

WADESWORTH:
(voice getting louder) You.

CHARLES:
(yelling) You.

(both lean towards each other with Willy between them)

WADESWORTH:
CHARLES:
(continue to exchange word 'you')

WILLY:
(with arms out sideways separate the two) All right...that's enough...back to your own corners.

CHARLES:
(pouting) He said he would play a game with me.

WADESWORTH:
(turn with nose in air, tidy up clothes) Spoiled rotten child.

FRED:
Lilly, may I ask you a question about... (point upward) ...heaven?

LILLY:
Sure Fred, I came back to help anyway I can.

FRED:
Does the man upstairs have a list...you know a good and bad?

DIVA:
Fred you're thinking of Santa Claus... (begin to sing) He's making a list and checking it twice...to see who is naughty or nice.

CHARLES:
I love Christmas...all the toys and games...I would get Wadesworth to play,

WADESWORTH:
Bah...humbug.

FRED:
A list of who gets beyond the pearly gates and who ends up in....

FRIDA:
Hell of a good place to be...if God was a woman all men would be damned and believe me Fred, you'd be on the list.

DIVA:
All men?

LILLY:
God should be a woman...and change a few things between the sexes. (say in a preaching manner)

DIVA: Like what?

LILLY:
(grand standing) Give P.M.S. to men.

(lightning flashes, thunder sounds)

LILLY:
Oops, I'm not supposed to take sides...l work for him now.

WILLY:
Is there a list...like Fred asked?

LILLY:
I'm not supposed to say...but I can tell you...he takes into consideration those that change their wayward ways.

FRIDA:
You'd better clean up your act Fred...or I'll be going to heaven alone.

FRED:
Well you sure don't make it easy for a guy to change.

LILLY:
Don't forget Frida, God is not a female... You may have to change too.

DIVA:
Which list am I on?

WILLY:
What about me?

CHARLES:
Surely, I'm on the privileged list.

WADESWORTH:
Satan's privilege list.
LILLY:
Oh...can't say...privileged information.

CRAB:
(reel in a bottle of wine, pop the cork, smell it, measure one eight with fingers, glance at others, look at bottle, shrug shoulders and drink contents, shake empty bottle upside down, put cork back on bottle and place back into water)

LILLY:
But some are higher on the undesirable list...Captain Crab what do you have there?

CRAB:
(show empty bottle, shaking nothing out)

CHARLES:
A bottle with a cork.

WADESWORTH:
Splendid deduction Master Charles.

CHARLES:
Don't you see...we can write a note and put it in the bottle... and set it adrift.

DIVA:
Someone will find it...read the note and come and rescue us.

WILLY:
It won't work...we are adrift...we can't put our coordinates down...because in five minutes we will be adrift to another position.

DIVA:
It's still worth a try.

FRIDA:
At least we can tell them we're alive...and to keep searching for us.

CHARLES: I have a solid gold pen with waterproof ink...(reminiscing)...a gift from Mommy... I've had it for years.

WADESWORTH:
(grab pen) For heaven's sake we will return it when we have completed our message. (take a pad of paper from Charles' pocket)

FRED:
What should we say?

DIVA:
Dear Talent Manager....I gained weight, but I lost it all and more...see you soon...I hope...

CHARLES:
Rescuers...look for a raft floating on water...seven people...one female ghost.

FRED:
We can't say that...we mention ghost and they will think the note is a joke.

WILLY:
He's right...only we can see the ghost.

FRIDA:
She has a name... it's Lilly.

LILLY:
Thank you, Frida. As a past member of this raft I think the note should read...To whom it may concern... castaways on a raft in need of rescue...please hurry.

FRED:
Good enough...you get all that, Wadesworth?

(Wadesworth tears off page and gives it to Fred, Willy holds bottle as Fred puts note into bottle and corks it. Wadesworth puts pen and note pad into his vest pocket, Willy leans over south of raft and puts bottle into water, all gather at south of raft to see the bottle off, Crab shakes head and goes on fishing.

WADESWORTH:
(in French accent) Bon Voyage. (waves handkerchief)

WILLY:
It's off... it's on its way.... there it goes.

DIVA:
It's not going away very fast,

WILLY:
Once the current catches it.

FRIDA:
I think it's sinking.

FRED:
It's not sinking...it's bobbing in the waves.

FRIDA:
Are you sure...did you put the cork in tight enough?

CHARLES:
You should have given it a helpful push to send it on its way.

WILLY:

I sent it off just fine.

WADESWORTH:
This is a large ocean...a journey will take time...just think of its journey as a letter delivered by Canada Post.

DIVA:
(lean over and blow) Help...if we all blow, we might get it going a bit faster.

(reluctantly all join in and blow until out of breath and light headed, each showing different effects)

LILLY:
(watching, stand straight up and look to the sky, others do not relate to her) How about a little wind to help these poor desperate...retching tokens of life's vicious and uncaring circumstances...taken from their joyous lives and cast unmercifully into the vastness of the deserted oceans and toyed with as if guinea pigs... (voice build showing a bit of anger)...to be pitted against nature and it's creatures that are waiting to devour them at any given moment without regard to their feelings...their loved ones...to be speared by a passing sword fish in the middle of the ocean...There was lots of room...it could have jumped over there...over there... but no...it had to jump right here...(point to middle of chest)...no it had to hit me...not a little gold fish but a large...very large...mean looking with a jagged dull sword nose...An agonizing...painful...just plain rotten way to go...and to make things even more degrading and sick...you let them devour every last morsel of me...(look at Crab) and they enjoyed it... but like a well behaved angel and without remorse...l...forgave them...why...l don't know...and now I ask for just a little wind...l don't think that is too much to ask for...after all I work for you... (a small wind begins, become angelic, clasp hands together at chest with an air of holiness gaze down on crew then look skyward with a little tilt of the head) Please...

(Diva is the only one still blowing, she takes one deep breath and gives one last big blow, with a quickness the lights dim a bit and a big wind begins to blow, the sound of a storm with thunder is heard with lightning flash, Lilly doesn't move, she holds her position through the storm, Crab rocks back and forth and from side to side, but never loses his seat on the east end of the raft and he continues to fish. Others in the raft are bouncing from side to side and up and down and colliding with each other, spurts of water are squirting towards the raft from the wings of the stage, just as quickly the rain and wind and the sounds stop and the lights come up full, slowly the crew crawl up on the south end of the raft a bit seasick looking, all slowly become aware of the floating bottle that did not float away.)

DIVA:
It's still with us.

CHARLES:
It followed us.

FRED:
Or we followed it.

LILLY:
(be discouraged and look up then look in all directions) Thanks...thanks a lot....

(a sudden lightning flash and thunder is seen and heard)

LILLY:
(cower with hands praying)

CRAB:
(wring out shirt and continue to fish a happy non-caring smirk on face)

WADESWORTH:
I am at a loss for words to explain this unpredicted situation of wind and rough seas with no measurable distance between us and our message in a bottle floating on the ocean.

FRED:
You sure spout a lot of words to explain nothing.

WADESWORTH:
Quite right Fred.

CHARLES:
So, what do we do now?

DIVA:
(start to give a little blow)

ALL:
(look to Diva) Quit that.

LILLY:
Remember what happened last time you did that.

FRIDA:
Yes dear...I, don't need all that salt water blowing on my face...it wrinkles the laugh lines on my baby soft skin...

FRED:
That's a laugh.

FRIDA:
Well you ain't much to write home about...not on this vacation.

WILLY:
It's too late, the last note in a bottle was mailed yesterday.

WADESWORTH:
And it has not left Canada Post mail sorting department.

(all sigh and hang over the side of the raft in a state of despair and watch the bottle go nowhere)

WILLY:
Eventually...we're bound to wash up on a deserted island filled with coconut trees...banana and mango trees...white coral sand beaches.

FRED:
A real vacation...eat and sleep on the beach, no malls...no city noises...no in-laws... (lean back on west end of raft)

FRIDA:
(stand over Fred and shake finger) Your relatives are like vultures hanging around waiting for a hand out of food and money.

FRED:
(smile) They won't be there on our deserted island either.

FRIDA:
That's... (begin to smile, lean back on northwest end of raft) ...That's good... real good.

DIVA:
No managers...no one telling me what to eat...swim and play all day long on the beach...the sand between my toes... (move to north end of raft beside Lilly)

CHARLES:

(turn from southeast of raft) We could play badminton on the beach...and collect sea shells.

WADESWORTH:
(move to northeast of raft between Charles and Lilly and Diva) Long moonlight walks on the beach... dining for two...a delicious meal of shrimp ala mode... candlelight...coconut wine...a maiden of beauty I shall recite love poems to...

CHARLES:
Not while I am with Diva... Wadesworth, I will need you to prepare my wardrobe and my household.

WADESWORTH:
Fat chance ole boy...I shall be too busy... (extend arm to Diva)

CHARLES:
(hold out two arms to Diva) Diva...I can offer you so much more.

WILLY:
(on south end of raft) No need for clothes...they will wear out anyway...what do you say Diva?

(Crab quickly turns and ogles Diva, Frida covers herself with her arms, Fred becomes wide eyed, Lilly puts a protective arm around Diva and extends other arm in a stopping motion)

LILLY:
Hold on boys...I, stress the word boys...I guess I have my work cut out for me.
WILLY:
Being a sailor, I know how to provide for her... Wadesworth can cook fancy food...but I can catch and find food... Charles... he knows only how to buy food.

CHARLES:
I will pay you Willy...to hunt and search for food...I'll double anyone else's offer.

WADESWORTH:
On a deserted island your wealth is of no value...I on the other hand can offer culture and experience in social manners.

WILLY:

She won't need no culture and manners to impress the sand crabs and tree monkeys aren't high on the society invitation list.

DIVA:
Well, you are all nice...and I like each of you in your own way...but why do I have to choose?

FRIDA:
It ain't right...you can't lead them all on...it ain't moral.

LILLY:
You may have to choose one...or refuse all...you ever thought of being a nun?

DIVA:
(shake head no) Don't nuns have to take a vow of chastity?

WILLY:
CHARLES:
WADESWORTH:
HEAVEN FORBID.

FRED:
CRAB:
(shake head no)

FRIDA:
Fred...you're married.

LILLY:
You're lucky I'm here...let's narrow this down...Fred for example is married to Frida...so he's out.

FRED:
Not much of a conciliation prize.

FRIDA:
(back hand Fred) If you're not satisfied...I... could leave and offer myself to someone else.

WILLY:
CHARLES:
WADESWORTH:
HEAVEN FORBID.

CRAB:
(make face and shake head)

LILLY:
Captain Crab...well he's...just too physically...worn out...too old... he's out.

CRAB:
(pout and turn back to fishing)

LILLY:
That leaves...Willy...Charles...and Wadesworth.

DIVA:
(smile and flirt) I like all of them.

LILLY:
You can't have all three.

(Charles, Willy, Wadesworth quickly put heads together then break)

WILLY:
CHARLES:
WADESWORTH:
WHY NOT.

WILLY:
I'm willing.

WADESWORTH:
A gentleman's agreement could be reached.

CHARLES:
A time share proposal.

FRIDA:
You, disgusting perverts. (back hand Fred)

LILLY:
This is perplexing... I'll have to discuss this with a higher power.

FRED:
You could...draw straws.

WILLY:

Sounds good.

FRIDA:
Shut up Fred... You're not helping.

CHARLES:
I am skilled at games.

WADESWORTH:
A one out of three chance...fair odds.

DIVA:
There won't be any hard feelings, will there?

(Willy, Charles, Wadesworth reluctantly shake their heads no)

LILLY:
Diva...what about love...marriage... commitment...children...yes children.

DIVA:
OOH...I never thought of that... (look at guys) ...we would need a whole bunch
of condoms.

(Willy, Charles, Wadesworth quickly search their clothing turning pockets
inside out, discouraged and a forlorn look in their eyes they gaze at Diva who
gives a tough luck kind of smile)

LILLY:
Diva...think of your dignity, your self respect...think girl think.
DIVA:
All I can think of is years and years and years stranded on a deserted island
with men drooling over my figure and they are trying to understand why I had
to take a vow of chastity.

LILLY:
It will be for the best...for everyone.

DIVA:
Lilly...I like sex.

WILLY:
CHARLES:

WADESWORTH:

ME TOO.

FRED:
For what its worth...sex ain`t all it's cracked up to be.

FRIDA:
What's that suppose to mean?

FRED:
I'm just saying that at our age...a good bowel movement...is sometimes ecstasy.

FRIDA:
Oh...I, know what you mean, l could use a little ecstasy right now.

WILLY:
Fred has a good idea...let's draw straws.

WADESWORTH:
Here Fred... I, have some matches.

CHARLES:
The longest one wins.

WILLY:
(pull up at pants) The longest what?

CHARLES:
The longest match will determine the winner.

LILLY:
Shame on you...Diva is not a piece of meat...or a prize to win on a whim, she should be able to choose ...for love...affection... romance...togetherness...friendship

DIVA:
And sex.

(Willy, Charles, Wadesworth nod their heads yes.)

LILLY:
Yes...Yes... Yes, sex...oh how I miss that little word that is rated with an X, there's no sex in heaven.

WADESVORTH:
That is a pity dear Lilly...but shall you deprive us mere mortals of a little pleasure here on earth.

LILLY:
Yes.

FRIDA:
Men have had the rule of the roost too long, it's about time a woman called the shots.

FRED:
Sorry fellas...what I've learned over the years is that women have made all the decisions and tell men what to do... they brainwash us into thinking we have control...they praise us for thinking of something they told us to do in the first place...we are but a ceremonial figure...(pause)...but just for the sake of the game...pick a straw.

(Willy, Charles, Wadesworth move closer itching to draw a straw)

FRIDA:
Fred's trying to use some kind of reverse psychology, but we are women...hear us roar.

FRED:
Quiet woman...we are conducting an important game here.
Everything is a game to them... hockey...football, gin rummy... women...

DIVA:
I like hockey.
LILLY:
Diva...denounce men...rise above them.

DIVA:
I wouldn't mind seeing...just for fun... who wins.

CHARLES:
Maybe...we should draw straws to see who goes first at drawing first for Diva.

WADESWORTH:
What...then maybe we should draw straws to see who goes first to draw first to see who is first to draw first.

WILLY:

68

Enny-menny-minny-moe...

CHARLES:
Who said you could go first to decide who goes first to pick first?

WADESWORTH:
One potato...two potato...

(Willy, Charles, Wadesworth speak at the same time)

CHARLES:
London bridges falling down, falling down...

WILLY:
Enny-menny-minny-moe...catch a girl by the toe...

WADESVORTH:
Three potato four potato more...

(Willy, Charles, Wadesworth repeat lines softly mumbling)

LILLY:
Typical men...they argue...they start a fight...go to war...kill each other...come home from a war...have a field day with all the women...produce an abundance of children, then the children grow up and argue...start a fight...go to war...it never ends...over and over and over.

(Willy, Charles, Wadesworth all grab for the matches in Fred's hands, they all examine the matches, then slowly compare them with each other.)

DIVA:
Who won, who won, who is to be the love in my life? (Become romantic)

FRIDA:
For ever and ever...through good or bad...sickness and health...for richer or poorer...

FRED: Hold your peace Frida...you ain't the preacher.

LILLY:
Until death do you part...Frida you forgot all the good stuff... PMS... temporary impotence...babies... diapers ...whining and crying...

DIVA:

Oh yhea, and no condoms... (Pause) ... I'd still like to know who won...just for the fun of it.

WILLY:
No one won.

CHARLES:
They are all the same length.

WADESWORTH:
Bravo...bravo...a fine deduction inspector Charles.

CHARLES:
That's it... (anger building) ...I've had enough of you...you are fired...get off of this raft immediately.

WADESWORTH:
quit...you cannot fire me... you... two-bit imposter of royalty.

WILLY:
You tell him...royalty...ha.

WADESWORTH:
Butt out...you son of a son of a sailor.

DIVA:
DON'T pick on him...you...you...fancy man.

LILLY:
GOOD GIRL.
DIVA:
Bug out Lilly...you started all of this.

LILLY:
Me... you were the one that was so hungry... that you needed to eat me.

DIVA:
Me... Frida ate the most of you.

FRIDA:
No, I didn't...Miss anorexia.

FRED:
Frida you pigged out...call a pig a pig.

FRIDA:
That's it...l divorce you.

FRED:
The sooner the better...it was your fault we left the ship and got into this raft.

FRIDA:
Me...it was Bonny Prince Charles.

CHARLES:
Me...it was Willy.

WADESWORTH:
There you go...always blaming someone else for your faults.

CHARLES:
I thought you quit...Fancy Pants.

WADESWORTH:
(take coat off, put fists up in English style boxing) Okay prune...you and me...right now.

LILLY:
Boys...Boys...no hitting below the belt...a technical knock out on the count of three.

CHARLES:
(hold up tennis racket in front of face) Not the face...l, need my good looks.

WILLY:
It ain't all that pretty.

FRED:
Give him a good one Wadesworth... an upper cut.

FRIDA:
(give a back hand to Fred) Charles... knee him low.

DIVA:
That's dirty Frida...l should bop you a good one right on the nose.

LILLY:
DIVA...one fight is enough...get some bandages ready...we may need them.

DIVA:
Don't tell me what to do Lilly....you're not my mother.

WILLY:
Quit prancing around...if you're going to hit each other...then swing.

WADESWORTH:
Stand still...so...I can bop you one.

CHARLES:
I am innocent...I, tell you innocent, ...it was Willy... WIlly helped us into the raft...He knew something was wrong....it was Willy...Willy...Willy...

WILLY:
Me... why me?

LILLY:
Yhea...why...you did not say... NOT to get into the raft.

DIVA:
Willy...are you hiding something?

FRED:
Speak up sailor.

FRIDA:
What was wrong with the boat?

WILLY:
Yacht.

WADESWORTH:
Whatever...yacht...boat... dingy, you and the Captain were on the raft alone...alone.

CHARLES:
Early in the morning.

DIVA:
Without us.

LILLY:
Speak up boy...or maybe you will be the next one they eat.

WILLY:
There was nothing wrong with the yacht...nothing wrong...

FRIDA:
You were sneaking away.

WILLY:
No... no... I swear... the Captain... the Captain just likes to fish from the raft each morning...he just likes to fish... (point to the Captain)

(all freeze then slowly turn to look at the Captain)

ALL:
FISH!

WILLY:
He just likes to fish.

CRAB:
(turn and nod and smile, make a cast and continue to fish)

(with exasperation everyone relaxes into their places on the raft, Fred leans on elbows on southwest of raft, Frida sits on northwest of raft, Lilly and Diva sit together on north of raft, Willy sits on north and below Diva, Wadesworth flops over south of raft, Charles pouts on southeast end of raft.)

(pause)

CRAB:
(sniff the air, stand on the east end of the raft and look from side to side, put hands together to form a telescope and put up to patched eye and move it all about, remove it from patched eye, blow on hand and wipe it as if it was a dirty lens, put it back to patched eye and again move it all about, take hands away and look at them, then it dons on you to move the patch to the other eye, put telescope to good eye and scan the ocean, turn to southwest, jump down and clamber over and past crew and stand on southwest end of raft and point like a stationary bird dog, when no one looks stress the point again, with no reaction point again with frustration then speak) ...LAND HO....ME MATES.

DIVA:
Land.

FRED:
Ho.

FRIDA:
Who said that?

WILLY:
Captain Crab.

CHARLES:
I thought he was a mute.

WADE5VORTH:
You fools, ...the Captain said land ho-me mates.

(All perk up and look at the Captain and the horizon.)

LILLY:
Captain... after all this time... why haven't you spoken to us before this?

CRAB:
(gesturing as you think) I... had nothing important to say until now.

ALL:
(except Captain Crab, in a jubilant rousing yell and scramble to Southwest end of raft) LAND HO!!!

(the lights black out instantly and the sounds of the ocean and gulls build)

THE END

MR. CHEEKS TOO SOFT
by
Richard E. Mousseau

STAGE:
THE STAGE SHOULD RESEMBLE A CAMP GROUND IN THE MID EIGHTEEN-SEVENTIES. A CENTRE FIRE-PIT CIRCLED BY ROCKS. AN OLD COFFEE POT HANGS OVER THE FIRE. AROUND THE FIRE ARE SADDLES AND VARIOUS COWBOYS, USED TO ADD ATMOSPHERE AND SOME NEEDED REACTIONS, MUSICIANS MAY DOUBLE AS COWBOYS. A HITCHING POST IS IN THE BACKGROUND, A HORSE IS HITCHED TO THE POST. MR. CHEEKS AND THE COWBOYS SHOULD BE DRESSED IN PROPER ATTIRE OF THE TIMES. ACTIONS SHOULD BE TYPICAL OF COWBOYS RESTING BY THE CAMP FIRE AT DUSK AFTER A LONG HARD DAY ON THE TRAIL.

SOUND:
BACKGROUND SOUNDS SHOULD BE CONTINUOUS OR AS NEEDED TO HIGHLIGHT ACTIONS ON STAGE. TYPICAL SOUNDS NEEDED ARE, RAIN, THUNDER, HORSE, STEER, FIRE AND WILD ANIMAL NIGHT SOUNDS.

LIGHTING:
DARK BACK GROUND LIGHTING, HIGHLIGHTING OF STARS AND MOON. FRONT LIGHTING CHANGING AS THE MOOD OF THE CHARACTERS AND STORY CHANGES. FIRE LIGHTING SHOULD BE SELF CONTAINED, BRIGHTENING AND DIMMING WITH A NATURAL FLOW.

NOTE:
IT IS POSSIBLE TO HAVE OTHER COWBOY CHARACTERS RECITING POEMS OR STORIES, EVEN THE SONGS MAY BE PERFORMED BY OTHERS ON OR OFF STAGE. MUSICIANS MAY BE PIT OR CHARACTERS ON STAGE.

CHARACTER LEAD
MR. CHEEKS TOO SOFT
MR. CHEEKS IS A SCRUFFY, LIGHTHEARTED COWBOY. HE SOMETIMES SEEMS TO BE ACTUALLY LIVING THE POEM HE IS RECITING. HE HAS LIVED HIS LIFE ON THE FRONTIER. MR. CHEEKS IS IN HIS MID FORTIES, HAIR AND BEARD GREYING. HIS DRESS IS RAGGED WITH AGE, BUT CLEAN. ACTIONS ARE OF A

MAN THAT HAS SPENT YEARS IN THE SADDLE AND COUNTLESS NIGHTS SLEEPING ON THE HARD GROUND.

COWBOYS
ALL OF THE COWBOYS SHOW THE VARIETY OF MEN THAT HAVE LIVED A COWBOY'S LIFE. THEIR REACTIONS SHOULD BE TO THE POEMS BEING READ. THEY MAY DISPLAY ANIMATED ACTIONS OF THEIR OWN TO SHOW THE CASUAL GATHERING OF COWBOYS AROUND THE CAMP FIRE. ALL SHOULD ACT OUT THEIR REACTIONS DURING THE RECITING OF THE POEMS.

MUSICIANS
IF POSSIBLE, ALL INSTRUMENTS SHOULD BE ACOUSTIC, GUITARS, BANJO, HARMONICA, STAND UP BASS, SNARE DRUM, AND FIDDLE. IF POSSIBLE, THE MUSICIANS SHOULD BE THE COWBOYS.

OTHER CHARACTERS REQUIRED

FOUR COWBOYS
ONE COWGIRL
COOK

SET AND PROPS
FIRE
COFFEE POT
ROCKS
SADDLES
SLEEPING BLANKETS
COWBOY HATS
SPURS
HITCHING RAIL
BRIDLES
MANNEQUIN HORSE
MANNEQUIN STEER
HOUND DOG
INSTRUMENTS
TIN COFFEE CUPS
TIN PLATES
FAKE BEANS AND BREAD IN PLATES
MOON AND STARS ON BLACK SCREEN BEHIND SET
GROUND, ROCKS, LOGS, CACTUS, STRAW
TREES
CHUCK WAGON

SONGS
Lyrics and Scores by
Richard Mousseau
A Cowboy's Lullaby
Copyright January 21, 1994
Dusty Trail Blues
Copyright January 21, 1994
Forsake Me Not
Copyright April 28, 1987

ACT ONE
The stage is black, the only light being emitted is that of the fire on centre stage. The house lights dim, the house music fades. Slowly heard are the sounds of the frontier with cattle calling and the sounds of horses arriving. From the stage is heard the clanking of pots, the cook is beginning to dish up the evening meal from his chuck wagon. Slowly the cowboys arrive, they are bantering among themselves. They place their saddles by the fire then retrieve a tin plate of beans, bread and a tin cup for coffee. When they settle down to eat, they slowly relax, placing their plates by the fire, a cowboy begins to hum, one by one the cowboys pick up instruments and begin an intro of a song. Mr. Cheeks Too Soft is the last to arrive around the fire, he stands back eating his plate of beans and listens to the music. The musicians begin to play the 'Cowboy's Lullaby' song.

Musicians:
(build music)

A COWBOY'S LULLABY

Lonesome nights on forgotten trails.
To you I tell of a cowboy's tale.
Of loved ones left back on the farm.
Angels keep from the devil's harm.

Many rivers we will cross.
A wandering calf will be lost.
A stampeding herd on a moonless night.
Do dare to hide this cowboy's fright.

Saddle up boys it's time to ride.
Find those lost steers that want to hide.
Sing a soothing song, a lullaby.
Move them out the cowboys' cry.

Lonesome times out riding alone.
My heart so sad, the cattle moan.
Your face I see upon the moon.
Forsake me not, coming home soon.

Musicians:
(fade music)

Cowboy:
(place a log onto the fire) Another cold night a-coming.

Cowgirl:
Didn't your grandma pack your long johns.

Cowboy:
I got both pairs on.

Cheeks:
(sit on a log at the head of the fire) I wish that I had packed extra clothing on
my first job. It was colder than this, I damn near froze. But I was inventive.
(fall into the poem)

GOOSE DOWN SLEEPING BAG

Old Bones and I were heading west.
By no means were we well dressed.
In a haste to leave it was blankets I did forget.
Bones promised that this mistake I would regret.

Wagon wheels waddled under freight stuffed to the hilt.
Fear not, this canvas covered wagon is Canadian built.
This is not a story of a wagon well-built,
rather poor old me with feelings of guilt.

On a hardwood seat sitting side by side,
I realized this was going to be a long ride.
Bones cursed relentlessly in my ear.
Come nightfall I could barely hear.

With a campfire ablaze, and the horses fed,
and stomachs full it was about time for bed.
"No sleep for you," Old Bones moaned, his voice low.
"Stoke the fire, recall the blankets you did not stow."

Old Bones hated the cold with a passion.
To keep him warm would be compassion.
Sticks and twigs I gathered in a monstrous pile.
Warm by the campfire Bones grinned a smile.

Come early morning after a good night's rest,
Bones said, "The fire so warm was the best.
"Each night it's your chore Cheeks-Too-Soft.
With your new job, no need to be too aloft."

I surely did not want the extra work.
My face expressed a tormented smirk.
The benefit of rest would I reap,
on endless nights without sleep.

Above in the cool spring air I heard,
geese flying on wing, oh my word,
honkers landing at every pond.
Of Canada Geese, I am truly fond.

Thinking of comfort at this moment,
and of their thick fluffy nest I lament.
Ten baby geese bundled warm and cozy.
Down covered butts and cheeks so rosy.

Snuggled in close Bones would fit right in,
cuddling right up smiling with a wide grin.
Warm as a northern flea on a south bound duck.
Inspiration hit hard, Bones and I were in luck.

While dreaming, scheming and planning all day,
Old Bones wondered why I had nothing to say.
Blaming me for not stowing Hudson Bay Blankets,
Bones questioned why I strolled off with a basket.

A mother goose stood by tall and leery.
"I am not after your chicks so be cherry.
I'd like to borrow a handful of down."
She looked at me with an angry frown.

Pinching fluff in hand off I scurry.
In flew a gander with frazzled flurry.
"Why bother peaceful geese for measly feathers,"
quipped Bones. "A softer pillow, that's Clever."

After months on the trail and a gunny sack full,
Bones noted, "Ground's hard, just darn pitiful."
I cleaned and fluffed the precious cargo,
worthy of gold carried by Wells Fargo.

At each stop our load of fright emptied a bit.
From the wagon's cotton canvas, I took and slit.
Bones questioned, "kind of a long pillow for one head?"
Paying no mind, I double stitched with horse hair thread.

One frosty Northern night, borealis danced.
Maple ambers smoldering created a trance.
With final stitches made the quilts were sweet.
Bones hollered, "Stoke up the fire, I need heat."

"Bones," I began to boast, "we won't need more heat."
Bones quipped, "My maker I do not want to meet?"
"Every night for months I stoked the fire.
You won't need it no more, I'm no liar."

A canvas quilt with goose down is my salvation.
"Bones you'll be as warm as a chick in incubation."
"If I wake up dead Cheeks, on frozen ground,
I'll take you and we will be hell bound."

Eyeing the quilts, Bones seemed puzzled.
Into the fluffy goose down quilt he nuzzled.
He pulled my quilt over his rickety old bones.
Cold and shivering by the fire I sat all alone.

"Cheeks, I feel a slight draft, I hate to nag.
Tomorrow please sew the sides into a bag."
He wants a sleeping bag, of all the gall.
Without a blanket by the fire I sprawl.

Next spring when heading freight out west.
I will have my own cozy sleeping bag to test,
filled with double the amount of soft goose down.
Across Canada from east to west, I will be renown.

Thee inventor of a sleeping bag of goose down.
Soft and warm when sleeping on cold ground.
"Hey Bones, would you mind sharing, I feel cold."
Bones mumbled, "Never, not for a coin of gold."

Cowboy:
(place another log on the fire) Would you care to share your sleeping bag, Cheeks, I don't snore.

Cheeks:
There are two things that I don't share. (with puzzlement begin to count on your fingers)

Cowgirl:
What's that Cheeks?

Cheeks:
My sleeping bag and my horse . . . maybe three things, my wife if I had one.

Cowboy:
If you need one, I have one back home I am willing to trade. I could use a new horse.

Cheeks:
Picked up my first horse when I was just knee-high to a long-legged grasshopper. (fall into poem)

HORSE TRADER

Five bucks read the for-sale tag.
I am not one to continuously nag.
It is a bit much for an old hag.
For profusely its belly does sag.

I will offer you one dollar for this old roan.
At this point in time it is just skin and bone.
I am able to give it a barn made of stone.
He is lonely, do you not hear him moan?

Everyday I will take him for a ride.
Over logs and hedges we will glide.
I will teach him to trot a gallant stride.
With heads high we will ride with pride.

Will you look at those big sad eyes liquefy?
Any moment now he just may start to cry.
For days, no one was willing to buy.
I have one dollar and I am your guy.

This honest to goodness horse trader I do endorse.
Accepting a five-year-old kid's bid, I have no remorse.
You win young cowboy, a done deal of course.
Partner, saddle up your antique hobby horse.

Cowboy:
(sniffle and blow nose into neck bandanna)

Cowboys:
(all choke back tears, all look into different directions)

Cowgirl:
What? I am surrounded by lily-livered mama's boys.

Cowboy:
It was sparks from the fire.

Cowgirl:
All of you, all at one time?

Cowboys:
(all nod heads at the same time)

Cook:
More beans?

Cowgirl:
Heck no Cook, full, had enough, good for another week, bloated enough for
the night.

Cowboy:
Here Cook. (hand two plates out to be filled)

Cheeks:
Your sleeping down wind tonight.

Cowboy:
Ah, Cheeks, do I have to? It is dark and . . . and . . .

Cowgirl:
Lonely?

Cheeks:

Lonely is a man heart broken, alone in the darkness of winter. A note we found in a cabin lay beside an old man telling of his last days. (fall into poem)

LOG CABIN DREAMS

At the cabin's door bite's winter's chill.
Warm in a down bed roll I lie stiffly still.

Flames of life burned bright in my youth.
Memories recalled are splinters of truth.

Among the stars, northern lights shimmer.
I see a figure's reflection, only a glimmer.

I am unable to wake from a sleeping slumber.
Early in life a love vanished, I begin to wonder.

When I felt Cupid's arrow from above.
I should have realized it was true love.

In my youth, I should have taken a dare,
asked a love of my life to joyously share.

From her father, for her hand I did not ask.
For her to be burdened with me, a great task.

Words of love and affection I never did deliver.
Emotions turn within, a raging serpent river.

For her to follow me into the wilds a great task.
Her tears on skin so soft were hidden by a mask.

A love I have forsaken in the years of my past.
This land in the north is empty, great and vast.

I hear a mouse and mate and their mating sound.
All creatures seem to share what I have not found.

All of me to her I did not truly give.
Without her love, I do not want to live.

I live in a cabin of logs built by lonely hands.
Not a home, a building resting on barren land.

Flames are extinguished in the hearth across the room.
A cold chill I feel creeping contributing to my doom.

No more do I toss and turn in extended sleep.
With eyes closed I'm no longer able to weep.

I lie stiffly still in a bed roll of eider down.
A cold body by a loved one will not be found.

Cowboy:
(place several logs onto the fire) I feel a slight chill in the air. Northern arctic air creeping along the ground. (place a hand onto the ground) Do you feel the chill?

Cowboy:
(pull blanket over legs) More hot coffee for me. (fill coffee cup)

Cook:
You are all a bunch of mama's boys, wimps, sissies, I remember being up north in the dead of winter, I froze to death, but I was tough and mean, I came back to life in the spring just for spite.

Cowgirl:
You should have stayed frozen.

Cook:
What? Who said that?

Cowgirl:
Put the coffee on the fire, it is almost frozen.

Cowboy:
(put coffee closer to the fire, sit a little closer and warm hands)

Cowboy:
Hey boss, why did you sign us on for a northern drive? At this time of year driving cattle down Mexico way would be nice.

Cowboy:
Warm weather, music, dancing girls.

Cowgirl:
You are too young for a woman. You can't handle a real woman. (stand, puff up chest) Boss, tell these tenderfoots what could happen to a boy that falls for a Senorita. Tell them about Lopez and Juarez.

Cheeks:
Lopez was in love with Senorita Martina, under a difficult situation. (fall into poem)

LOPEZ AND JUAREZ

Beneath the golden sun of Mexico, they ran,
Lopez and Juarez, friends since time began,
blood brothers, kin only to their sombreros,
crusaders of the west fighting the caballeros.

Not yet fifteen, for young maidens they cared not.
A herd of wild horses, it was them they sought.
To stake life and limb they were willing,
for life on the vast plains was thrilling.

Lopez and Juarez dreamed days away,
of riding Spanish barbs, they did pray.
Thoughts were of capturing a steed.
To last breaths they vowed to succeed.

Below the gorge rimming a snaking river,
horses drank slow making the water quiver.
Lopez and Juarez rested beneath the noon day sun,
then with beating hearts on bare feet they did run.

Bold and brave, Lopez was first to lead,
seeking a horse displaying strength in deed.
A horse with flowing mane he would claim.
Pacos would be the white stallion's name.

Juarez favoured a young sleek black mare.
A prancing stride she displayed with flare.
Sanora, her anointed name held his rapture.
This young spirted filly he would capture.

Lopez and Juarez on the run let lariats fly.
Lassoes carried by angels from on high.
Dust rose from stamping horses through the gorge.

On their mighty steads into history they would forge.

Filling their throats was the red desert dust.
Across sand and water, the amigos were thrust.
Dragging behind they put up a good fight,
as daylight was bidding them a goodnight.

As tough as leather their hearts were willing.
Dust caked eyes peered at a sight so thrilling.
Morning found them still clinging to ropes,
tethering two steads fulfilling their hopes.

In dreams they would duel the caballeros with verve.
These young amigos, the horses would willingly serve.
Pacos and Sanora for ever more would be true.
Lopez and Juarez toasted their adventures anew.

Conquistadores of fame their names became.
For one's misfortune whom shall we blame.
Years of high adventure too quickly passed,
for into a heart came a love from the past.

Into town rode Lopez on the back of a trusted steed.
Juarez, a companion at his side, a man of good deeds.
Like a Don Quixote, his hero Lopez mimics,
crusading the west with laughter and frolic.

Lopez's devoted love of a dark-haired girl was a sin.
In the night, Lopez rode away from her vengeful kin.
Under a Mexican moon their passion went array.
Lopez escaped in the night down to ole Monterrey.

Lopez feared not the edge of a Spanish blade.
His talk of a dark-haired beauty did not fade.
Lead shot would never catch fleeting feet.
Vengeful caballeros Lopez would defeat.

In Fort Worth, Lopez lingered letting sorrow wallow,
his wanting heart with Senorita Martina in Amarillo.
Juarez mingled with ladies in Madam Mae's bordello,
letting the night pleasures of Madam's ladies crescendo.

Through Santa Fe and Monterrey, they strayed.
Behind barred windows Martina felt betrayed.

Spanish blades would not stop Lopez from a date.
On his steed, this night, Lopez would face his fate.

Of Martina's vengeful kin, Lopez feared not.
A derringer beneath a pillow echoed a shot,
when into a room, he presented himself to her.
Lopez's heart flowed red, her face a dark blur.

The lead of shot caught Lopez's fleeting feet.
His body lies beneath fields of golden wheat.
No more will Lopez fear a cold Spanish blade.
In time Juarez's memory of Lopez will fade.

Lopez and Juarez feared not a cold Spanish blade.
In Amarillo beneath a tall weeping willow's shade,
by a campfire, Juarez tells tales of Lopez's lore.
Beside his grave Martina weeps forever more.

Cowboy:
See, see, they were in love.

Cowgirl:
The moral of the story is, do not sneak up on a woman, especially when she
has a shooter. (grab a hold of your pistol making a warning suggestion) I am
going to water the lilies, and I have an itchy trigger finger. (head off into the
dark)

Cowboy:
I piety the critter that sneaks up on her.

Cowgirl:
I heard that.

Cook:
Women hear everything, even the thoughts in a man's head. I have no
thoughts, so I am exempt. I don't have women-problems. Now Cheeks, he's
had a few.

Cowboy:
Boss, have you a girl back home?

Cowboy:
A sweetheart?

Cheeks:
(shake head no, stand and shuffle feet in the ground shyly) Nah, I am destined to give my life to the trail.

Cook:
Cheeks was sweet on a girl once, a pretty-little thing, a vet.

Cowboy:
You was sweet on her?

Cowgirl:
Who's sweet on who? (slide pistol up and down in your holster) No one had better be sweet on me. I'll fill the critter with lead. Who is sweet on me?

Cook:
No one is sweet on you. No one in his right mind would live in a house where two people wear the britches. It is bad enough that I have to do the cooking, I ain't a-gonna start doing your laundry too. (clang pots and mumble, continue to clean up)

Cowboy:
Boss, who were you sweet on?

Cook:
Tell them Cheeks. Miss Anita, that's who.

Cheeks:
(in a dream state fall into poem)

MISS ANITA

A pretty little gal, is Miss Anita the vet,
though not well endowed with a big set.
I was sure tickled pink on the day we first met.
"Not your type," the boys sassed, "wager a bet?"

Now old Doc Good use to come around,
that's when he was a virile young hound,
but I can't say that I miss the old coot.
Someone must have gave him the boot.

I must say folks, that I am a bit perplex.
This situation could become complex.
For you see, each year come early spring,

88

Doc Good, with some tools, he'd bring.

People doctors back in them good ole days just were not around.
With a youngin a-coming many a Pa rejoiced when Doc was found.
By-Joe, I think ole Doc was there when I was a-coming.
He sure done good, for I'm still here and still humming.

Let us not linger, that is another story.
When Doc's working, he is in his glory.
He checked Buttermilk my old mare.
I stood next in line somewhat bare.

As if nothing different he checked my withers,
then casually said, "fancy a game of checkers?"
Once a year, every year this was the ongoing situation.
For what ails me, Doc gave me caster oil for lubrication.

This spring it was pretty Miss Anita the vet.
I sure fancied her my type, I'd wager a bet.
I was tickled pink, I blushed, she said, "I'm glad we met.
Bring in them horses Mr. Cheeks Too Soft, I'm all set."

One by one, all in a row, in came a horse.
At the end of the line I stood of course.
The old timers watched intently from around the checker board.
Will she, or won't she, they wagered hoping to claim a reward.

Next came I, my teeth just a chattering.
In long-johns would she find me flattering.
"Open wide," said she. "I'll check your teeth."
Raising each bare arm, she checked beneath.

A hush fell among the menagerie in the barn.
I hope you all don't think this is just a yarn.
"You're in fine shape," smiled Miss Anita the vet.
My eyes were transfixed on this pretty brunette.

I could speak not a responsive word.
The other old guys, yes them I heard.
"Well make your move," they chimed.
Without spoken words, I pantomimed.

With love struck eyes my heart did pound.
Comments from the guys were sure to abound.

Flowers from behind my back to her I gave.
Rubbing my face, I realized I needed a shave.

"That's sweet of you Mr. Cheeks Too Soft."
My blood pressure rose, my heart was aloft.
"Here is some caster oil for whatever ails you."
This wasn't what I expected, this is surely true.

I spoke not a word as the sun began to set.
In the distance rode away Miss Anita the vet.
I sure fancied her my sweet Miss, and I'll wager you a bet.
Come next spring, I'll ask her to be my Mrs. Anita the vet.

Cowgirl:
(sniffle, blow nose into a long red hanky) It's a fall cold, I feel winter coming on.

Cowboys:
(with open mouths stare at cowgirl)

Cowgirl:
(wrestle with pistol in the holster) I said winter is coming and the sniffles are the first sign of a cold coming on.

Cowboys:
(all nod heads in agreement)

Cook:
A little Cheyenne pepper in your coffee will cure a cold. (dump pepper into cowgirl's cup)

Cowgirl:
(hesitate, then force down coffee, make faces) A fall cold.

Cowboy:
(begin to play your harmonica soft and low)

All:
(listen for awhile)

Cheeks:
Sure, is sweet music. It has been a few years, but I remember that long winter when Sourdough got that harmonica for Christmas. (fall into poem)

COWBOY'S CHRISTMAS

Two old cowboys we were, trail pals for near on ten years.
Every winter about this time, Sour Dough expresses cheers.
Sour Dough somehow knew when it was Christmas time.
On the Eve, he'd hang cow bells hoping to hear a chime.

All kinds of big, little, round and square bells he'd string on a line,
from Birch tree to Poplar, Oak, Maple and around a big Scotch Pine.
How he knew exactly which day it was supposed to be on, I don't know.
For a man pushing forty, he was still waiting for you know who to show.

There were times he had me a-going with stories of gifts under a tree.
He told me of a time when young in England sitting on Santa's knee.
A big guy all dressed in red, trimmed with fur and a long white beard.
On Christmas Eve down chimneys he comes, sounds somewhat weird.

This year we was camping on the trail, sixty miles north of Dawson City.
With the stars over head we huddled by a fire, Sour Dough sang a ditty,
something about flying reindeer, I was thinking he was off his rocker.
I hear tell, for cabin fever they toss people in the river, a real shocker.

Sour Dough seemed pretty normal to me, except at Christmas.
He was just a kid, anxious, pretentious, sure to create a ruckus.
There he was, knee deep in snow, hanging up cow bells all in a row.
I said, "Are you trying to capture that guy who says Ho, Ho, Ho?"

Sour Dough stared and said, "I know I am getting old,
but before I meet my maker, Santa Claus has to be told."
"What in tarnation do you need to tell a guy hog tied in cow bells?"
Sour huffed, "I got to tell him it weren't me who plugged the well."

"I've been cow-poking for forty years and I've been a good boy.
"Santa ain't ot-ta punish me, under a tree I'd like just one toy."
"Tarnation," I said, "this guy ain't brought you no gift in how many years?"
Sour Dough nodded, I scratched my beard of white, I thought I saw a tear.

"So, you plan to catch this Santa guy and explain your legal case.
If he thinks you're a good boy, under a tree a toy he will place?"
"Yup," Sour Dough acknowledged, clearing a place under a baby pine tree.
He was elated with anticipation, a young fella filled to the brim with glee.

Night time fell, the campfire sparkled, I began to hum a lullaby.
Sour Dough settled down, yawning then fell asleep with a sigh.

No doubt dreaming of being a boy back in old England town.
I though of snow and the cold, the bells, I can't let him down.

In long-johns I braved the bitter cold and quickly tied a string to the bells.
Under the tree, I placed a paper wrapped gift, Sour would not find swell.
At the first of dawn I was supposed to yank the string with force.
Bells clanged a chime, what a ruckus, I awoke in bed of course.

Darn near gave Sour Dough a heart attack, what was he to think.
He called out Santa's name, noticed the gift and was tickled pink.
For the first time, I saw Sour Dough cry, bringing a tear to my eye.
Sour Dough gazed into the sky and slowly gave his gift a good try.

Music flowed from a new harmonica, a tune sweet and low.
Near on twenty years I've rode the trails with old Sour Dough,
and every night is like Christmas when he plays the sweet music,
despite my intended pleasure of placing a lump of coal as a trick.

Two old cowboys we were, trail pals for near on twenty-year,
and every winter about this time, Sour Dough expresses cheer.
A year don't go by that he and I don't get in mood at this time,
to hang cow bells from tree to tree hoping to hear them chime.

(cowbells and cow sounds drift into the camp building in volume, the cowboy
continues to play his harmonica soft and low)

Cook:
Git out, git back to where cows belong, it's bad enough I slave all day to fix
meals for these ya-ho cowboys then have to feed mangy steers. I have a good
mind to put one of you steers on a spit over the fire and have you for supper.
Ahh . . . another cow-patty. You critters have thousands of miles on which to
plop down your cow-patties. No, you visit my chuckwagon and leave your
calling card. I am a renown chef. I could have any job I want in Montreal, but
no, I dish up breakfast, lunch, supper and snacks for ungrateful cowboys.

Musicians:
(as Cook is rambling begin to play the into to the song 'Dusty Trail Blues')

DUSTY TRAIL BLUES

You mangy old cows get-along,
Ain't no time to sing a sweet, sweet song.
To the stock-yard you're all bound.
Hanging at the butcher's you'll be found.

At fourteen-dollars a head, a head,
That's a-lot of take-home bread.
At night we'll sing our lament,
This cowboy life it is a strife.

Dusty old trials are long and hard.
Sour-dough biscuits are made with lard.
Beans cooking in the iron pot.
Keeping them down is a battle hard fought.

Sleeping under the stars is for the birds,
And farting sounds of cattle-men is heard,
And cowboys' moan and groan about,
This cowboy life it is a strife.

Saddle-sore blisters grow from day one.
The cattle boss asks are we having fun?
Chocking down dust is a regular meal,
And working for a dollar a day is a deal.

Snakes under foot and critters in the beans.
Without a bath in weeks, no-one is clean.
Long-johns stand on their own two legs.
This cowboy life it is a strife.

(The melody of the song continues, sounds of cows and horses build, the stage
lights dim, the curtain closes, house lights come up)

THE END OF ACT ONE

ACT TWO
The house lights dim, the only light being emitted is that of the fire on centre
stage. Cow and horse sounds fade. The stage lights come up on the characters
around the camp fire. The melody of the song 'Forsake Me Not' begins to
build.

Musicians:
(build music)

FORSAKE ME NOT

I am lonely as tumbling tumble weeds.
On lonely trails rustlers I heed.
I sing to soothe the cattle so wild.

And I dream of memories of my child.

Lonely nights in the saddle mile after mile.
I can't seem to recall your dimpled smile.
If I could write a letter, I would entrust.
Delivery to you on forsaken winds of dust.

By our campfire skyward I stare.
To angels I tell a tale of woe I share.
Of ruthless rustlers and cattle so lost.
Your picture, I hold, they did accost.

Forsake me not, oh my love this harm.
To never return to your loving arms.
To my children give a loving touch in lieu.
Forsake me not if I bid adieu.

Lead burns deep into my flesh.
Still, onward a hundred miles we thresh.
With cold winter storms the mountain pass may close.
A season may pass to find our bodies froze.

In defeat to the night I softly sing.
As if near my children I still cling.
Angels on high oh please hear my cry.
Bring to my love, my sad goodbye.

I no longer feel the burning pain.
Our campfire is doused by pelting rain.
Eyes search for loved ones I no longer weep.
Angels carry me home while I sleep.

Cook:
(pickup dialogue and feel of the moment form your last entry, walk to the fire and place a big pot on the fire) You guys do not know what good food is. You don't care that I am up hours before the sun thinks about getting up, just so that I can have a good breakfast waiting for your sorry, tired old bones. You don't deserve my good cooking. (mumble on)

Cheeks:
(lean over the fire pit and look into the pot that Cook had just placed there, sniff then make a face)

All:

94

(everyone lean closer in wonderment of what could be stewing in the pot)

Cheeks:(fall into poem)

WEEK OLD SOUP

"Hey, Cook what's a-simmering in your pot?"
"Something mighty special, enough for you lot.
When you taste this, it will hit the spot.
Now don't touch that, the handle is hot."

Sour Dough backed quickly before he received a swat.
One more inch and Sour Dough would have got shot.
Just-the-Cook was a mean tempered French-Scott.
When Just-the-Cook is cooking don't touch the pot.

Just-the-Cook looked like any other cattle man.
At forty yards shoot the label off a tomato can.
He'd always say, 'The road to good health is plenty of bran.'
Rumours where he learned cooking in a place called Japan.

I don't rightly recall what is his real name,
but he is renown, with world wide fame,
a genius at making a hearty meal out of any old wild game.
If you ever get sick, take my word, him you better not blame.

Just-the-Cook is might sensitive, he just loves favouritism.
He say's, 'Food should be devoured with candle light romanticism.
Close your eyes and let its taste remove any scepticism.'
No matter how fast a draw you are, don't offer criticism.

I know, for I was once warned not to speak my mind.
The boys all said, 'Cheeks-Too-Soft say something kind.'
When them words left my lips, I knew I was in a bind.
I felt rock salt from Cook's twelve gage hit my behind.

It was not that I didn't enjoy trail side gourmet cooking,
but swimming in my tin plate were critters, I ain`t joking.
Mexican jumping beans with legs grabbed whiskers with their hooks.
Like a wild bronking horse I bucked and shook and shook and shook.

Cowboy profanity profusely rambled freely from my lips.
Just-the-Cook took exception to my literary verbal quips.
With lightning speed sprang up the shotgun from Cook's hip.

Stinging rock salt tingled the flesh of my butt as away I did skip.

Now when Cook asks, I quickly recite, 'Mighty fine.
There is no greater honour then to sit here and dine.
With campfire light, cowboy chatter and day-old cactus wine.'
Word spread quickly that Mr. Cheeks-Too-Soft has no spine.

Many a cowboy has wondered what kind of special ingredient,
Just the Cook adds to his daily soup to make eyes glow radiant,
or wonder what Cook is picking on the plains that are so nutrient.
No one will ever say to his face, 'That Just-the-Cook is deviant.'

Sitting around the campfire late at night we all contemplate,
if it is snake or worms or grasshoppers into the soup he grates.
Cowboys ain't scholars, some stutter but all join in on the debate,
and wonder if we are long for this earth or is it boot hill our fate?

Then one day the trail Boss said his son was a-joining the cattle drive.
We all thought the new Tender Foot was one we should want to deprive,
of ingredient knowledge of Just-the-Cook's cooking and see if he survives,
and if he asks what's in the pot, if no gun shots then Tender Foot's alive.

"Go on Tender Foot ask the cook what he puts in his soup?"
Us cowboys hid behind a sage bush in a tight little group,
like a bunch of old clucking hens afraid to come out of the chicken coup.
Tender Foot marched right up to Just-the-Cook, a typical nincompoop.

"I was wondering," said Tender Foot. "What makes your soup so delicious?"
We all cringed knowing that Just-the-Cook could become quite vicious.
Now what I am truly about to relate is not anywhere near friction-us.
A few more mumbled syllables then Tender Foot said, "It is nutritious."

Surely shotgun rock salt would be flying, but Cook stood there with a smile.
He sucked in his belly, brushed back his beard, for a cook he looked virile.
Cook seemed somewhat proud, almost pleased, no sign of being hostile.
"Sit down Tender Foot, let Cook explain culinary delights for awhile."

Tender Foot sat on a block of wood and held out a dented tin cup.
Cook grinned and poured black coffee for the kid, an innocent pup.
Cook rambled out tales of cooking for royalty. Tender Foot said, 'Yup.'.
Those stories were so good we decided to join them, from hiding we got up.

Just like little cowboys at bedtime we hung onto every word said.
A few tales were so heart felt that a few of us had tears to shed.

Just the Cook told us of a fellow who swallowed a goat's eye then dropped dead.
A lady that gave up wayward ways because of his cooking, him she wanted to wed.

Long into the night Just-the-Cook lamented, cattle were being lulled to sleep.
Sour sighed delightfully. We all felt that Just-the-Cook was not an old creep.
Tender Foot asked, "How do you make your soup." Silence, no one made a peep.
We held our breath, did Tender Foot make a mistake, we were ready to leap.

Cook scratched a critter out of his beard then proceeded to rub his nose on a sleeve.
"Well," Cook grumbled. "Plenty of experience is needed before one can happily achieve,
a great taste, smiles of satisfaction, applause and money you guys never leave,
but a great gourmet cook should always say, I am great, in myself I do believe."

"Then you get yourself a great big thick-walled cast-iron pot three feet round.
Build a good hardwood fire, use buffalo chips, there's plenty on the ground.
Use water, preferably swamp water, it has a bit of an edge, best I've found.
You need meat, so-what if it has been chewed up by a hungry blood hound."

"Throw in some wild root, wild rice, some noodles I picked up in Japan.
Keep the campfire going, we need really hot coals, use your hat as a fan.
Chop up rattle snake, pinewood grubs, Cheyenne pepper then fry it up in a pan.
Just keep cooking, add what-ever's at hand, there's no need to have a recipe plan."

"Every day just add something new, never ever let the pot go dry.
Add what-ever is left over from last month, any day that's gone by.
If need be wash out the coffee pot and tin plates in the soup, I need not lie.
It adds taste, you guys lack a sense of good taste, you'd rather see beans fry."

At about that moment there weren't a cowboy around to hear them words.
Every Tom, Dick and Harry scattered wilder then a stampeding cow herd.
I tell you the chirps us cowboys made weren't the sweet sounds of southern song birds.
To die of thirst or trampled by steers or snake bite us cowboys would have preferred.

Now I wouldn't say Just-the-Cook was a-trying to put every cowboy in Boot Hill,
but everyone came to the conclusion, that there was poison a-brewing in his swill.
Tender Foot said he was too young to have growing on his grave a bunch of daffodils.
"Tom, Dick and Harry you hold Just-the-Cook down, that pot of soup we need to spill."

Just as Cook's twelve gage hammers clicked up stepped the cattle Boss.
"Boys let the cook go, Cook, your speciality of pot soup will be your loss,
but after six weeks of your soup I'm filled to the brim, your soup we must toss.
I'm laying down camp law, don't cook anything that tastes like swamp moss."

For awhile things cooled down, I wouldn't say the cook was being mean.
Of his cooking, we all found tolerable, the flavour and substance a bit lean.
Around the campfire on cool evening nights our antics created quite a scene,
if you can imagine forty cowboys after digesting fired up beans, beans, beans!

Cook:
(step closer to the fire with a frying pan) Anyone want more beans, I've got plenty, enough for you lot.

All:
No thanks Cook, we've had our fill, full, stuffed, can't eat another bite, best beans we've ever had.

Cook:
You lowdown cowboys wouldn't know what good food is. If it ain't burnt and greasy, you finicky critters won't eat it. (stir beans and head away and mumble)

Cowgirl:
That was close. Boss, was that a true story about Cook?

Cheeks:
Well, Cook does get carried away with his soup.

(the sound of a horn sounding in the distance echos, a haunting sound)

Cowboy:
What was that, did you hear that sound? A bugle?

Cowboy:
That is tin Horn Jack.

Cowgirl:
Who is Tin Horn Jack? I haven't seen anyone following us.

Cowboy:
You won't, he's dead, a ghost, a spirit that haunts lonesome cowboys.

Cowgirl:
(reach for pistol in your holster, itching to draw) He'd had better not sneak up
on me, I'll fill him full of lead.

(the sound of the horn mixes with the sound of cattle)

Cheeks:(fall into poem)

LONELY IS THE HEART

I will tell you this story from the start,
a tale of one's lonely broken heart.

The winter of eighteen-sixty to be exact.
Each detail related is God's honest fact.

Where should I start, the beginning is best.
Jack built a log cabin up in the north-west.

Ilene, Jack's true love was back east waiting with patience.
She figured this waiting around in the city was a hindrance.

After all they were married, the calendar had six months marked.
It was the lonely absence of Jack, surely a debate was sparked.

'Stay home,' pleaded Ilene's folks, 'wait until spring.'
It was now that Ilene wanted to go, she twisted her ring.

There was no convincing a head strong girl in love.
No guidance came when the folks prayed to God above.

Off Ilene was by stage, dog sled and a few miles by canoe.
One last hill, Ilene was getting use to her big snowshoes.

As nightfall fell a candle flickered from Jack's cabin door.

What would her true love think of the clothes she wore.

In Jack's eyes a sight to behold, her face radiant, all aglow.
Together in each other's arms as the snow fell, I do know.

I was trapping oh about four miles up from Tin Horn Jack,
a nick name because of a musical horn hung on a moose rack.

When the wind was cold and haunting there came a strange sound.
Across the lake, I could hear its echo, echoing for miles around.

Before the heavy snows fell, I passed by the cabin from up on a ridge.
A happy couple doing chores, I never crossed over their river bridge.

I felt I would be intruding, interrupting the newly weds.
I sure felt hungry when smelling her fresh baked breads.

With night falling and the northern lights fading I made tracks.
I pushed on homeward as dark snow clouds followed my back.

Without my dogs a howling I would never have made it home.
Their sounds guided me in and for six days we did not roam.

With snow drifted to the door's header we had to dig ourselves out.
The landscape had changed, no sign of earth anywhere close about.

'Well dogs,' I said as I tried to figure out where I left the woodpile.
Cutting exposed branches from the trees should last for a long while.

Sure, the clouds cleared for a day or two then the cold winds came.
Tin Horn Jack's horn began to play, I lost sleep, him I would blame.

I acquired a strange feeling when the horn would not stop its plea.
Dreaming abstractly in hallucination, Jack was somehow calling me.

Through the night my malamutes strained to pull my sled.
Jack's cabin looked cold, to find the worst I would dread.

The wind stopped, a silent hush, the horn no longer screamed.
Almost tranquil, the snow untouched around the cabin it seemed.

I knocked lightly on the door, no answer as I slowly stepped in.
Life's emptiness filled the abode, a devil would create this sin.

Slowly on bended Knee Ilene rocked in front of a log-less fire.
Almost lifeless beyond the cold's shiver her eyes ready to expire.

Her shoulder ice cold to my touch, she turned, our eyes met.
A dry voice said, 'Jack you are here.' My eyes began to wet.

Tin Horn Jack was nowhere about, Ilene hugged my hand so tight,
as cold as ice and bitter cold to the touch, like a hungry dog's bite.

Quickly a fire I built to thaw the reaper's hold on Ilene's soul.
Slowly by hour the cold vanished, her life from the devil I stole.

In Ilene's eyes, I was no other than Tin Horn Jack, her love so true.
But where was Jack, I began to search relentlessly, no useful clue.

Up in the north-west is a land of change, a land of misfortunes.
Snows came and went, never again did the tin horn blow a tune.

Thirty years passed and willingly I assumed the life of Tin Horn Jack.
Ilene did forget that winter and never mentioned the mound out back.

Ilene passed away this past spring, I recall her last whispered words of
reflection.
She said, 'I've always loved you Tin Horn Jack, you are a man of my
affection.'

When the winter thawed in the spring of eighteen-sixty and one,
I found Tin Horn Jack frozen beneath a tree, hands gripping a gun.

Frozen to death hunting for the food of life he never attained.
Ilene planted flowers on the turned earth mound, still retained.

Today they lay side by side, Ilene loved Jack so and somehow her he.
To Ilene I was Tin Horn Jack, no questions asked, was it meant to be?

Alone I now rock on a chair of oak on a cabin porch at night,
dreaming of a love so true, love as pure as these northern lights.

To our grandchildren, I tell a story from the start,
a tale of my life and Ilene the love in my heart.

As I grow older, I wonder when I head to heaven's gate,
will Ilene be arm in arm with Jack, will I be too late?

On this porch, I tell a story of my lonely broken heart,
a story of losing my true love, a tale told from the start.

(the horn sounds a long haunting blow that blends in with the moo of a calling steer, all of the cowboys stare out into the audience until members of the audience turn to see if anything in there)

Cowboy:
Is . . . is . . . is that Tin Horn . . . horn . . . Jack?

Cowgirl:
Of course, it ain't mama's boy. (keep a tight grip on your pistol)

Cowboy:
(place another log onto the fire) A bit chilly to night.

Cowboy:
We started out with a native fire, small and stay close for warmth. Now we have a white-man's fire, big and stay far way to keep cool. The bottoms of my boots are drying up and curling from the heat.

Cowboy:
(take hat off and mop forehead with bandanna) Boss, when are we going to take a herd into warmer climates?

Cheeks: When this drive is over, we will be heading down south of the Canadian border.

Cowboy:
(begin to sing) Where the deer and the antelope roam. Home, home on the range. (sing off key)

All:
Bad, terrible, where did you take singing lessons, any more of that and the cattle will stampede.

Cheeks:
We will be heading into Slim Jim Sarn's territory. Stuttering Slim Jim Sarns. (fall into poem)

BALLAD OF STUTTERING SLIM JIM SARNS

I had been on the snake bite trail for days on end,
just me and four horses, a dog and an old friend.

Jim stuttered bad, each sentence started with but.
I figured his tongue was stuck in a wagon rut.

Eventually he said what he had to say, darn if I could figure the story out.
Then he began to shout, something about being a scout suffering the gout.

Now he may need a doctor but there was no way I was a gonna turn about.
"But, But, But," Slim Jim shouted with restrain. "This land is a drought."

I reckoned we was riding for three days under a scorching sun,
taking Jim near on seventy-two hours to get them words undone.

For a man that stutters bad, simple communication is a frustration.
When Slim Jim began singing, diction of words was a salvation.

I remember a time in ole Cheyenne and a high noon gun fight.
Jim was a-trying to tell the sheriff to head to the main street site.

Darn if Jim didn't start singing to the tune of 'Mary had a Little Lamb'.
Slim changed the words to suit the situation, the Sheriff said, 'Damn.'

Town folk began gathering around, not the gun fight but around Slim Jim.
"Mighty fine singing strange." Stuttering Jim decided to go out on a limb.

It didn't matter if it was a sad or happy song or a spiritual hymn,
Jim added fancy yodelling, thus generating a nick-name for him.

From then on folks began calling him yodelling Jim Sarns,
though not to be confused with old man Yodel Jim Barns.

Jim was tall and skinny, and became Yodeling Slim Jim Sarns.
Plenty of Folks around to ask, so don't think this is just a yarn.

Now come to think of it, I cannot recall the gun fight's outcome.
One guy was Billy, just some kid, the other Rango, Billy's chum.

That was just about the time I met up with Stuttering Slim Jim.
For a partner on the trail, I asked for his company on a whim.

I figured with him a singing, I wouldn't have to do all that much talking.
If complaining about my cooking, well his singing would be fine balking.

Once he found his voice, Yodelling Slim Jim never seemed to stop yapping.
He would rattle on for hours singing, I showed my appreciation by clapping.

The funny thing was, I recognized all of those fine old western tunes.
Words were slightly different, whatever he was thinking he'd croon.

Never interrupt Slim when he's a singing, I once made that grave mistake.
I thought he asked a question, I answered, he stopped and began to shake.

He just stopped singing for hours, stuttering his complaints, he was sore.
I was disappointed for I had become fond of his renditions of folklore.

"But, but, but, but, but." I reckoned that his words were stuck in a big deep rut.
In-between buts, Slim used profanity quite well, I figured that he called me a nut.

I pleaded for forgiveness between buts, in unison the pack horses tried to apologize.
Suddenly Jim slid off his horse and wandered into the sage brush, I began to theorize.

To be civilize one must not antagonize, one must surmise to compromise,
refrain from interrupting an artist's tune, for you, he may want to vulgarize.

The sun was setting on the horizon while Jim was wandering through the brush.
Tumbling tumble weeds tumbled on by and the air suddenly had a queer hush.

Slim Jim was way off yonder, I could no longer hear him stutter and cuss.
We were all in agreement, me, horses and dog that Jim was making a fuss.

We was on the trail for near on four or five days and I made only one mistake.
Who would figure that interrupting the singing would cause Jim a headache?

Observation is a big part of preservation of man's life in the wide-open spaces.
Villains, vultures, one could die of a lingering thirst leaving no tangible traces.

The pony express was a hundred or so miles north of the bad land's locale,
and ain't no way to send a letter to kinfolk, no messenger pigeon to corral.

The sun was setting, and I was getting worried about Slim Jim wandering off.
It was getting late to make camp, I planned to cook his favourite, stroganoff.

Putting on my specs, I only use them when I need to see something important.
This was the time to observe any of Jim's peculiar irregularities of movement.

There behind a weather-beaten sage brush next to a dried-out cactus,
and what I am about to say is the truth and is truly real and factious.

Slim removed suspenders and gun belt and mooned the desert critters.
Some men have their morals when nature calls and Jim was no exhibitor.

Maybe he was a little constipated from eating my gourmet cooking.
I organized camp, Jim did not need an audience to keep a looking.

A fire crackled and the setting sun set the horizon a blaze in an orange hue.
Wojo the dog yawned, the horses neighed, I commenced stirring the stew.

Hours later from way out yonder came Jim with a hoot and a bellow.
I sensed some kind of pain in his voice, I felt sympathy for this fellow.

Why? I had no idea, Slim was jumping and hollering, his britches hanging down.
He looked like a clown, he rolled on the ground, his face had a gruesome frown.

"But, but, but, but, but what? You have a cut, you hate my mutt?"
"Gut, you hurt your gut, butt, butt, butt, bite your Lilly white butt?"

Well, I looked at dog, he looked at me, the horses turned away from us three.
Cowboys have a code of honour to oblige when a friend calls, but why me?

We could have been there all-night a-trying to make sense out of stuttering Slim Jim.
For without a clear understanding of what he was saying, I wasn't a-gonna bite him.

"Sing it Slim, sing it out loud and clear, give me just the facts."
Jim yodelled that it was snake bit poison he needed to extract.

Well, I looked at dog, dog wandered off, Slim looked hopelessly towards me.
Jim got down on bended knee and to the tune of Amazing Grace began to plea.

"But, but, its your butt," now I began to stutter uncharacteristically.
Thinking I mumbled, "I am allergic to snake bite," said hypercritically.

There is a code of the west all cowboys do abide by from time to time,
and I am never one to take an oath or pledge to a lodge, it is no crime.

So, shoot me for leaving Slim Jim with a bite on his butt from a snake.
On his next birthday, if it comes, I will bake him a butter biscuit cake.

Ah heck, Jim's butt was swollen for a week, it was a little wee baby snake bite.
Not even one rattle, Jim rode side saddle, but this snake bite gave him a fright.

From that day forward ole Slim stuttered twice as bad, and as jumpy as all get out.
Every once in awhile when nature's call is necessary, into the brush he would shout.

Jim is a bit bashful and reluctant to give up his privacy behind the sage.
I guess battling a snake ain't worth betting the outcome of a yearly wage.

Over time Jim won a few hands and lost a few to the side winders.
He became immune to snake bite, but once in awhile got a reminder.

Slim Jim's singing is sweeter than ever on the trail, to Jim just wave.
Do not stop to talk if you're not needing some precious time to save.

It has been near on ten years riding the trails for days on end.
Just me, four horses, a dog and Slim Jim Sarns, my old friend.

Cowboy:
(slowly get up and begin to move saddle and bed roll looking for snakes and other unwanted critters)

Cook:
(run around camp in a slow-motion stomping at something, pick up the critter and secretly put it into your cook pot)

Cowgirl:
If it weren't for us women, you big bad cowboys would be cowering behind your mother's apron stings.

Cowboy:
I ain't no mama's boy.

Cowgirl:
There, there, a spider on your boot. (point to a boot)

Cowboy:
(jump up shaking your boot as you dance around the camp)

106

All:
(all cower away from the frantic cowboy, twitch as if there might be something falling onto you)

(from the background in a far distance a sound of a cry, almost human, echos across the distance, all become still as if the hairs on the backs of their necks are standing up on end, again the sound of a loon echoes)

Cowgirl:
What is that?

Cowboy:
A baby.

Cowboy:
A calf calling for its mother.

Cowboy:
A baby, that's a baby's cry.

Cheeks:
That is the call of a lost sole, a lonesome call. (fall into poem)

LONESOME CALL

Erringly haunting, sounds a wild loon's call.
An abandoned child lost gives a forsaken bawl.
Men, brave, fearless have mistakenly sought.
To a mother's bosom a wee child is brought.

A sky hidden, a tree at every turn, so dense.
A call from which direction, nerves intense.
As scattered as rain drops on shifting sands.
Lakes dot abundantly on these northern lands.

Native folk lore recites this sacred tale.
In a mother's heart a piercing cry impales.
Wed-less, shame, distraught, arrives a newborn child.
Wrapped in comfort on soft moss, a cry in the wild.

Clear heavenly skies illuminate with northern lights.
Echoed cries of hunger, painful tears, a child's plight.
From valley to ridge to valley and beyond still waters,
a cry, whine, whimper, silence of a sleeping daughter.

Elders of a long-house sit gazing on in silence.
A child's mother cowers, eyes wet with grievance.
In battle a worrier fell, his brave soul taken.
Of lost love in a dream she does not waken.

Outstretched hands had offered a promise to wed.
A Warrior rests on burial grounds, tears are shed.
Words unspoken, a new life growing within.
Chastity lost, without marriage she carries a sin.

Crimson runs a stream flowing by a village.
Born this day a brave and maiden's lineage.
Returning to the long-house she arrives alone.
Mistaking a natural loss for a child all moan.

A baby's body and soul they must prepare.
A loss of one's self is a burden to openly bare.
She cries in shame for a child she abandoned.
A child born out of wedlock left in the hinterland.

Rain falls heavily on silken green moss,
upon an unwanted trinket one would toss.
A child lays waiting, hoping to be retrieved.
Silence in the night, only creatures to bereave.

A lone wolverine sniffs the air with glee.
A baby is only sleeping, unable to flee.
Tiny birds of a feather shrill out a call,
a warning, squirrels bark hoping to stall.

A thundering flapping of wings come forth.
Of two mates, as majestic as the wild north.
Silent was once a northern loon's mute voice.
Created by their maker, a reason of choice.

A strange being lays by their nest on shore,
not to be a meal for a vicious carnivore.
With survival instincts, they attack with bravery.
Repelled to flee retreated a creature so unsavoury.

Hours turn to days, a baby's cry began to weaken.
With a remorseful cry in the night a mother wakens.
People of the village have searched in agonizing vain.
Through advancing years surely heartache will wane.

All of earth's creatures are blessed with a soul,
mouse, deer, loon, squirrel, down to a small mole.
To warm and care for this infant is their quest.
Helplessly they watch, all gather around a nest.

Man, questions nature's need to be so cruel.
What comes to pass is Mother Nature's rule.
A last faint sigh, a child sleeps for ever more.
Thus, the beginning of this native folklore.

With respect the silent loons begin to cover with moss.
Bit by bit until hidden from sight they bury one's loss.
Humans endlessly search the land of lakes.
For lost ones, never to be found a heart aches.

Suddenly a faint cry is heard from the nest.
All creatures gather and heard, they will attest,
human cries from a young loon, a whimper, a whine.
The spirt of the child's cry crossed over, it was a sign.

For centuries, the loon was mute, this was its fate.
For reasons unknown, a cry was given to its fate.
On lakes of the north haunting cries are heard.
A haunting human voice crying out take my word.

Old and grey is the native mother now.
Her tragic story recited at a pow-wow.
There is a cry in the distance across a lake,
of an echoing cry of a child heard, not a fake.

At dawn or dusk she searches the northern woods.
At every mossy mound over the years she has stood,
recalling if this is the place her child lay,
'not this spot' the Great Horned owl will say.

If you ever hear a cry coming from places afar,
and think a human cry heard in woods is bizarre,
it is a loon with the spirt of someone's loss,
a native, a boy, a girl, a baby laying in moss.

A long echoing cry will chill you to the bone.
Look around every similar tree, you are alone.
Every sound is louder, lost here you wish not to die.
From across the fog covered lake you will hear a cry.

Erringly haunting, sounds a wild loon's call.
Imitating a lost child crying, a forsaken bawl.
A spirt lays, waiting, hoping to be retrieved.
Silence in the night, only loons to bereave.

Cowgirl:
(man like, take out your hanky and sniffle into it then loudly blow your nose)

Cowboys:
(each in turn stare at the cowgirl then at each other then begin to sniffle and blow your noses into hankies, bandanas and sleeves)

Cowgirl:
What? You sissies, I have a cold coming on, it is the weather, the dampness. What?

Cowboys:
(nod heads as you all continue to sniffle)

Cheeks:
(take a small hanky and dab at your eyes)

(the sound of the loon echoes in the distance)

All:
(in unison, all begin to blow noses and sniffle, wipe eyes, then begin to take it to an exaggeration)

Cook:
(enter from the shadows) What's all the sniffling about?

Cowboy:
Ah . . . the Boss told us a story about the cry of the loon.

Cook:
Oh that story. (turn to walk away, pull out a hanky, blow and sniffle as you head away)

Cowgirl:
Just as I thought, nothing but sniffling mama's boys. Who on earth would marry any one of you?

Cheek:

There is always someone for everyone, even you young Miss. There is a cowboy out there for you. You just have to meet someone, just like Slim Pickings. (fall into poem)

SLIM PICKINGS

Samuel Pickenpaw, Slim Pickings, him we did call.
He was always hungry, skinny and just plain tall.
Eat three helpings, ask for more in a cowboy drawl.

Fellow farmers thought he was a good old sport.
Many a pa shook a head when Slim asked to court,
daughters who turned him down, he was an odd sort.

Just cooking all day for Slim is not a good life.
Single girls stated that cooking in heat is a strife.
We all kidded Slim for bad luck in finding a wife.

Slim was getting up in age, almost pushing twenty.
He wished for a farm, cattle and youngins aplenty.
Growing old alone, Pickenpaw felt was a certainty.

There was homestead land in the Red River valley.
We all urged Slim to go, do not sit and dilly dally.
"You may find a wife out there," said sister Sally.

No more was Slim going to feel like a circus clown.
From his face, Slim wiped away a wrinkled frown.
There's girls in the big city, Slim headed to hog town.

Slim packed up bags and headed south to big town Toronto.
A wagon train was leaving soon, a wife he needed pronto.
Whether she be homely, he needed a magician to say presto.

"Slim, just slim pickings," Slim said to himself.
Alone on a bench, Slim sat like a book on a shelf.
Such low esteem made Slim feel as small as an elf.

"It is nice to meet you sir, is it Mr. Slim Pickings?"
A voice so sweet tickled Slim just like the dickens.
Greeting her sweet smile, Slim heard bells ringing.

Good teeth, big bones, deep blue eyes and a bit of a rump,
almost an old maid at eighteen, this luck he would not dump.

Long days on a wagon seat, she would need a padded rump.

'With pickings slim, you get what you get,' pa always said.
'If a woman can keep you warm on cold nights and well fed,
my boy, waste no time for that kind of girl you had best wed.'

This rosy cheeked dumpling of a girl to Slim spoke.
"You are famished, weak, skinny and ready to croak.
I will fix you a meal, fill you up, come meet my folks."

After Slim and Dumpling wed, their honeymoon did start.
With families on a pioneer wagon train ready to depart.
The Pickenpaws were a lovely couple on a Red River Cart.

Slim doted on Dumpling endlessly that long first week.
Heating warm water for her soft features, Slim did seek.
He boasted, "Nothing too good for Dumpling my sweet."

Third week out, Slim rested, fiddle his fiddle for awhile.
Dumpling cooked, hauled water, fire wood she did pile.
Dishes were washed, warm rocks in bed, Slim felt virile.

Slim and Dumpling watched the setting sun, who could ask for more,
maybe a small home in Red River Valley, something nice to adore,
and maybe a youngin running around, feeding him would be a chore.

By the end of the month Slim and Dumpling's honeymoon was over.
No more days for young love birds to lounge in the fields of clover.
Slim was a married man, Dumpling put an end to him being a rover.

Rain poured down heavily, Ox carts raced to beat a flood.
Low and behold, Slim's cart got stuck in the river's mud.
"Time for team work," hollered Slim to oxen chewing cud.

Slim pulled hard on the leads, the leather stretched the oxen's snout.
Over pelting rain, the oxen's bleated, the heavens heard Slim's shout.
"Push a bit harder my sweet precious Dumpling, we are almost out."

From the shores of the flooded river all of the pioneers lent a hand.
No longer was Dumpling a city folk, with the best she would stand.
The cart pulled free but not Dumpling, "I'm stuck," was her demand.

On rolling plains of golden grass, the Red River Valley came into view.
A year of long hard miles were left behind, every man and woman knew.

People grew old, youngins were born, by unmarked trails rested a few.

Slim Pickings sat proud in his cart while cradling a first born.
Dumpling was expecting again, the hard trail she did not morn.
"This is our home Slim," Dumpling said. "Now go plant corn."

With winter coming, Slim and Dumpling built their first sod hut.
Come each spring there would be another youngin proudly to strut.
Each fall Slim added a room, even a hut for the four-legged mutt.

With kids working the farm, Mr. and Mrs. watched from the porch.
Slim touched callused aging hands, in his heart burns a loving torch.
"Without a woman to love me, my life would have been scorched."

"If it weren't for women like me, there would be no one well fed.
If women weren't helping with plowing, there would be no homestead.
Need I mention the youngins, and not to mention who warms your bed."

"My dear, I don't know why you put up with an old Piccadilly."
Dumpling patted his hand, "After all our memories don't be silly.
If you and I were not sitting hear we would not enjoy our family."

No, Slim never had, slim pickings

Cowgirl:
I ain't gonna be cooking and cleaning, having youngins' and doing all of the farm work for some no good lazy good for nothing layabout loaf who doesn't appreciate a good woman when he sees one. (grumble on) Ask for my hand in marriage.

Cowboys:
(pause, then all say at the same time with a bite of sarcasm) No one has asked you.

Cook:
(stumble into the light with arms full of plates and cups) Whose turn is it the clean these dishes?

Cowboys:
(all look at each other and slowly shake heads no then point accusing fingers at the cowgirl)

Cowgirls:

Tarnation! Even out here in the vastness of the west a woman's work is never done. Okay Cook, I'll do my chore. (sit there as Cook deposits the plates and cups in your lap)

Cowboy:
If women are all going to be like you, why should a cowboy bother.

Cowboy:
It is hard enough just trying to find a girl to court. It ain't easy, there is a lack of feminine type women in the west.

Cowgirl:
What? You saying that I ain't feminine?

Cowboy:
We think of you as one of the fellas.

Cook:
Mr. Cheeks thought that finding a woman to hitch up with was a problem, until one day he was inspired.

Cowboy:
What did you do boss?

Cheeks:
Finding a true love is hard to find, but don't let my story discourage you form searching for your own true love. (fall into the poem)

MAIL ORDER BRIDE

I was talking one day to the holy guy above,
about that day in May when I met my true love.
It was about this time I was mending my ways,
rejecting saloons and boudoirs where I would stay.

Abstaining from my fill of whisky straight,
rather those hangovers that I truly did hate.
After a night of gambling and dance hall girls,
a cowboy's mighty fist sent me flying in a whirl.

I sailed through the air, my head landing with a thud.
I sniffed an aromatic smell, dung not a pillow of mud.
I lay there contemplating an existence in this universe.
A stranger dressed in black said, "You need a hearse?"

114

You could say I saw the glow of hallelujah angels in the night.
It dawned on me I was laying in mud in morning's first light.
Whatever the reason I swore off liquor for the rest of my life.
That's about the time I became free of a drunkard's strife.

I stood tall as possible with my boots stuck in the muddy street.
Ladies of morals walked quickly by, me they would not greet.
For new clothes, a bath, a hair cut and shave, six bits was lacking.
Many nights were spent in a town jail, the walls needed shellacking.

"Not here to be incarcerated sheriff, I'm seeking meagre employment.
I'll polish the bars, paint the walls, mend curtains for your enjoyment."
He was apprehensive but I truly promised to be a new upstanding citizen.
With an oath on mother's grave, I swore never to be an inmate in this prison.

Quickly passing saloon doors a whiff of liquor filled the air, I hesitated.
'No,' I said, a hot bath is required, to Harry Woo's steam baths I gravitated.
Near on three years since I last soaked old bones, I requested a two-bit bath.
"Well Harry Woo, I have changed my ways, I'm heading along a new path."

"Where you go, what you do, you no cook?' Woo babbled, "You need a girl mate."
Soaking in that tub of hot water I did contemplate, what I first needed was a date.
"Take too long, too much work." Harry Woo pointed to an add in the daily news.
Lose your blues, a slightly used mail order bride, no guarantee, you can't lose.

Well to my arousal the idea was just dandy for alone one should not sleep.
A pick of a blonde, brunette or red head from back east did not come cheap.
With a thought of a mail order wife occupying my mind I now had a real-life goal.
Old man Barns offered a job, buck-board, a nag, and a winter fixing fence poles.

Winters can be mighty long and cold out on the Ontario Manitoba boarder.
Every night by campfire light I read that add and wished to place an order.
With the cold north wind blowing I hugged my Hudson Bay blanket a bit.
I'd try to cuddle up to Buttermilk the old mare, she thought I was a twit.
Not much body warmth from four spindly legs, not much to hug.
After moving from leg to lanky leg she stomped on me like a bug.
In dreams, I dreamt of a blonde, brunette and red headed vison of beauty.
I had six months to come up with one hundred bucks, this was my duty.

Springtime finally arrived, I was no worse for ware thanks to my old mare.
I taught her to lay down to keep me from freezing, warmth I would share.
I did not mind her big lips or even her tongue licking me behind the ear.
Several times she'd roll over me and wouldn't move until I called her dear.

We came out of the dry gulch rolling hills a pitiful sight in the early spring.
Old man Barns felt sorry, he gave me Buttermilk, pay and extra for a ring.
Though I smelled bad a bath could wait, I high tailed it to the telegraph office.
I placed my order for the only girl left, a plump dance hall girl from Memphis.

I ain't much for dancing, maybe a slow waltz, they did say she was a red head.
Whispered word spread quickly that my bride was bringing a four-poster bed.
On a little plot of cleared land outside of town a small cabin I began to build.
'Ain't big enough the fellows all said.' At beds and buildings, they were skilled.

Well not to get in the way I sat back and watched as the cabin became a house, with an entrance, parlour, social room with a piano, all for me and my spouse.
There on the boardwalk in front of the stage office I waited in my Sunday best.
By noon time a crowd gathered, mostly fellow men all waiting to be impressed.

There she was a vision of beauty, fifty mouths fell open, a lilac smell filled the air.
What a sight, the mayor declared a holiday, with all this attention did I have a prayer?
Did I mention the main street parade, eight men carried the bed on their shoulders?
She rode like a queen on a down filled throne, I hung to a post like a discarded bolder.

That night it was a gay affair, music, men dancing with men and my soon-to-be wife.
She was supposed to be my wife, but the preacher was a bit late, another fate in my life.
At about twelve o'clock my Memphis bell shocked all and happily gave a rousing speech.
I quote, 'There are too many men that needs a woman and the preacher ain't here to preach.'

Come sun up I found myself with old Buttermilk as cozy as can be snuggling in the hay.

On the cabin door a freshly painted sign said, 'Madame May's.' Men were hooting hurry.
I was told to get in line, me, the man who had ordered a red headed bride to be.
There was no need for the likes of me to want to plea for thee on bended knee.

At about noon after Buttermilk nibbled behind my ear, I decided to hit the trail.
I realized you just can't buy true love or order a bride via the Canadian mail.
In my broken down old buck-board and Buttermilk leading the way,
the sun began to set on the prairie in eighteen-sixty, the month of May.

Oh, I love the smell of spring flowers, the wide-open spaces of the range,
northern lights, skies of blue, freshly fallen snow and no need for change.
I had me a long heartfelt talk with you know who, the holy guy up above,
and thanked him, Buttermilk neighed, for a cowboy's life is my true love.

(sounds of the horses and cattle are heard in the background, all of the cowboys and cowgirl take a deep breath and sigh, one by one the cowboys relax and begin to get settled in for the night, the stage lights dim, the fire light builds as another log is added to the fire, the stars and the moon in the background become brighter)

MUSICIANS:
(slowly the music begins to build, everyone singing and building on the end section of the song)

A COWBOY'S LULLABY

Lonesome nights on forgotten trails.
To you I tell of a cowboy's tale.
Of loved ones left back on the farm.
Angels keep from the devil's harm.

Many rivers we will cross.
A wandering calf will be lost.
A stampeding herd on a moonless night.
Do dare to hide this cowboy's fright.

Saddle up boys it's time to ride.
Find those lost steers that want to hide.
Sing a soothing song, a lullaby.
Move them out the cowboys' cry.

Lonesome times out riding alone.
My heart so sad, the cattle moan.
Your face I see upon the moon.
Forsake me not, coming home soon.

(instrumental music continues as the stage lights dim, slowly the fire light also dwindles, the curtain closes)

THE END

My Beau
Copyright May 1, 1996
by
Edmond Alcid

STAGE:
AN INTERIOR OF A RETIREMENT HOME, ON CENTRE STAGE IS A
ROCKING CHAIR, ONE OTHER ROCKING CHAIR ON STAGE LEFT
WITH A LAMP, A BRIGHT LAYOUT, A SMALL TABLE BESIDE
ROCKING CHAIR, ON AND AROUND FLOOR ARE A SCATTERING
OF MOVIE, GLAMOUR, TRUE ROMANCE MAGAZINES, A FLOWERY
HOOK RUG IN THE FRONT OF ROCKING CHAIR, A RADIO IS ON
THE TABLE, TO THE SIDE IS A CUPBOARD WITH FLOWERS,
KNICKKNACKS AND MEMENTOS, SONYA OCCUPIES THIS AREA,
ON BACK WALL IN MID AIR HANGS A BRIGHT PAINTING OF A
BEACH SCENE.

TO THE OTHER SIDE OF THE STAGE IS AN ARM CHAIR, BIG DEEP
AND CUSHIONED IN EARTH COLOURS, ELIZABETH'S SIDE OF THE
ROOM, EARTH TONE HOOK RUG, PLAIN LAMP BEHIND CHAIR,
BESIDE CHAIR IS A SMALL TABLE WITH A RADIO AND BOOKS
NEATLY STACKED, AGAINST THE WALL IS A BOOKCASE FILLED
WITH BOOKS AND FLOWERS ARRANGED ON AND AROUND THE
BOOKCASE, ON THE BACK WALL HANGING IN MID AIR IS A
PAINTING OF A DARK MOUNTAIN SCENE.

SOUND:
RADIO SOUNDS, BIRD SOUNDS,

LIGHTING:
EARLY MORNING, DAYLIGHT AND NIGHTTIME LIGHTING,
DIFFERENT INTENSITIES TO GIVE THE FEELING OF A DAY
PASSING.

FIRST LEAD: ELIZABETH.
SECOND LEAD: SONYA.
THIRD LEAD: EDMOND.

CHARACTERS:
ELIZABETH, A WOMAN IN HER EIGHTIES, TALLISH, TOM BOYISH
IN HER YOUTH, SHE IS THE YOUNGER SISTER, SHE WAS ALWAYS
THE ONE THAT RECEIVED ALL THE HAD-ME-DOWNS, THE ONE
TO BLOSSOM LAST, THE ONE PICKED ON BUT SHE FOUGHT FOR
EVERYTHING SHE GOT, HER HAIR IS ALL WHITE AND HANGS

FREELY WITH THE SIDES PULLED BACK AND CLIPPED AT THE BACK, SHE WEARS LONG MEN'S PYJAMAS COVERED WITH A PLAID HOUSECOAT, LEATHER SLIPPERS, HER DAILY DRESS IS A TAN TOP AND SLACKS WITH A BAGGY STYLE AND A WOOLLY PULLOVER SWEATER.

SONYA:
A WOMAN IN HER EIGHTIES, THE OLDER SISTER, SLIGHTLY PLUMP AND RAVISHING IN HER YOUTH AND IN HER ADVANCED YEARS, THE GIRL MOST WANTED IN HER YOUTH, THE GIRL THAT WANTED EVERYTHING AND GOT WHAT SHE WANTED AND NOT REALLY CARING WHO SHE HURT ALONG THE WAY, HER HAIR IS SHORT, A PLATINUM BLONDE, HER FACE IS ALWAYS MADE UP, SHE WEARS A MID LENGTH NIGHTGOWN WITH MATCHING LONG COVERING AND FLUFFY SLIPPERS, HER DAILY DRESS IS A DRESSY PANTSUIT AND JEWELRY THAT IS WORN AT ALL TIMES.

EDMOND:
A GENTLEMAN IN HIS EIGHTIES, THE BEAU OF BOTH SISTERS, A TALL SLIM MAN WITH A LOT OF PEP BUT AGE HAS SLOWED HIS MOVEMENTS, AN ATHLETE AND A CHARMER WHEN YOUNG, A LOST SOUL WHEN YOUNG AND IN HIS OLD AGE IS SEARCHING FOR WHAT HE FEELS HE HAS LOST THROUGH THE CARELESSNESS OF HIS YOUTH, HE WEARS BAGGY TAN PANTS AND HIS FAVOURITE HUNTING SHIRT, RED PLAID. HIS HAIR AND BEARD IS SHORT, NEAT AND WHITE.

BASIC STORY LINE:

ELIZABETH AND SONYA SHARE A SENIORS CITIZEN APARTMENT ONLY BECAUSE THEY ARE SISTERS IN BLOOD AND HAVE NO OTHER FAMILY MEMBERS OF THEIR OWN, AS SISTERS THROUGH THEIR LIVES THEY HAVE HATED, LOVED, LOATHED AND CHERISHED EACH OTHER, JUST BECAUSE OF THEIR ADVANCED AGE IS NO EXCUSE TO REHASH THEIR LIVES OVER AND OVER AND THEY MAKE SURE THEY DO FROM THE FIRST THING IN THE MORNING TO THE LAST GOOD NIGHT AT BEDTIME, THE CENTRE OF ALL THEIR CONVERSATIONS REVOLVES AROUND EDMOND, THOUGH HE HAS PASSED ON, HE SEEMS TO BE CONSTANTLY THERE AMONG THEM, INTERTWINED BETWEEN THESE THREE OCTOGENARIANS AS THEY RELIVE THE SAD, HUMOROUS, DISAPPOINTED AND HAPPY MOMENTS IN THEIR LIVES IS A LOVE TRIANGLE.

SET AND PROPS:
ARM CHAIR
TWO ROCKING CHAIRS
CUPBOARD
BOOK SHELF
LAMPS
HOOK RUGS
PAINTINGS
SMALL TABLES
FLOWERS
BOOKS
MAGAZINES
KNICKKNACKS
CARDS MEMENTOS
TWO RADIOS

PART I

STAGE:
THE STAGE IS DARK, ALL ONE SEES IS THE FAINT OUTLINE OF
THE SET, THE SOUNDS OF EARLY MORNING IS HEARD, BIRDS ARE
CHIRPING, A FEW SOUNDS OF POTS CLANKING AND A KETTLE
STEAMING AS THE LIGHTS BUILD TO GIVE THE FEELING OF
EARLY MORNING. ELIZABETH ENTERS CENTRE DRESSED IN HER
MENS' PYJAMAS, PLAID HOUSECOAT AND LEATHER SLIPPERS.
HER HAIR IS NEAT AND PULLED BACK AT THE SIDES AND
CLIPPED AT THE BACK. ELIZABETH MOVES SLOWLY TOWARDS
HER CHAIR AS SHE WORKS OUT AN OLD BASEBALL INJURY IN
HER BACK. TAKING HER SEAT, SHE DOES SEVERAL STRETCHING
EXERCISES.

EDMOND ENTERS AT THE BACK OF THE ROOM BEHIND THE
HANGING PICTURES. HE IS DRESSED IN HIS BAGGY PANTS AND
HIS FAVOURITE PLAID HUNTING SHIRT. EDMOND STOPS AND
WITH BOTH HANDS HELD TOGETHER IN FRONT IS LOOKING
TOWARDS THE FLOOR AS IF DEEP IN THOUGHT.
ELIZABETH TURNS HER RADIO ON, THE SOUNDS OF THE BIRDS
FADE AS THE SOUND OF AN ANNOUNCER IS HEARD ON THE
RADIO.

RADIO ANNOUNCER:
(music fades) It is another fine morning . . . and we at C.F.R.M. 100 on the
F.M. dial bid you a good morning . . . the time is six-thirty with an expected
daily temperature of 20 degrees Celsius . . . For your listening pleasure we

bring to you a golden oldy for those of you that can still remember being young in the good old days.

(a big band begins to play; a crooner begins to sing a love song)

(Edmond nods his head and with a faint smile on his face begins to waltz a few steps)

(Elizabeth forcibly turns off the radio, Edmond looks up wondering where the music has disappeared to)

ELIZABETH:
(talk to radio) I do remember being young . . . and it wasn't the good ole days . . . How old are you? . . . Good old days . . . what are you . . . maybe twenty . . . you have not even lived yet . . . The good old days . . . they were not good . . . (pause) . . . and he was not a great singer either.

(Sonya enters dressed in her nightgown and matching cover and her fluffy slippers, her curly hair is a bit tossed, she is wearing her jewellery, she stops behind her rocking chair)

SONYA:
(sway to the music as if it was still playing) I could dance all night to that kind of music . . . why did you turn if off? (move to rocking chair and sit down and turn dial on the radio) What station was that on? . . . (pause) . . . Elizabeth!

ELIZABETH:
I don't know, Sonya.

SONYA:
You were just listening to it.

ELIZABETH:
I can't remember.

SONYA:
Well look at the radio dial dear.

ELIZABETH:
I don't have my glasses. (turn away)

SONYA:
(turn towards Elizabeth) You don't wear glasses . . . (turn to radio and move dial until the music starts) . . . that's it . . . oh how wonderful . . . he was a great

crooner in his time . . . (lean back dreaming) . . . I remember nights that seemed to go on forever . . . Edmond and I would waltz . . . as if on a cloud.

(Edmond again begins to waltz around, there is a smile on his face)

ELIZABETH:
(turn to radio, a frown on face, turn dials) You and Edmond . . . You and Edmond . . . Edmond and you . . . There was also Ed and I.

(Elizabeth's radio blares out a rock and roll song)

(Edmond stops suddenly and questionably looks at the back of each woman)

SONYA:
Elizabeth, please!

ELIZABETH:
Please what?

SONYA:
Edmond and I loved this music.

ELIZABETH:
Edmond and you. (begin to turn radio volume up)

(Sonya in frustration fluffs up her gown cover then turns the volume up on her radio, at the slight increase in sound Elizabeth turns her radio up. As both gather more anger each turns up their radio twice more. Out of desperation Elizabeth gets up at the same time as Sonya. Elizabeth walks behind her lamp towards Sonya's radio. Sonya walks in front of chairs towards Elizabeth's radio. At the same time, they turn the radios off, the music ends. Sonya turns to go back to her chair, but comes face to face with Elizabeth. After an awkward pause Sonya throws her gown cover closed and turns and walks around Elizabeth's chair and lamp towards her own. When both are at their own chair, they give each other a slight look then they sit down. Sonya begins to tidy up by brushing her hair. Elizabeth picks up a book and begins to read)

(Edmond shakes his head from side to side as he begins to enter area between Elizabeth and Sonya. Sonya has her hand up and out as she looks at her nails. Edmond softly takes her hand in his and bends and ever so slightly kisses her hand)

EDMOND:
Good morning my dear.

SONYA:
Oh . . . I should have my nails manicured today.

(Edmond moves towards Elizabeth and with an open hand touches her grey hair, he bends down and kisses the top of her head)

EDMOND:
Good morning my love.

ELIZABETH:
I read in a magazine that modern day witches use pencil sharpeners to do their nails.

SONYA:
That is interesting.

ELIZABETH:
Where is your . . . pencil sharpener?

SONYA:
Oh . . . it must be put away some . . . where . . . maybe in the closet with your army boots.

(Elizabeth turns the pages of her book faster than she is able to read them. Sonya strokes her eyebrows looking into a hand-held mirror. Edmond shakes head humorously and begins to sit in his rocking chair. He changes his mind and stands and walks towards the audience.)

EDMOND:
Sisters . . . (laugh) . . . they truly love each other . . . they just don't realize it yet . . . do you know they cannot stand the sight of each other . . . (pause) . . . I've been gone for a while . . . departed . . . kicked the bucket . . . passed on . . . . I reside in the afterlife . . . (pause) . . . what? . . . (listen to audience) . . . dead . . . yes that too . . . but I will tell you heaven ain't all it's cracked up to be . . . yes, it's clean, comfortable . . . hell it's too damn boring up there . . . so every day I come down here and visit the two women of my life.

ELIZABETH:
Drop dead sister!

SONYA:
After you dear.

ELIZABETH:

By all means . . . you first.

SONYA:
Please . . . please . . . go first . . . I insist.

(Elizabeth continues flipping pages, Sonya continues to put her make up on)

EDMOND:
There is never a dull moment in this old folk's home . . . (look at audience) .
. . excuse me . . . advanced aged facility for those wishing to indulge in
handicrafts day in and day out . . . after six months of that crap you're ready
for the loony bin . . . (pause) . . . There is plenty of excitement with these two
women . . . I guess it started . . . oh . . . about eight years ago . . . Elizabeth
and Sonya both applied for a senior's apartment . . . right here in this building
. . . it was some bureaucrat that figured that because of a shortage of
apartments . . . (move to rocking chair) . . . and the fact that they were sisters
. . . heck why not put them together . . . then . . . all hell broke loose.

ELIZABETH:
First . . . you have never let me go first . . . I applied for this apartment first. .
.

SONYA:
Is that the subject you wish to start the day off with?

ELIZABETH:
. . . but you came along . . . wiggled your butt for the administrator and the
next thing I know your junk is crowding mine.

SONYA:
The heel of my shoe was loose.

ELIZABETH:
That is not the only thing that is loose.

SONYA:
What does that mean?

ELIZABETH:
You know.

SONYA:
Know what?

ELIZABETH:
Do I have to spell it out?

SONYA:
The administrator fixed my shoe . . . you were there . . . you watched him fix my shoe.

ELIZABETH:
You are a floozy eighty-year-old woman . . . a loose woman . . . he had a heart attack in your bed.

SONYA:
He was smiling . . .

EDMOND:
Disgusting.

SONYA:
. . . are you jealous? . . . you are jealous of me . . . that at my age I am still able to get a man excited.

ELIZABETH:
This apartment should have been mine . . . mine alone.

SONYA:
When was the last time you turned a man on?

EDMOND:
That is not a nice question to ask.

ELIZABETH:
If you had not wiggled your way back into my life and this apartment . . . that administrator would still be alive.

SONYA:
He died two years later . . . a city bus ran over him.

EDMOND:
OUCH!

ELIZABETH:
You helped him along . . . if you had not given him a heart attack . . . maybe he could have avoided the speeding bus.

126

SONYA:
A Boy Scout pushed him.

EDMOND:
Sometimes it is better to go quickly . . . at our age a lingering death sometimes
drags on for years . . . It is better to go fast . . . get it over with . . . I remember
when Saint Peter called on me . . . he said Ed . . . you . . .

ELIZABETH:
A likely story . . . I am sure you could invent a more colourful story than that.

SONYA:
You're jealous . . . jealous that men still find me desirable . . . I would just bet
you were the one that hired that Boy Scot to bump the administrator off.

ELIZABETH:
I wouldn't waste good money on the likes of you two.

SONYA:
What you need is a man . . . preferably alive . . . a long night of hot passionate
love.

ELIZABETH:
No, I don't.

EDMOND:
(look at Sonya) What are you getting at?

SONYA:
Sex, Elizabeth . . . plain old sex . . . it does wonders . . . it keeps one alive . . .
revived . . . rejuvenated sex may just wipe that grumpy frown off your face.

ELIZABETH:
What . . . end up like you . . . word is getting around this place.

EDMOND:
What . . . I haven't heard. (look at Elizabeth)

ELIZABETH:
For a loony just call Sonya . . . I could afford Lobster everyday just answering
the phone for you.

SONYA:
When was the last time you had a man?

ELIZABETH:
You took the only man I ever loved away from me.

EDMOND:
(nod head)

SONYA:
That was a long time ago . . . since then has there been a man in your life?

(pause, Elizabeth is silent)

SONYA:
Not even one man?

ELIZABETH:
(show pent up anger) Even if a man was to be interested in me . . . sooner or later you would come wiggling along and steal him away from me . . . the same way you stole my first beau.

SONYA:
(defensive anger) He was not just your beau . . . he came into our lives at the same time . . . (show a happy remembrance) . . . remember that day . . . I was nine . . . you had just turned eight . . . (move toward dresser) . . . I was on the porch swing . . . dressed in a pink fluffy dress . . . my doll . . .

ELIZABETH:
Dolls . . . all your useless dolls . . . daddy gave me the best birthday present of all . . . a real baseball glove . . . real genuine oiled leather . . . (get up and pretend to punch hand into a gloved hand) . . . glove . . . not kid's plastic . . . a real ball . . .

SONYA:
You were a Tom-Boy.

ELIZABETH:
. . . A slugger's bat . . . the grass was cool on my toes as I bounced the ball off of old man Barton's side fence . . .

SONYA:
He was a spooky old man . . . he died that winter and the new people were ready to move in at any moment.

ELIZABETH:

Old man Barton didn't like kids . . . he built that big solid fence that went on for ever and was as high as the sky . . . Old man Barton was dead, so it was okay to bounce the ball off the fence . . . with one mighty throw the ball sailed over the fence . . . I thought it was lost for good . . . (reach up with both hands) . . . then the ball came back over . . . high in the sky.

EDMOND:
(cups hands around mouth) Catch the ball.

ELIZABETH:
. . . I caught the ball then threw it back as high as I could.

SONYA:
You and that boy played that silly game of catch for hours.

ELIZABETH:
It wasn't silly . . . it was fun . . . (back into a dream-like state) . . . Then all of a sudden, the ball did not come back . . . I could hear a rattling on the other side of the fence . . . as I pressed my ear against the white washed wood . . . a clanking . . . rattling . . . then there was a voice above me.

EDMOND:
May I come over to your side of the fence and play?

ELIZABETH:
Sure . . . we can try out my new baseball bat . . . it's a big-league slugger.

SONYA:
(With a happy reminiscent voice step forward to face the back of Elizabeth) A skinny tall boy . . . not at all like the other boys in the neighbourhood that were a head shorter than the girls. (sway a bit and fluff nightgown)

ELIZABETH:
One . . . one lousy throw of the ball and then he noticed you . . . (turn to face Sonya) . . . wiggling your butt on the porch . . . he forgot all about me.

SONYA:
(show off charm and figure) Well I guess I had what it takes to hold a man's attention . . . and I still do.

ELIZABETH:
I met him first . . . he was interested in me first . . . you stole him away from me.

SONYA:
He made up his own mind . . . I did not twist his arm . . . I was the one that asked him his name. (with a French emphasis in voice) A romantic French name . . . Edmond . . . there was passion in the way he talked.

ELIZABETH:
His name was ED . . . just plain ED . . .

(Elizabeth resumes her game of baseball, Sonya parades in her flowing gown)

EDMOND:
(rise and step forward to audience) I liked them both . . . there was absolutely no way I was able to choose one over the other . . . Elizabeth and I were chums . . . we played ball . . . hiked up Buttermilk Hill . . . she put her own worm on her fishing hook . . . (move towards Elizabeth) . . . we did all kinds of stuff together . . . we were real pals . . . I did not think of her as a girl . . . Not like Sonya . . . (turn towards Sonya, gesture with arms) . . . she was a girl . . . we would sit and talk for hours about everything . . . I felt comfortable . . . as if she sincerely cared about me . . . If only the two of them were one . . . my problems, and all the problems I caused over the years would not have been such a burden.

(Elizabeth and Sonya slowly move face to face during the following sequence)

SONYA:
He was the first boy to kiss me . . . right on the lips.

EDMOND:
I did not.

ELIZABETH:
He didn't want to . . . you made him do it.

EDMOND:
She did not.

SONYA:
He wanted to.

EDMOND:
I did not.

ELIZABETH:

130

He liked me.

EDMOND:
Yes, I did.

ELIZABETH:
More than he liked you.

EDMOND:
I like you . . . the both of you equally.

SONYA:
He would do anything for me.

EDMOND:
Yes, I would.

ELIZABETH:
We went skinny dipping.

EDMOND:
Yes, we did . . . no we did not.

SONYA:
No, you didn't.

ELIZABETH:
Yes, we did.

SONYA:
You didn't.

ELIZABETH:
Did . . . too.

SONYA:
Didn't.

ELIZABETH:
Did.

(as Sonya and Elizabeth stare face to face, Edmond walks between them towards audience)

EDMOND:
It's not true . . . not the way they said it happened . . . I kissed Sonya on her cheek . . . it was her birthday . . . my Mom made me . . . and . . . and . . . skinny dipping no way . . . we had our underwear on . . . I was too young to know . . . (pause) . . . if I only knew then what I know now . . . (walks towards Elizabeth's dresser)

SONYA:
Did not.

ELIZABETH:
Did too.

(pause)

SONYA:
What did you not do?

ELIZABETH:
(thinking) I did something you said I did not do.

SONYA:
Which was?

ELIZABETH:
Give me a minute . . . I will remember.

(Elizabeth stands thinking, trying to remember what they were arguing about as she pretends to toss a ball into a glove, Edmond examines a picture on the bookshelf, Sonya moves towards her dresser and gathers a towel)

SONYA:
I think I will use the bathroom . . . do you need to use it first?

ELIZABETH:
No.

SONYA:
I will take a shower first . . . do up my nails . . . my hair . . . do my toe nails . . . moisturize my face . . . add pre-makeup . . . do my eyebrows . . . eye lashes . . . cheeks . . . lips . . .

ELIZABETH:
(turn with angered frown) I don't need to know every little detail.

SONYA:
. . . wrinkle cream for my legs . . . (exit) . . . you should try some.

ELIZABETH:
(voice building) I will need to pee in about an hour.

SONYA:
(loud voice from off stage) Yes dear.

(Elizabeth paces around her side of the room in anger and frustration, Edmond turns from picture and walks across to centre as he speaks, then moves to rocking chair)

EDMOND:
For an eight o'clock date with Sonya I would tell her I would pick her up . . . oh . . . about six thirty . . . then I would show up around five thirty and visit with Elizabeth . . . Mrs. Muscotti was sure to feed a skinny boy like me . . . Then oh . . . about eight thirty Mr. Muscotti would say I would have a few minutes more to wait . . . "a game of chess would be just about right." he had said

ELIZABETH:
(walk towards bookcase, touch the face of Edmond in the picture) Such a sweet smile . . . with playfulness in those brown eyes . . . Other people would say all they saw was a sternness . . . with emotion hidden way back deep inside yourself . . . I saw that emotion . . . felt your tenderness . . . and all of your love . . . why . . . why . . . did I not marry you . . . why did I say no . . . why did I call all of the arrangements off so close to that one special moment in a girl's life.

EDMOND:
Why?

ELIZABETH:
Why . . . why . . . I ask myself every day . . . Why I did not ignore what Sonya said . . . ignore what everyone said . . . married you anyway . . . maybe we would have been happy . . . (move to centre of stage and look skyward with your hands clinging to picture) Ed . . . I've been lonely all these years . . . I've missed your company . . . there is no one . . . and there has never been anyone else . . . no children . . . who said your eighties are your golden years . . . I share an old folks' apartment with Miss . . . never get old . . . who thinks she is in her sixties . . . (look to area where Sonya exited, raise voice) . . . You are older than me . . . you, old hag . . . (look tearfully at picture, move to bookcase and place picture back to its spot) . . . There was no one at your wake when I

arrived . . . slowly I walked to the front and sat on one side . . . A picture of you by an urn was all I was granted to see . . . you were gone . . . gone from me . . . and I missed the chance to say I was sorry and forgive you . . . then behind me I hear high heels clipping along the floor . . . (raise voice) . . . and there she was . . . my sister . . . the bitch that came between us . . . she sat across the aisle . . . we glanced at each other . . . she had the nerve to ask how I was . . . After fifty-five years of not talking to each other she has the nerve to ask how I was . . . My sister Sonya . . . the neighbourhood tramp . . . the one that prevented us from getting married fifty-five years ago . . . she says, "how are you?"

EDMOND:
Maybe it was her way of trying to patch things up . . . It was I . . . the dust particles stuffed into a spittoon that brought the two of you together . . . It was time to mend the past.

ELIZABETH:
She wormed her way back into my life . . . I was vulnerable . . . filled with grief at the passing of Ed . . . there was no fight left in me . . . I did not fight her off . . . I let her back into my life and this apartment . . .

EDMOND:
To cherish and love her as a sister.

ELIZABETH:
. . . so, I could make the rest of her life a living hell . . . for eight years . . . (move to Sonya's side of the room near her rocking chair) . . . I've argued . . . put her down . . . called her names . . . burnt her food . . . and she is still here. (walk back to your side of the room frustrated) And not once in eight years has, she mentioned what she did to you and me . . . or said she was sorry . . . she goes about as if nothing ever happened . . . (pause, a sorrowful voice) . . . well it did happen. (walk to Sonya's rocking chair, with loud voice yell) . . . I have to PEE NOW! (walk back to your chair)

SONYA:
(from off stage) All right dear . . . I am just applying wrinkle cream to my legs . . . it is applied in small circular motion starting from the ankles to the knees . . . to . . .

ELIZABETH:
(walk to back of chairs and stop behind Edmond, stand with arms folded) I don't need to know the details with moment to moment descriptive dialogue . . . I have to PEE . . . NOW.

(Sonya enters all dressed and carrying her make-up, towels, etc. to her dresser, Elizabeth storms by and exits, Edmond slowly rocks)

SONYA:
The lavatory is all yours dear.

ELIZABETH:
After you've used it . . . . it is more like Ma and Pa Kettle's out house. (exit)

SONYA:
You are so witty Elizabeth dear. (go about putting things away)

EDMOND:
(rise and look at Sonya admiringly) Sonya you are still a ravishing woman . . . your glow has not diminished . . . that same glow I saw from the top of old man Barton's fence is still with you.

SONYA:
(look into hand mirror) OOOH . . . a wrinkle . . .

EDMOND:
Just a laugh line.

SONYA:
Oh, it is just a laugh line . . . (giggle) . . . old sour puss could use a few laugh lines . . . (in a thinking manner) . . . I try and try to remember Elizabeth and I as little girls . . . but I can't . . . it is . . . as if we did not exist . . . until Edmond moved into old man Barton's house . . . our existence in life started from that moment Edmond climbed over that tall white-washed fence . . . (smile and give a little girl giggle) . . . We were happy all of the time . . . we laughed . . . played . . . Elizabeth -had a great smile . . . we were sisters . . . had problems like sisters . . . we both adored Edmond . . . in our own way . . . but we got along, Elizabeth and I . . . then . . . (smile fades, walk over to bookcase and softly touch picture of Edmond)

EDMOND:
Then the world we knew caved in . . . Elizabeth . . . Sonya and I parted.

SONYA:
Then all hell broke loose . . . I opened my big mouth days before Elizabeth's wedding . . . Elizabeth called everything off . . . she would not talk to me . . . she misunderstood . . . . she would not let me explain . . . (hold picture) . . . Edmond . . . I am so sorry . . . but . . . I thought if I let things slide and try to forget what happened . . . maybe everything would work out.

EDMOND:
Sonya . . . it did not work out.

SONYA:
(quickly walk back to your side of the room) It did not . . . everything was a
shamble . . . after fifty-five years it is still a shamble . . . I cannot bring myself
to explain it to Elizabeth . . . I can't have her rejecting me again . . . I know
her . . . she would throw me out of her life and out of this apartment . . . I love
her so dearly . . . all those years apart hurt . . . I missed her in my life . . . (turn
and point to Edmond's picture) . . . and I missed you Edmond . . . (put hands
to mouth). I never found the right time to explain . . . you up and died on me
. . .

EDMOND:
Yeah, I did . . . it wasn't my choice to join the dearly departed club . . . (wander
about) . . . after a stint in the waiting room between heaven . . . and hell . . .
us new recruits get to look over life's transcripts . . . it is mandatory reading .
. . a huge book . . . all of life is in there . . . boring reading . . . oh there are
some hot spots . . . Marilyn Monroe . . . Mae West . . . and then I came across
our moments in history . . . (with compassion) . . . Sonya I know of all the
details . . . you don't have to seek my forgiveness . . . It is Elizabeth that needs
to know . . . and she will need you . . . and all of your love.

SONYA:
Yes, there is time left to explain all of it to Elizabeth . . . today . . . today I will
tell her . . . if she will listen.

EDMOND:
She will.

ELIZABETH:
She did not seem to be in a good mood this morning . . . maybe I will tell her
tomorrow.

EDMOND:
Today.

SONYA:
Tonight.

EDMOND:
This morning.

SONYA:

After lunch.

EDMOND:
Next year . . . next May . . . on a Tuesday.

SONYA:
Yes today, after a nice lunch.

EDMOND:
Have it your way.

(Edmond heads to his rocking chair, Sonya is deep in thought as she mills about the area between her rocking chair and her dresser, Elizabeth enters dressed in day clothes, she heads to the bookcase, Sonya notices her and begins to stare)

ELIZABETH:
What are you staring at?

SONYA:
(caught off guard) Oh . . . I was . . . just . . .

ELIZABETH:
You have something on your mind?

SONYA:
Well . . . yes.

ELIZABETH:
I don't have time for you to beat around the bush . . . say what you have to say.

SONYA:
Did you have a nice pee?

ELIZABETH:
(pause, build to dramatics) It was the best pee I have had in years . . . exquisite . . . almost as gratifying as a good bowel movement . . . do you want to discuss crap?

SONYA:
I was reminiscing . . . about you and I . . . trying to remember if we were friends . . . if we had shared any special moments . . . before Edmond moved in next door.

(a light, laugh-filled sequence)

ELIZABETH:
I was eight . . . I could spit as far as any boy . . .

SONYA:
You wanted to be a boy . . . Mom had a hard time with you . . . all those nice dresses . . . each one ruined in just one day . . .

ELIZABETH:
. . . Sliding into home plate ruined them . . . mud and sand up in my drawers. (wiggle like a child)

SONYA:
Mom spent hours trying to comb out the tangles in your hair . . . then you took six inches of hair off one side . . . all jagged . . . you had used Mom's hemming scissors . . . (laugh)

ELIZABETH:
(laugh) I begged you to try and fix it so it looked nice . . . a little more off I said . . . just a little more . . . each time I looked at the floor . . . a little more was on the pile.

SONYA:
And Daddy at suppertime . . . he sits down . . . looks at you and says . . . (use deep voice) . . . hello there . . . then calls three times for you to come to the table for supper.

ELIZABETH:
He looked right at me . . . right into my eyes and says . . . (use deep voice) . . . You must be new to our neighbourhood . . . tell me . . . what is your name son?

SONYA:
Mom comes in with a platter of spaghetti and screamed at the top of her lungs . . . the chandelier shook.

ELIZABETH:
Daddy did not look very nice with spaghetti in his hair.

SONYA:
Not a word was spoken all through supper . . . at bedtime I could hear Daddy say to Mom . . . it will grow back . . . even the bare patches . . . I was just nine, my first hair cutting job.

ELIZABETH:
But boy could I run . . . and sliding into home plate was easy in boy's pants .
. . like Mom said . . . if you're going to look the part . . . you should dress the
part.

SONYA:
You looked just like a boy.

(Sonya and Elizabeth begin to laugh)

EDMOND:
I don't remember that . . . it must have happened before I moved into old man
Barton's house.

ELIZABETH:
And you . . . that bright idea you had . . . surprise Mom and Dad on their
anniversary.

SONYA:
That was a great idea.

EDMOND:
I read about that in your life's transcripts . . . what a chuckle that gave me.

ELIZABETH:
Sonya, you could not cook.

SONYA:
And I still can't.

ELIZABETH:
There you were standing on the step stool at the counter dishing out orders.

(Sonya and Elizabeth move to centre of stage and stand side by side, Sonya
gives instructions, Elizabeth moves about around Sonya, Edmond slowly
stands and moves for a better view, his laughter building, Sonya and Elizabeth
display the minds and hearts of children, their bodies conduct themselves as
eighty-year-olds)

SONYA:
I need a big, big, big bowl for mixing . . . that bowl . . . that one . . . that one
and that one for ingredients.

ELIZABETH:

A big stick for stirring.

SONYA:
It is called a spatula . . . and I will need that cranking thing.

ELIZABETH:
What cranky thing?

SONYA:
Not cranky thing . . . cranking thing . . . that contraption Mom uses . . . you know . . . you turn the big wheel with a little handle and the two little bird cages go round and round . . . and fluff up everything.

ELIZABETH:
Mom lets us lick them when she is finished (stick tongue out, pretend to lick little bird cage)

SONYA:
You got your tongue stuck between the wires . . . we had you laughing and crying at the same time.

ELIZABETH:
I was making whipped cream bubbles . . . I could not stop laughing . . . crying . . . laughing.

SONYA:
Crying.

ELIZABETH:
Laughing . . .crying . . . laughing
SONYA:

ELIZABETH:
What are we making for Mom and Dad?

SONYA:
Everything they like to eat . . . Canadian bacon with eggs . . . crepes` . . ..

ELIZABETH:
With pure maple syrup.

SONYA:
Big thick flap jacks.

ELIZABETH:
With ice cream.

SONYA:
Two frying pans . . . toaster . . . oven set at five hundred . . . a tray for the fresh biscuits.

ELIZABETH:
Don't forget the cake with thick icing and the fancy lettering . . . you misspelled anniversary.

SONYA:
I was busy cooking . . . the eggs were frying.

ELIZABETH:
Burning.

SONYA:
The crepes were golden in colour.

ELIZABETH:
Stuck.

SONYA:
The biscuits browning.

ELIZABETH:
Black.

SONYA:
The cake . . . did not rise.

ELIZABETH:
Flat as a pancake.

SONYA:
The flap jacks were thick.

ELIZABETH:
They were not cooked.

SONYA:
Open a window . . . it is smoky in here.

ELIZABETH:
It was a great idea.

SONYA:
Yeah . . . Mom and Dad liked the shredded wheat and milk.

ELIZABETH:
With a big strawberry on top.

SONYA:
They looked happy together in bed . . . Daddy said it was the best breakfast in bed he had ever had.

ELIZABETH:
What's all the white stuff on your clothes Mom asked . . . you were quick and smart for a blonde.

SONYA:
Stay in bed until noon . . . Elizabeth and I will clean the house from top to bottom . . . we will call you when we are done.

(Elizabeth and Sonya lean against each other as if exhausted from all their work)

ELIZABETH:
We got the whole kitchen cleaned up . . . it was a mess . . . it took forever . . . Mom was pleased with us . . . we were the best girls ever . . . she would never trade us in for new daughters. (a happy sigh)

SONYA:
(giggle) Every day for weeks Mom would say . . . I thought we had eggs . . . no more flour . . . where's the ice cream . . . I am sure I had bought Canadian bacon.

ELIZABETH:
That was weeks and weeks ago Mom. (giggle)

SONYA:
See . . . we were sisters and friends . . . and we did a lot of things before Edmond came into our lives.

ELIZABETH:
When Edmond came into our lives, we did a lot more.

SONYA:
We had fun . . . all of the time.

ELIZABETH:
Then we began fighting over him.

SONYA:
That's what happens when hormones start to infiltrate the mind and body.

ELIZABETH:
Ed was in the middle of our tug of war.

SONYA:
We must have made his life miserable . . . Edmond stuck by us . . . he was always there for us . . . remember our last year of high school . . . it was spring just before the spring formal . . . we did something awful to him . . . what was it. (walk away, move into a reminiscing state)

ELIZABETH:
It was spring . . . a hot humid day . . . the three of us were sitting at a table at the Bob Inn Soda Shop (walk to your side of the room)

SONYA:
The Bob Inn . . . oh I loved that place . . . everyone hung out at the Bob Inn . . . the place to be.

ELIZABETH:
We were talking . . . nothing out of the ordinary.

SONYA:
Boys . . . all the boys in their team sweaters would drop by . . . every girl in the place would flirt.

ELIZABETH:
Just talking . . . then the happy mood changed . . . either you or I said something.

SONYA:
To be the team captain's girl . . . to wear his pin . . . or his sweater.

ELIZABETH:
You were eyeing one of the guys from the team . . . right in front of Ed.

SONYA:

Edmond was not on the team.

ELIZABETH:
He was injured at the start of the season . . . they dropped him from the team.

SONYA:
The captain of the team came by our table.

ELIZABETH:
You winked at him . . . in front of Ed.

SONYA:
I would love to wear the team captain's sweater.

(Sonya and Elizabeth both fade back to the time at the Bob Inn)

ELIZABETH:
You are making a spectacle of yourself . . . acting the flirt . . . people are watching us . . . and you are embarrassing Ed.

SONYA:
Well we are just friends . . . it is not as if we are going steady or anything . . . he has never asked . . .

ELIZABETH:
PLEASE!

SONYA:
Please what? . . . You are jealous that Edmond just might . . .

ELIZABETH:
People are watching . . .

SONYA:
. . . might be more interested in me than you . . . and with the prom coming up you may be sitting and sulking at home while I am dancing the night away.

ELIZABETH:
Who cares about the prom and dancing?

SONYA:
You care . . . because you can't dance.

ELIZABETH:

I can too.

SONYA:
Edmond . . . ask her to dance . . . right now . . . go ahead show me.

ELIZABETH:
Ah . . . ah . . . the music . . . it is not the right kind.

SONYA:
Not the right kind . . . wooo . . . you are all talk . . . no action.

ELIZABETH:
This is not the right place or time . . . and quit talking to me like that.

SONYA:
I will talk any way I like.

ELIZABETH:
But not to me you won't.

SONYA:
I will not talk to you.

ELIZABETH:
Then don't.

SONYA:
I won't.
ELIZABETH:
You are.

SONYA:
I am not.

(Edmond gets up and starts to walk towards the back of the room)

ELIZABETH:
Now see what you've done . . . Ed is leaving.

SONYA:
Me! . . . what about you.

ELIZABETH:
I am not talking to you. (turn back on Sonya)

SONYA:
I am not talking to you either. (turn back on Elizabeth)

(Edmond slowly walks to front of stage while Sonya and Elizabeth try to ignore each other)

EDMOND:
Prom night was just days away . . . (turn to face girls) . . . I liked both of them . . . I was going crazy . . . which one should I ask . . . I was hoping someone else would ask one of them first . . . Then I'd be off the hook . . . I was not able to choose between them . . . and the prom . . . just days away.

SONYA:
My prom dress is beautiful . . . with cleavage to accentuate my bosom.

ELIZABETH:
Excess baggage as far as I am concerned.

SONYA:
At the prom I will dance the night away . . . with every boy there . . .

ELIZABETH:
With advertising like those there will be a waiting line . . . and with boys' mouths wide . . . salivating . . . (show a grimace on face)

SONYA:
Prom night is days away and no-one has asked to escort me . . . not even Edmond.

ELIZABETH:
I don't want to go . . . it is a waste of time . . . I don't need an escort . . . dancing is a waste of time.

(Sonya and Elizabeth mope with their backs to each other and slowly move to their sides of the room, Edmond walks towards his rocking chair, then turns towards the front, all three are to be present in the past)

EDMOND:
(raise hand and pretend to knock on a door, pause) Hello . . . Mrs. Muscotti . . . yes, I am fine . . . fine . . . ah . . . may I speak to your daughters please . . . yes the two of them . . . together . . . at one time . . . yes, I will wait here. (Edmond rocks back and forth on his heels with his hands clasped behind his back, Elizabeth and Sonya with girlish mannerisms turn and slowly walk towards Edmond)

ELIZABETH:
Hi Ed, . . .

SONYA:
Oh . . . hello Edmond.

ELIZABETH:
How you been?

EDMOND: Fine . . . just fine . . . (your eyes shyly dart from one girl to
the other) . . .. Good . . . good . . . fine . . . and you?

SONYA:
Good.

ELIZABETH:
Fine.

(pause)

EDMOND:
Sonya . . . Elizabeth . . .

(pause, all three are in an awkward moment, all attempt to speak feeling they
are interrupting the other)

EDMOND:
Would . . .

SONYA:
Yes . . .

ELIZABETH:
What's up Ed . . .

EDMOND:
Would . . . you like . . .

SONYA:
Yes.

ELIZABETH:
Yes.

EDMOND:
What? (startled)

SONYA:
You were about to say something.

EDMOND:
Yes . . . I know that this is short notice . . . and if you have already been asked . . . to the prom.

ELIZABETH:
Nope.

SONYA:
No . . . not as of yet.

ELIZABETH:
I'm not up to dancing . . . and dressing up all fancy.

EDMOND:
(a firm voice, stand tall) I would like to escort the two of you to the spring prom . . . the band is hot . . . jive music . . . slow waltzes . . . the night will fly by . . .

(the music builds, a jive style, Sonya and Edmond do a early jive style dance, music fades into a waltz, Edmond gently takes Elizabeth's hand and they begin to waltz, music fades, Edmond steps back, Elizabeth and Sonya are in a state of awe, both move towards each other at centre stage and each holds out a hand as if Edmond was there to hold them, Elizabeth holds out a left hand with palm down, Sonya holds out a right hand with palm down)

SONYA:
The evening was grand . . . everybody's eyes were on us . . . I swirled . . . shimmered . . . I floated on air . . . like dancing on a cloud.

ELIZABETH:
Ed kissed our hands goodnight.

SONYA:
Weren't we something on the dance floor . . . Edmond and I . . . we sure turned some heads?

ELIZABETH:

Ed kissed my hand . . . a kind of tingling shiver went up my spine . . . I cannot explain it . . . it is as if . . . for a moment baseball meant nothing to me . . .

SONYA:
Betty Ohanlin and Wilbur Crabtree were the wrong picks for prom King, and Queen, I can tell you . . . I think they envied Edmond and me.

ELIZABETH:
. . . There was something strange happening to me . . . my heart fluttered . . . I wanted Ed to kiss my hand again.

SONYA:
(drop hand and rub both over hips and slightly push up bosom, speak in a bragging voice) If I was a teenager today . . .

(both return to the present)

SONYA:
. . . Edmond and I would have made out behind the football bleachers.

ELIZABETH:
(with disgust step away and slap the air with your left hand) What . . . and do just like Betty Ohanlin . . . they didn't call her Betty Boobs Ohanlin for nothing . . . Talk went around that she was under the bleachers the night of the prom . . . six months later she could not hide the basketball in her stomach.

SONYA:
Talk was . . . it was Wilbur Crabtree's baby . . . .it was funny that Wilbur and Mildred were married a couple of months after the prom.

ELIZABETH:
And you wanted to do the same thing.

SONYA:
Not with Wilbur Crabtree.

ELIZABETH:
What! . . . with Ed?

SONYA:
Why not . . . he was sweet on me.

ELIZABETH:

(not responding to Sonya, rub the top of your left hand with emotion and tenderness) But Ed kissed my hand . . . I had changed that night . . . as if I suddenly developed into a woman.

SONYA:
(an uncaring attitude) Ah he kissed my hand plenty of times.

ELIZABETH:
That was no hand kissing at the train station . . . Ed only gave me a peck on the cheek . . . you . . . you he kissed on the lips . . . a French kiss . . . more slobbering than a St. Bernard.

SONYA:
Edmond was joining the army . . . the best thing I could give him before he left . . . something to remember . . . an . . . enticement to return.

ELIZABETH:
And the night before he left . . . I saw you sneak out of the house . . . and your high heels waiting at the end of the walk way . . . were you planning to give him a little extra . . . something more to remember . . . Betty Ohanlin has something to remember from under the football bleachers . . . was it Ed . . . my Ed.

SONYA:
Your Ed . . . he was not your Ed! . . . Edmond was sweet on me . . . only after he joined the army is when we parted ways . . . you and he only got romantic three months later when he was on leave . . . I was not interested in Edmond then.

ELIZABETH:
And just when everything is going my way . . . when I start to get my share of happiness . . . you . . . you . . . pick that moment in time to inform Mom and Dad . . . the whole damn world that you were KNOCKED UP!

EDMOND:
(quickly stand) Elizabeth how could you say that with such words . . . . Sonya's feelings . . . you should not hurt her feelings.

(Sonya emotionally breaks down inside, she moves to her rocking chair in distraught, Elizabeth with built up anger begins to work an imaginary ball and glove together)

EDMOND:

You don't know the whole story . . . no one wanted to listen fifty-five years ago and you have made no effort to listen all these years . . . Elizabeth, you and I were in love . . . engaged to be married . . . then our world fell apart . . . if only you would have listened to Sonya's side of the story . . . listen with an open mind . . . let your heart forgive . . . (pause, walk between Elizabeth and Sonya) I had to kick the bucket . . . shuffle off to the great beyond to read life's chronicles to find out the truth . . . I wish I could tell you . . . I wish you could hear me . . . (pause, put a hand on Sonya's rocking chair) Sonya is the only one who can tell you what really happened . . . please listen to her . . . Elizabeth.

ELIZABETH:
Quit your sniffling . . . when you get into one of your moods . . . it drives me crazy . . . most people ball their eyes out . . . five . . . ten minutes then blow their nose and it's over . . .

(Edmond moves to his rocking chair, Sonya blows her nose)

ELIZABETH:
. . . no, you carry on and on . . . (pause) . . . and on . . . (pause) . . . and on . . . and on . . .

SONYA:
I get the point . . . (dab eyes, put handkerchief away) . . . I am all finished now . . . (a happier mood) . . . Elizabeth dear . . . would you be so kind and make me something to eat . . . I would like a tomato sandwich on whole wheat toast.

(Elizabeth winds up liken to a big-league pitcher and follows through with exaggeration as if throwing the ball towards Sonya)

ELIZABETH:
Bean the batter . . . bean the batter . . . if only I had my ball and glove . . . (thinking) . . . whatever did I do with my old ball and glove.

SONYA:
Have you gone off your rocker . . . are there a few screws a little loose upstairs?

ELIZABETH:
Mom hid my ball and glove on me that first year of high school . . . she said . . . (mimic mother) . . . you have to act like a young lady in high school.

SONYA:

(mimic mother) You cannot go around acting like a Tom Boy all of your life . . . you cannot play . . . with boys the way boys play . . . (pause) . . . They have other things on their minds . . . (turn to Elizabeth as Sonya) . . . And so, did I.

ELIZABETH:
I really needed my glove . . . Ed said the ball team needed me . . . the Colts were one win away from finishing first at mid-season . . . That's when Wilbur Crabtree pulled a groin muscle and could not pitch the game.

SONYA:
I bet Betty Ohanlin helped him pull that muscle.

ELIZABETH:
We were lucky Mom was at bingo that day you cut my hair short for the second time.

SONYA:
You almost looked like a boy in that baseball uniform . . . just a little eye shadow added to your upper lip and side burns to look like hair and . . .

ELIZABETH:
Then Dad knocks on the door and you have to say come in . . . and me standing there all decked out . . . except for that sports cup I was holding in my hand.

SONYA:
(laugh and stand up and act like the father) I found your ball and glove in my sock drawer . . . I was wondering . . .

ELIZABETH:
I froze holding that thing with straps . . . and Dad's words slowed right down . . . a little lip grin . . . just like Elvis had.

SONYA:
(act like the father) . . . if you might need . . . (pause) . . . ball game . . . Wilbur Crabtree is out . . . You are in . . . well dear . . . ah son . . . you will need to wear that . . . that protector in order to look like a boy . . . and don't forget to scratch every once-in-a-while.

ELIZABETH:
A jock strap and a tin cup . . . it felt more like a medieval chastity belt . . . put a lock and key on it and Betty Ohanlin wouldn't be in the fix she was in.

SONYA:

152

Oh, that reminds me I need to watch my soap opera . . . Jenny's daughter's best friend is going to have a baby by Jenny's husband's business partner.

ELIZABETH:
Who cares!

SONYA:
Today is the day Jenny's daughter is going into labour . . . but doctor John is worried about the daughter's deep coma.

EDMOND:
(listen intently) Tragic . . . life at times is so cruel.

SONYA:
Jenny's daughter's friend may never wake up to see her new baby.

EDMOND:
That is so sad.

SONYA:
And . . . Jenny's daughter's friend's Mother has a restraining order to keep Jenny's husband's best friend from knowing about the baby.

EDMOND:
Legalities.

SONYA:
But two days ago, Jenny's daughter told her Dad's best friend about her friend being pregnant and, in a coma, . . . he said that it didn't matter . . . he was in love and wanted to marry Jenny's daughter's best friend.

EDMOND:
True love.

ELIZABETH:
(speak like an announcer) Yes, another episode of as you make my stomach turn.

EDMOND:
Sonya dear . . . is there going to be a wedding?

SONYA:

Elizabeth . . . just picture it . . . a bedside wedding in the hospital and a miracle may happen . . . Jenny's daughter's best friend wakes from her coma in time to say I do. (a happy sigh)

ELIZABETH:
When the preacher asks if anyone knows why these two people should not be joined in holy matrimony . . . (build up volume and anger) . . . you yell out . . . I am carrying his baby . . . just like you did before my wedding.

SONYA:
(with shock and visible hurt) Elizabeth . . . I never meant for it to happen that way . . . I . . .

ELIZABETH:
It was no secret . . . everyone knew you and Ed were a couple . . . months before he joined the army. . . the two of you spent all of your waking hours together . . . many a night I would hear you sneaking into the house . . . hours after midnight . . . how many non-waking hours did you spend together?

EDMOND:
I would never do that . . . Sonya . . . and I were just very close friends . . . as you and I were.

SONYA:
It was never like that Elizabeth.

ELIZABETH:
For months you kept quiet . . . not uttering a word . . . you even helped on all of Ed and my wedding plans . . . there was not one hint of a problem . . . or even an inclination that you were pregnant . . .

(Edmond lowers head slowly moving it from side to side, Sonya withdraws into herself with her hands busily fussing)

ELIZABETH:
(move to the side of your bookcase) . . . our house . . . our family house dressed in bows, ribbons and fresh flowers . . . a fresh smell of spring flowers flowed from room to room . . . (breath in the smell) . . . Dad had just finished giving the inside and outside of the house a fresh coat of paint . . . he was wiping off his hands as he gazed up the stairs to where I stood . . . there was a glint in Dad's eyes . . . Mom was bringing in another vase of flowers . . . my layered lace gown hung lightly from my bare shoulders . . . Sonya you fussed behind me . . . removing any wrinkle . . . or speck of dust . . . a flawed thread . . . though I was just trying it on . . . it was as if a church full of eyes teared

up . . . I was not the Tom Boy they remembered . . . the only time I truly felt a like female . . . I belonged in that wedding dress.

(Sonya looks up with a smile on her face, one hand is lightly trembling against her lower lip and chin)

ELIZABETH:
Dad wiping his hands at the bottom of the stairs . . . and smiling . . . Mom holding those baby breaths and ferns . . . her hand on Dad's arm . . . I wanted what they had . . . fulfilment . . . togetherness . . . friendship . . . and the true love that binds one's dreams and wishes together . . . more than anything else in life . . . if only a taste of what they had . . .

SONYA:
(with your hands grip the arms of the rocking chair tightly) Elizabeth . . . you did deserve to have that . . . and a lot more . . . you could have overlooked what I said . . . took a chance . . . let your heart decide . . . why didn't you let your heart lead you?

EDMOND:
(stand and step forward and slowly extend a hand) Elizabeth . . . my heart was there for you . . . and for you . . . only you . . . all you had to do was reach out your heart for mine.

ELIZABETH:
Was I meant to understand . . . (turn to Sonya) . . . how could I understand . . .? everything was racing through my mind . . . everyone around me became strangers . . . I could not take all the confusion . . . everyone was talking at one time . . . talking about different subjects . . . (put your hands to your ears, pause) . . . Why at the moment did you need to confess . . . was it some spiritual thing . . . redemption . . . forgiveness . . . you needed to steal the spotlight away from me?

(Edmond sits back down, Sonya shakes head no)

ELIZABETH:
You sure made a grand stand presentation at the rehearsal luncheon . . . instant silence . . . everyone heard the word pregnant . . . piercing self-righteous eyes focused on me . . . then on you . . . then on Ed . . . there was no need for words . . . the evidence was etched in everyone's mind . . . whispers, gossip . . . everyone's mouth flapping in the wind . . . I could picture all the different scenarios . . . (use different dialect) . . . Oh the three of them always together . . . oh I heard . . . and so and so told me . . . that Sonya . . . such a flirt . . . Ed . . . I heard from Mrs. Ohanlin . . . and that Elizabeth . . . such a Tom Boy

... who would think she would be interested in boys ... let alone ... marriage ... she was too much into baseball ...? baseball this ... baseball that ... did you hear that she once dressed as a boy just to play on that high school team ... baseball ... baseball ... baseball ... baseball ... (exit characters, become excited) ... Turn the TV on, there is a baseball game on, what time is it ... I don't want to miss the opening pitch ... (move about with imaginary ball and glove)

EDMOND:
Ball game ... at a time like this ... we were just breaking the edge ... we were making progress.

SONYA:
Elizabeth ... (stand with excitement) ... baseball ... a game is a game ... just a game ... my soap opera is life imitating real life ... I need to find out about Jenny's daughter's best friend's unborn baby.

ELIZABETH:
(wind up arm to give a pitch) It is the bottom of the ninth ... mighty battling Beth is at the mound ready to deliver a fireball pitch ...

SONYA:
Dr. John is being paged to hurry to Jenny's daughter's best friend's room ... friends and family are crowded around the bed as moans are heard above the panicked voices ...

ELIZABETH:
... first the slow wind up ...

SONYA:
... her heart beat is increasing ...

ELIZABETH:
... a pause at the pinnacle of the pitch ...

SONYA:
... SHE IS STARTING LABOUR shouts Dr. John . . ..

ELIZABETH:
... the baseball is hurled towards the plate ...

SONYA:
... she is one hundred per cent dilated ...

(Elizabeth follows through with the pitch, Sonya extends her hands down as if accepting a delivered baby)

ELIZABETH:
. . . a perfect delivery.

SONYA:
. . . a perfect delivery.

ELIZABETH:
. . . strike three . . . you're out.

SONYA:
. . . it's a boy . . . a baby boy.

ELIZABETH:
Mighty battling Beth saves the game again . . . and it takes a woman to get things done right in a man's world.

SONYA:
Only a woman suffers pain and emotional abuse . . . then rises above it all and bring into this world another male of the species.

(Elizabeth and Sonya freeze in position)

EDMOND:
Now hang on there a minute . . . I must protest . . . as a man . . . I speak for most . . . we do our part in life . . . forage for food . . . work our youth away . . . struggle to please the woman we love . . . and what happens . . . we are the first ones to kick the bucket . . . and you women live on . . . enjoying life . . . (move to the bookcase and the picture of you) . . . oh yeah . . . every once-in-a-while, you dust an inch of dust off my picture . . . a few soothing words . . . then my image is left to linger trapped behind a blur of glass.

(pause, silence)

ELIZABETH:
That is food for thought.

SONYA:
Speaking of food Elizabeth dear.

ELIZABETH:

Okay Sonya . . . okay . . . I will manage to fix you something to eat . . . I wouldn't want you to wither away by starvation.

(both exit back centre between the paintings)

(pause, Edmond wipes dust off his picture)

EDMOND:
I come here every day to visit and listen to the both of you . . . (turn and no one is around, walk away, pause then turn back to the picture) . . . typical . . . when a man has something important to say . . . women . . . just vanish.

(lights fade)

END OF PART 1

PART 2

THE STAGE IS DARK AND FROM OFF STAGE THE SOUND OF A GRANDFATHER CLOCK IS HEARD CHIMMING TO SIX O'CLOCK AS THE LIGHTS SLOWLY BUILD TO REVEAL EARLY EVENING.
EDMOND IS STANDING BY THE BOOKCASE WIPING DUST OFF OF HIS PICTURE FRAME.
ELIZABETH AND SONYA ENTER FROM BACK CENTRE BETWEEN THE PAINTINGS, BOTH ARE DRESSED IN THEIR NIGHT CLOTHES. THEY WALK TO FRONT CENTRE STAGE, AS THEY ADJUST THEIR NIGHT CLOTHES EDMOND NOTICES AND HE THEN RESTS HIS ARM ON THE BOOKCASE, ELIZABETH AND SONYA FREEZE IN POSITION.

EDMOND:
As I was saying before you both decided to desert me for the rest of the afternoon . . . (shake and get back into mood) . . . I come here every day to visit and listen to the both of you . . . that is all I can do . . . I cannot feel your touch . . . smell your fragrance . . . there is a hurt of wanting in my heart . . . in eternity it is very lonely . . . I miss your love . . . but from the tone and meanness of your conversations . . . I wonder if you both ever wanted me around.

ELIZABETH:
A man's world.

SONYA:

We just let them think of it that way . . . it is us women that really run the show.

EDMOND:
(show anger) You two ran the show from the beginning . . . and look where it got you.

SONYA:
A good man listens to what a woman says.

EDMOND:
You did not listen to me for one moment . . .

ELIZABETH:
(laugh) Then jumps and does the job right away.

EDMOND:
Neither one of you is married.

SONYA:
A good man is always at a woman's beckon call.

ELIZABETH:
With flowers and whispers of sweet nothings.

EDMOND:
One of you enjoyed every man that came along . . . (look and gesture to Sonya then gesture to Elizabeth) . . . the other gave up on men . . . couldn't even be bothered looking for a lasting love.

ELIZABETH:
A good man should always be around and silent.

SONYA:
Always ready and willing . . . a puppet on a string.

EDMOND:
Two old maids living together . . . can't stand each other . . . but living together . . . and . . . and I am still in love with both of them . . . (move to rocking chair and sit down)

SONYA:

It is not hard to rap a man around your baby finger . . . you just need the right material . . . (with your hands shape an outline of your figure) . . . well the material is a little weathered.

ELIZABETH:
A little . . . a drought . . . wind and rain has left us looking like misshaped dough boys with skin crinkled like dried out shoe leather.

SONYA:
I am not that bad yet . . . anyway the men I see have bad eyesight and they can't remember what a good woman looks like.

ELIZABETH:
Of all the men you have dated . . . you have never had a lasting relationship . . . surely one man was good enough for you . . . one you wanted to share a marriage with.

SONYA:
There were plenty . . . they all had good qualities . . . but there was not one man that had all the qualities in one . . . (smile as you reminisce) Francios . . . (speak in a French dialect) . . . was a great passion in bed . . . he snored.

ELIZABETH:
You scratched him off your list.

SONYA: (nod head) Omar . . . dashing . . . dancing at all the hot spots . . . champagne . . . he flashed his money . . . tipped everyone . . . he gambled in Atlantic City . . .. Vegas . . . Monte Carlo . . .

ELIZABETH:
He gambled more on the tables than on you.

SONYA:
Right . . . then I hit rock bottom with Frank the plumber . . . he had money . . . a big house . . . a big Italian family . . . no night life . . . his idea of romance was a sausage sandwich in bed . . . five minutes of heavy breathing . . .. then snoring on and off while Carson was on T.V.

ELIZABETH:
That lasted about a month.

SONYA:
A month too long . . . I have no idea what I ever saw in him . . . I ran into him at a senior's bingo . . . he was widowed . . . had ten kids . . . dressed twenty

years out of style and was hitting on every widow in the place . . . the disgusting thing was he left with Rosie . . . a retired hooker.

ELIZABETH:
I guess she did not retire.

SONYA:
It seems I spent my whole life searching . . . every time I found someone, I was already looking for someone better . . . I was never satisfied . . . never fulfilled . . . and now in my old age I feel like I have accomplished nothing in life . . . do you know Elizabeth I have held a job almost as long as I have held onto a man.

ELIZABETH:
We received all of your letters back home . . . they were filled with pictures and stories from exotic places all over the world.

SONYA:
I did travel . . . had a hell-of-a-good time . . . not always the lap of luxury . . . one day in Monte Carlo there I am sitting with royalty . . . a fur collar . . . diamonds . . . a pearl necklace . . . the next day after Omar left . . . there I am dressed in a blue cocktail waitress gown . . . swallowing my pride as I wait hand and foot on the same royalty that I was hob-knobbing with the night before.

ELIZABETH:
That was not in your letters.

SONYA:
Do you think I was going to write that to Mom after the stories Mom wrote to me about you?

ELIZABETH:
(shocked) Mom wrote to you?

SONYA:
She wrote . . . (walk to centre of your side of the room with head down) . . . but never once in her letter did she forgive me . . . .. every letter she somehow managed to bring up the evil deed I had done at your wedding rehearsal . . . then on and on she would list all of your accomplishments.

ELIZABETH:
(still in shock) Mom wrote to you.

SONYA:
(in anger) Yes, she wrote . . . that is the only way I found out what was going on in our family . . . Mom never mentioned Edmond . . . I was in Spain when Dad died . . . the letter was three weeks old . . . then soon after the letters stopped . . . I had a strange feeling something was wrong with Mom.

ELIZABETH:
(inch toward Sonya) I had no way of knowing where you were . . ..

SONYA:
That's okay . . . (wave off Elizabeth's advance) . . . I called Cousin Eva . . . she told me everything.

ELIZABETH:
Cousin Eva never mentioned you . . . ever called.

SONYA:
I made her swear not to tell anyone . . . I guess I was still angry towards you . . . why . . . I don't know why . . . maybe it was the fact that you were a success . . . (dramatic expression) . . . a big-league baseball player.

ELIZABETH:
Famous . . . hardly . . . it was just that there were only a few Canadian girls playing in the American female league during the war.

SONYA:
One of the best players.

ELIZABETH:
My world seemed to fall apart after the doomed wedding. I sulked in my room . . . it seemed like ages . . . I did not go back to work . . . I avoided all of my friends and family . . . I put on a few unwanted pounds . . . I stopped talking to Mom and Dad . . . every once-in-a-while, I would grunt . . . Neanderthal style.

SONYA:
And Dad put up with that . . . I can't see him . . .

ELIZABETH:
. . . I got away with it for about a week . . . after several grunts one morning dad knocked on my door . . . he entered and as he flipped through a magazine he said . . . a nice morning to toss a baseball . . . he found what he was looking for . . . bent back the page and placed it on my bed then said as he left without raising his voice . . . I'll be out in the back yard . . . if you come to your senses.

SONYA:
Is that all he said?

ELIZABETH:
That was all . . . (move to centre of your half of room) . . . I starred at the open magazine . . . then like a big old gorilla I grunted and reached for the opened page . . . over and over my eyes scanned the page . . . nothing registered in my brain . . . nothing . . . I scanned the page again . . . then shooting stars flashed before my eyes . . . it was just a little add . . . very little . . . little . . .

SONYA:
Yes little . . . what did the little add say?

ELIZABETH:
Not much . . . it said try-outs, female baseball league, travel, Saturday . . . Saturday was two weeks away . . . how could I be ready . . . I was ready to leave home . . . the town . . . leave all my troubles . . . my thoughts . . . my emotions and Ed behind . . . but two weeks . . . I was out of shape . . . (pause, turn as if to look out of a window) . . . I could see Dad in the backyard tossing a baseball into his glove.

SONYA:
Mom wrote to me of minute by minute of your progress.

ELIZABETH:
Progress . . . sure and drastic pain . . . every muscle hurt . . . Dad worked me twelve hours a day . . . no snacks . . . it was all worth it . . . I made the team on the first round . . . I travelled . . . played ball . . . made . . .

SONYA:
The front page of the town newspaper . . . a picture of you sliding into home plate.

ELIZABETH:
Some picture . . . all you see is my butt sticking up in the air.

SONYA:
I would know that butt of yours anywhere.

ELIZABETH:
Thank you very much . . . you know they put that same picture in the baseball hall of fame . . . it was great seeing all the girls at the reunion . . . those were the best years of my life.

SONYA:
Years without Edmond . . . you never looked for another fella . . . no one ever caught your eye?

ELIZABETH:
I was too busy . . . then time seemed to pass by . . . after the league closed down, I did some coaching and training for the Canadian team . . . baseball was all I knew, and it consumed my life . . . I . . . I never thought . . .

SONYA:
Thought about anyone else but Edmond.

ELIZABETH:
It was a lot of years . . . I never even thought about Ed . . . .

SONYA:
Years! . . . Edmond was always in my mind . . . even when I was with all those other men . . . some of them I don't recall their names.

ELIZABETH:
Not until I retired . . . then Ed began to creep into my thoughts . . . .and I truly wonder what if . . . what if we got married anyway . . . what if . . .

SONYA:
You would have been happy . . . you would have made a great couple.

ELIZABETH:
. . . what if . . . a home . . . some kids . . . maybe enough for a whole baseball team . . . live in a big old-style house . . . a back yard . . . a pond . . . some ducks . . . (pause) . . . that dream was never to be . . . no kids . . . no house . . . just this apartment . . . old age . . . and you . . .

SONYA:
I am old . . . and alone . . . and I live with you. (beginning of insults and sarcasm bantered back and forth with humour)

ELIZABETH:
You keep better company than I do.

SONYA:
What . . . are you saying I don't make you feel good . . . make you laugh . . .

ELIZABETH:
You are not . . . what I would call funny or humorous.

SONYA:
I can tell you . . . you are not a barrel of laughs.

ELIZABETH:
You trying to get into a barrel would be a hoot.

SONYA:
I am a perfect size eight . . . when I was a young girl I could . . .

ELIZABETH:
Fit into anything . . . after you stretched the life out of the material . . . then you handed them down to me.

SONYA:
Even if you had the prettiest dress in town you would still look like a Tom Boy . . . messy hair . . . cleats . . . stinky old cleats . . . (hold nose) . . . even our dog would cover his nose.

ELIZABETH:
Smell . . . you want to discuss smell . . . you take a bath with strawberry bubble bath . . . you wash your hair with Aloe Vera . . . cactus juice shampoo . . . wrinkle cream for your hands and feet . . . extract of Emu oil . . . cold cream for your face . . . lilac and apple blossom nectar . . . Oil of Olay for the rest of your body . . . then you soak your finger nails in Palmolive . . . lemon scented dish soap . . . all of that before you even put on deodorant and perfume . . .

SONYA:
One must pamper one's body.

ELIZABETH:
I've seen bees congregating on the roof . . . they are confused . . . you can hear them talking . . . one bee says to the other bee . . . (abstract voice) . . . Billy Bob . . . I think there is a colony of wasps using some-kind of chemical warfare . . . a big balloon disguised as a human.

SONYA:
Oh . . . you make me laugh . . . you are a real Joey Bishop . . . what ever happened to him away . . . you should go on the road . . . maybe a car will knock a smile onto that sour puss of yours . . . you old . . . old bag lady.

ELIZABETH:
Sticks and stones may break my bones, but names will never hurt me.

SONYA:
Give me a stick . . .

ELIZABETH:
You wouldn't beat me, would you?

SONYA:
It would be my pleasure.

ELIZABETH:
You are one of those people that use whips and chains and leathers for kinky sex.

SONYA:
I have indulged in the art of sex . . . I am sure I can compare you to a fruit that has never been picked.

ELIZABETH:
I am saving myself for the right man.

SONYA:
With some of the old fellows around here . . . you could be naked as a jaybird . . . and they wouldn't remember what to do . . . and if you got a rise out of them, they'd be so plum tuckered out from the exertion they'd be wasting your time.

ELIZABETH:
Who needs men anyway . . .? I've done fine all these years without them.

SONYA:
Everybody needs sex . . . it is a fact of nature . . . a man needs a woman and a woman needs a man . . . I will prove it to you . . . take a little test . . . (pick up a magazine) . . . there is a short test in this here Playgirl magazine.

ELIZABETH:
A test . . . I don't need to take a test.

SONYA:
Humour me.

ELIZABETH:
I thought I was.

SONYA:

(do not listen, search a page for a question) . . . Are you grouchy all the time and hardly ever smile when you meet people?

ELIZABETH:
(with frown on face think about question)

SONYA:
Don't bother . . . I can answer that question for you . . . a definite yes . . . while sleeping do you dream about men in the nude . . . and when you look at yourself are you wearing heavy winter clothes?

ELIZABETH:
One has nothing to do with the other . . . you know that since I was a kid, I was always chilly . . . even in hot weather.

SONYA:
Another yes.

ELIZABETH:
You don't know what I dream.

SONYA:
Do you have a hard time saying the clinical names of the male anatomy?

ELIZABETH:
They don't come up in a conversation too often at tea.

SONYA:
Go ahead say a name . . . just for the sake of the test.

(Edmond stands and takes a step forward)

ELIZABETH:
(attempt to speak with a faint Pe . . . sound) . . . Pe . . .

SONYA:
You can't do it can you . . . go on say it . . . there is no one here but me.

ELIZABETH:
(another attempt) . . . Pe . . . Pe . . . pencil . . . give me a pencil I will write it down.

SONYA:
No way . . . this is a verbal test . . . another yes.

(Edmond sits back down)

SONYA:
When there is a sex scene in a movie or on T.V. do you complain and get agitated if the scene goes on and on . . . do you change channels?

ELIZABETH:
You don't need sex all the time.

SONYA:
But every now and then . . . sex is good . . . it makes one happy . . . relaxed . . . puts a smile on one's face . . . an internal and external glow.

ELIZABETH:
All those tests are rigged . . . I could find a test that says too much sex is no good . . . and you are a perfect candidate. (pick up a baseball magazine) Here . . . here is a test in this magazine.

SONYA:
A baseball magazine . . . what do a bunch of jocks know about sex . . . all they want to do is score . . . other than that they are clueless

ELIZABETH:
It is not that way anymore . . . sure there are a few duds in the group that make millions . . . but there is a science behind sports now . . . (find proper page)

SONYA:
Go ahead test me.

ELIZABETH:
Are you tired and drained after having sex several times?

SONYA:
Well who wouldn't be?

ELIZABETH:
That is a yes . . . do you pay for sex?

SONYA:
Pay . . . I don't have to buy affection.

ELIZABETH:
For you that should read . . . do you receive payment for sex.

SONYA:
Never . . . never . . .

(Elizabeth questioning glares at Sonya)

SONYA:
. . . okay . . . there was one time . . . years ago . . . there is no question like that.

ELIZABETH:
Do sexually transmitted diseases prevent you from participating in your sport?

SONYA:
All those questions are irrelevant . . . I don't play sports.

ELIZABETH:
The point is you indulge in sex too much.

SONYA:
Jealous . . . you are jealous.

ELIZABETH:
Vamp.

SONYA:
Prude.

ELIZABETH:
Hussy.

SONYA:
Virgin.

ELIZABETH:
Solicitor.

SONYA:
Virgin.

ELIZABETH:
Street walker.

SONYA:
Virgin.

ELIZABETH:
(attempt to say whore) Wh . . ..

SONYA:
Ha . . . you cannot say it can you? . . . A simple word . . . you will use a hundred words to say what one word describes exactly what you are thinking of me.

ELIZABETH:
I do not . . . but if you act the hussy and solicit as a street walker then you are a wh . . . wh . . .

SONYA:
Thanks a lot Sister Mary Theresa . . . the last living virgin.

ELIZABETH:
Don't call me that . . . I am . . . there have been other men in my life . . . other men . . . other than Ed.

SONYA:
I know for a fact Edmond was out of the picture . . . and he did not seduce you . . . so who and when?

(Elizabeth paces back and forth thinking of a way to get out of this situation, Edmond comes forward and begins to pace with her, Edmond is also wondering who and when)

SONYA:
Well when?

EDMOND:
And who . . . who was the guy . . . if he's not dead yet . . . I can arrange it . . . I know a few people upstairs . . . (stop and look up) . . . okay . . . okay it was just a thought . . . If I get the guy's name will you check the big book and tell me if he's headed for heaven or to the agonies of hell.

SONYA:
Who was the guy . . . do I know him?

ELIZABETH:
No, you don't . . . I don't.

EDMOND:
What do you mean you don't?

SONYA:
You messed around with a fellow and never bothered to know him . . . you never bothered to get his name?

ELIZABETH:
We were not together long enough to exchange names.

EDMOND:
Fooled around . . . but had no time to exchange names . . . I can't believe it . . . (walk back to rocking chair) . . . I don't want . . . I am not going to listen to this.

SONYA:
This is getting interesting . . . you have my attention . . . do not leave out any details . . . not one.

ELIZABETH:
You relish in any kind of smut . . . and this is something you will hold over my head until I am in my nineties.

SONYA:
It cannot be anything worse then what I have accomplished in my life . . . go ahead dish out the details.

ELIZABETH:
(stop pacing, stand flat footed) . . . Chicago . . . the seventh game of a winning streak . . . I was hot . . . every pitch was a strike out until Chicago . . . I lost everything . . . my slider . . . my fast ball . . . my whole form . . . I couldn't hit the broad side of a barn . . . and at bat I was worse . . . even on a forced walk I was tagged out between first and second.

SONYA:
Who cares about baseball . . . what about this stranger and the fling?

EDMOND:
Hush . . . I would rather hear about the outcome of the game.

ELIZABETH:
I am leading to the point by justifying my actions to this sordid affair.

EDMOND:
You were out at second . . . continue.

ELIZABETH:
I let the team down . . . we lost the game because of me . . . I was down as far as I could go . . . I was worse than depressed . . . shattered . . . my confidence was shattered . . . I had no more tears to shed.

SONYA:
You needed a drink . . . a tall glass of sympathy to drown your sorrows in.

EDMOND:
It was just one game . . . it was only baseball . . . losing someone you love is worse than a game of baseball . . . are you saying this game was more earth shattering then the demise of our failed wedding plans . . . did you not shed one tear then?

SONYA:
Finally, every disappointment in life caught up with you . . . you needed a . . . (stress big) . . . big drink.

ELIZABETH:
I needed several drinks . . . after the girls settled into the motel rooms several of us sneaked out after curfew . . . I lost track of the number of drinks I had, and I lost track of the other girls . . . so . . . I decided I needed a man . . . a real man.

EDMOND:
I could have been that real man.

SONYA:
And then you gazed across the bar room and there leaning against the doorway was a tall dark handsome man . . . his steel blue eyes swept you off your feet . . . a Prince charming had nothing on this guy.

EDMOND:
What . . . was I not her prince charming?

ELIZABETH:
Hardly . . . I was in no condition to walk . . . I tapped a guy's shoulder at the next table . . . finally I shook him awake . . . he wiped a drool from his face . . . scratched his pot belly then arm in arm we staggered out of the bar.

SONYA:
Just any guy you picked up . . . how uncouth.

ELIZABETH:

It got worse . . . we staggered a few yards out past the back door and rolled down an embankment . . . it was all in a flash . . . he pulled at my dress . . . I yanked his belt . . . (pause) . . . then it was over . . . it was morning when I awoke and crawled up the little hill . . . I was not inclined to look back . . . no need to compound my shame.

EDMOND:
DISGUSTING!

ELIZABETH:
SHAMEFUL!

SONYA:
That was your romantic interlude in life?

EDMOND:
A revolting revelation . . . none of the guys in the army would ever relate a story like that.

ELIZABETH:
SHAMEFUL!

SONYA:
Yes shameful.

EDMOND:
Shame on you.

SONYA:
Shameful . . . shameful . . . shame---full.

ELIZABETH:
The worst thing . . . no matter how many times I've played the events over and over in my mind . . . I just can't remember if I enjoyed myself.

SONYA:
(laugh) . . . I doubt very much if your fellow remembered either.

EDMOND:
Shameful . . . shameful . . . you two women are shameful . . . if I wanted to hear this sort of talk, I would haunt Sneaky Pete's bar instead of being here . . . I am supposed to be here to help the two of you forgive each other and become loving sisters.

SONYA:
A one-minute affair . . . I can't believe it . . . (begin to laugh)

(Elizabeth's mood begins to change to distraught and anger near the end of her dialogue)

ELIZABETH:
I could not live with myself . . . what if Mom and Dad found out . . . what if I got pregnant . . . by a total disgusting stranger . . . my life would have been ruined . . . it was hard enough putting the fiasco of my intended wedding behind . . . I would never be able to show my face in town again . . . it would be more gossip for folks to talk about . . . Poor little Elizabeth. . . .. jilted at the alter . . . had to quit baseball . . . impregnated by a total unknown stranger . . . headline news

SONYA:
It was always about you . . . you . . . you, you . . . you are always thinking about yourself . . . why . . . (talk like Elizabeth) . . . .why is this happening to me . . . why are they treating me this way . . . don't you think that life's misfortunes . . . heartaches and pain sometimes befall on other people . . . like me maybe.

ELIZABETH:
You . . . you're the pretty one . . . the one that lives life in the fast lane of life . . . enjoying every moment.

SONYA:
All of that is only on the outside . . . that is what I wanted people to see . . . but inside . . . inside I was torn apart . . . my world was collapsing in one me . . . and there was no one to comfort me . . . no one was there for me.

ELIZABETH:
There was Dad and Mom . . . you could have come home . . . come home to me.

SONYA:
Dad . . . how could I go to Dad . . . we had nothing in common . . . he was interested in sports . . . you fulfilled his time and affection in that area . . . Mom . . . Mom wanted everything to run smoothly with no bumps in life's travels . . . how could I go to her with my problems . . . she would shut it out . . . pretend it never happened . . . she would tell me not to make waves.

ELIZABETH:
There was me . . . I am your sister . . . I would have been there for you.

174

SONYA:
No . . . No . . . I could not confide in you . . . you were planning your wedding . . . that was your moment in life . . . something special for you . . . I could not go to you with my problem.

ELIZABETH:
You could not come to me, but you were bold enough and not too shy to bellow to everyone that you were pregnant . . . during my special moment . . . talk about a special day going out the window with old garbage.

SONYA:
I could not help it . . . it was as if my emotions and thoughts came to a boil in my head . . . I could no longer hold it inside . . . yes it was the wrong time to shock everyone with my predicament . . . (pause) . . . Cousin Irma was the one that began whispering Edmond's name . . . everyone started speculating . . . no one listened to me . . . especially Mom . . . she went to the kitchen and began wrapping up the food and doing the dishes . . . You ran up to your room . . . everyone's mouths were flapping open and closed like a school of pregnant salmon going up a river . . . (with your hands begin to open and close them to simulate the mouths of fish) . . . all bragging that there was only one fish bold enough to be the proud father to be . . . (pause) . . . out of the corner of my eye I saw Dad with his hand gripped firmly on Edmond's arm escorting him out of the front door . . . something was lost in Edmond's eyes . . . hurt . . . sadness . . . bewilderment . . . that was the last I saw of Edmond . . . until that day of the wake . . . then it was only his picture with his ashes.

ELIZABETH:
Touching story . . . you still cannot convince me that my life was not ruined because of your actions.

SONYA:
Yes, I did put a bump in the road of life for you.

ELIZABETH:
A bump . . . an ant hill is a bump . . . a pot hole in a road is a bump . . . you excavated a pit . . . a meteorite crater . . . Lake Superior without water . . . a hole so deep . . .

SONYA:
I get the point . . . my life had the same big gaping hole of hurt also . . . I had to suffer my fate . . . but you Elizabeth could have took a chance . . . act a little like Mom and ignored the bad and go on as if nothing happened . . . (pause) . . . you should have married Edmond . . . even elope if you had to.

ELIZABETH:
Elope with a man that slept with my sister . . . and got her pregnant.

SONYA:
It was not Edmond.

(pause, Elizabeth with bewilderment tries to piece together the past and present situations and questions)

SONYA:
Edmond was not the man . . . he was innocent.

ELIZABETH:
After all this time you expect me to believe you . . . if it is the truth why didn't you tell everyone before . . . why did you let it go on for so long?

SONYA:
I was an outcast . . . who was going to listen . . . I was ashamed of what I did . . . and small-minded people continued to shame me . . . so . . . with vengeance I kept silent.

ELIZABETH:
My wedding?

SONYA:
I am sorry.

ELIZABETH:
Mom and Dad?

SONYA:
Forgive me.

ELIZABETH:
Ed . . . they are all gone . . . they died not knowing the truth . . . Ed died feeling guilty after all those years of . . .

SONYA:
Please . . . I beg of you to forgive me . . . after all these years I have truly paid for my sins . . . you are the only one left . . . without your forgiveness I cannot go on knowing what has happened to my baby . . . (fall onto knees)

ELIZABETH:

We know what happened to the baby . . . we read your letter over and over . .
. Dad said having a baby that was stillborn was for the best . . . mom nodded
in agreement as she rocked in her rocking chair . . . the same one you now
use.

SONYA:
The baby did not die . . . I gave it up for adoption.

(Elizabeth reaches for Sonya wanting to comfort her and willing to forgive
but holds back. Sonya hides her head and tears in her hands)

SONYA:
I dream over and over every night and it haunts me . . . I pray I could have
changed everything . . . start over again . . . (pause) . . . remember when we
were living the innocence of our youth . . .

(Elizabeth nodes in agreement, again she stretches her hand to place on
Sonya's head but pulls back)

ELIZABETH:
Maybe if on that day . . . that one day it was not Ed that jumped over old man
Barton's fence . . . but a girl . . . Edwina . . . Edwina jumped over the fence.

EDMOND:
(jump up concerned) A girl . . . you would rather have me be a girl?

SONYA:
(get up from knees and wipe away a laughing crying tears) Edwina . . . three
girls . . . she would be just like a sister.

ELIZABETH:
Sonya . . . Elizabeth and Edwina . . . we would grow up as the best of friends.

EDMOND:
I hate that name . . . don't call me Edwina.

SONYA:
If Edmond was not around . . . who else was there?

ELIZABETH:
There you go again . . . you and Ed.

SONYA:
Well you had your chance and you blew it.

ELIZABETH:
It is back to that again is it . . . well who was it that let everything that happened slide for all these years . . . whom let whom share this apartment.

SONYA:
We both applied for this apartment at the same time . . . because we were family . . . sisters . . . it made sense to share . . . after all we have no family of our own.

ELIZABETH:
And whose fault is that?

SONYA:
Whose fault . . . are you saying it is all my fault? . . . after I begged for forgiveness . . . and told you the truth . . . have I not suffered as much as you . . .

(Elizabeth bends down and begins to draw a line down the centre of the floor)

SONYA:
. . . What are you doing?

ELIZABETH:
This is a line . . . do you know what a line is?

SONYA:
Well I can make a line too . . . this is my apartment too . . . I pay rent.

(Sonya bends down and begins to draw a line over Elizabeth's line)

EDMOND:
What are you two doing . . . what is this . . . why . . .? . . . (straddle both lines)

(both women with pretend paintbrushes paint a line over the other's line, both push and bump all the time making comical angry faces to each other)

ELIZABETH:
This is my side of the apartment . . .

SONYA:
And this is mine . . . mine . . . mine . . .

ELIZABETH:
. . . and don't you dare step one inch across this line . . . or else . . .

SONYA:
I will be guarding this border day and night for any infiltrations . . . the perpetrator will get a shampoo squirt right between the eyes.

ELIZABETH:
Oh yeah!

SONYA:
Yeah.

ELIZABETH:
I could bean you between the eyes with a baseball at thirty feet . . . do you want to test my skill?

SONYA:
(in slow motion make dodging moves as if to cross the line) . . . Can you hit a moving target?

ELIZABETH:
No problem . . . (search the floor for an imaginary ball)

SONYA:
(toss imaginary ball in air) Can't find your baseball . . . oh this one looks familiar.

ELIZABETH:
(slowly look up) That's mine . . . (move towards line) . . . give me my ball so I can bean you with it.

SONYA:
No, no you don't . . . (put up hand to stop Elizabeth) . . . remember the border.

ELIZABETH:
(stop, then attempt to step on line, pull back and put an angry pout on face) I . . . hate you.

SONYA:
I hate you first.

EDMOND:
(step behind Sonya) Sonya.

ELIZABETH:
I hate you more.

EDMOND:
I love you.

SONYA:
I can't stand you.

EDMOND:
(step behind Elizabeth) I love you.

ELIZABETH:
I despise you.

SONYA:
You are despicable.

ELIZABETH:
You are despicable first.

SONYA:
Tom Boy;

ELIZABETH:
Hussy.

EDMOND:
(step behind Sonya) I love you.

SONYA:
I . . . hate you.

EDMOND:
(step behind Elizabeth) I love you.

ELIZABETH:
I . . . hate you.

EDMOND:
(step between the two women) Ladies . . .

SONYA:
I hate you.

ELIZABETH:
I hate you.

SONYA:
I hate you.

ELIZABETH:
I hate you;

EDMOND:
(with fists clenched and body and face tense, with a big build up step forward centre and yell) . . . I LOVE YOU!

(pause, Elizabeth and Sonya with faces tense begin to drain their emotions and begin to seek the other's needed affection)

SONYA:
I . . . do love my sister.

ELIZABETH:
I've . . . always loved my sister first.

(Pause, Edmond with bright hopeful eyes walks behind the women and with intent and bewilderment examines the faces of Elizabeth and Sonya, Elizabeth and Sonya with self-conscious bewilderment they gaze at each other with mouths open, each longing to reach out to hug the other, long pause)

EDMOND:
That's it now . . . now hug each other . . . (gesture for both to hug)

(slowly with emotional facial expressions and movements both begin to hug the other, Edmond with happiness walks towards the front as the women continue to mouth words of love and affection, Edmond dabs a hanky to his eyes as he continues to talk to the women, slowly the two break away from each other, Elizabeth heads for her chair and sits, then begins to read a magazine, Sonya moves to her rocking chair and sits then begins to file her fingernails)

EDMOND:
Well . . . if took a while . . . a lot of hard work . . . (look up) . . . maybe the big guy will give me a medal or something . . . I wouldn't mind tasting a pizza . . . with the works . . . (look up again) . . . what's that . . . (look at watch) . . . Yup . . . I am on my way . . . (turn and walk towards back centre of stage, stop at Elizabeth, bend and kiss her on the top of the head) . . . Goodnight Elizabeth my love . . . (as Sonya extends hand to look at her nails stop and tenderly kiss her hand) . . . sweet dreams my love.

(Edmond walks towards back centre of stage, as he reaches a point between the two hanging paintings he stops and pauses, Elizabeth turns on her radio, slow dance music of a big band begins to play, pause, the music plays then fades slightly)

SONYA:
I remember Edmond and I would dance away the night to that sweet music.

ELIZABETH:
Edmond and you . . . always Edmond and you . . . there was an Ed and me you know.

(build then fade in volume)

SONYA:
Edmond and I.

ELIZABETH:
Me and Ed.

SONYA:
Edmond and I.

ELIZABETH:
Me and Ed.

EDMOND:
(loud voice, look up) . . . On second thought big guy . . . my work is not quite finished.

(build in volume)

SONYA:
Edmond and I.

ELIZABETH:
Me and Ed.

SONYA:
Edmond and I.

ELIZABETH:
Me and Ed.

LIGHTS GO TO INSTANT BLACK THEN AFTER A SLIGHT PAUSE THE SOUND OF THE BIG BAND MUSIC BEGINS TO PLAY.

THE END

Publisher's Note:

My Beau had a run of fourteen performances at the Village Theatre in Qualicum Beach, British Colombia by Echo Players.
This play was their entry into the North Island Drama Festival.
Out of eight presentations by other theatre groups, Echo Players' presentation of My Beau placed second overall.
Their efforts and talent garnished a total of seven honourable mentions for; achievement by female actors in a leading role, achievement in set design, costume design, lighting, sound, graphic promotion and ensemble acting.
This was a great success considering that this play was given its first debut, up and against other well-known and established plays.

The Author, Edmond Alcid, and this Publishing House give a rousing round of applause to the ensemble and the crew of Echo Players for their success.

ON WITH THE SHOW
Copyright April 1, 1997
by
Richard Mousseau

STAGE:
ON CENTRE OF STAGE IS FOUR OR FIVE ROWS OF THEATRE
SEATS ON AN INCLINE. ON EACH SIDE OF THE SEATS ARE DARK
RED-CARPET RUNNERS. SURROUNDING THE STAGE IN AN OVAL
PATTERN IS A DARK GREEN BLACK CURTAIN WITH TWO EXITS
AT A FORTY-FIVE DEGREE ANGLE TO THE CENTRE OF THE
SEATS.

SOUND:
TYPICAL THEATRE SOUNDS OF CROWDS, CLAPPING, STAGE
MOVEMENT.

LIGHTING:
TYPICAL THEATRE LIGHTING, SEMI DARK THEN BUILDING TO
GIVE EQUAL LIGHTING FOR VIEWING.

ACTING PARTS:
FIRST LEAD:	JACK
SECOND LEAD:	SANDRA
THIRD LEAD:	INDIGO
FOURTH LEAD:	CISTA
FIFTH LEAD:	EASTMAN
SIXTH LEAD:	GERTRUDE
SEVENTH LEAD:	KISCALL
EIGHTH LEAD:	ALLBURT
NINTH LEAD:	BILL
TENTH LEAD:	SIR TREVOR
ELEVENTH LEAD:	DAME EDNA

CHARACTERS:
JACK: A TALL CLEAN CUT FELLOW IN HIS MID FORTIES, WEARS
A TRENCH STYLE COAT WITH COLLAR TURNED UP, ALSO WEARS
DARK SUNGLASSES, A MAN WHO IS OUT SEEING HIS MISTRESS
(SANDRA), A MAN OF PASSION AND MYSTERY, A MAN OF FEW
WORDS, HIS ANTICS AND GESTURES SAY ALL THERE IS NEEDED
TO SAY, JACK IS A WANT-TO-BE SILENT FILM ACTOR.

SANDRA:

A GOOD-LOOKING WOMAN IN HER LATE FORTIES, SHE WEARS A LONG WINTER STYLE COAT AND DARK SUNGLASSES, SHE IS OUT TO SEE HER BOYFRIEND JACK. UNDER HER COAT SHE HIDES HER PET DOG, ALL THE OTHERS THINK SHE IS PREGNANT, SHE IS A LONELY HOUSEWIFE SEEKING ANOTHER VENUE IN LIFE.

INDIGO:
A YOUNG GIRL IN HER TEENS, SHE IS DRESSED NICELY FOR A NIGHT OUT, BUT ALSO WEARS THE ACCESSORIES OF THE PUNK CULTURE, HER MANNERISMS AND TALK AND DICTION IS THE SOUND OF AN INCOHERENT PUNKER. SHE IS THE BOLDER FRIEND OF CISTA.

CISTA:
A YOUNG GIRL IN HER TEENS, SHE IS DRESSED IN A DRESS FOR A NIGHT OUT, SHE DOES NOT WEAR THE PUNK ACCESSORIES, SHE FITS THE LOOK OF THE NICE GIRL NEXT DOOR, SHE IS A FOLLOWER AND LIKE HER BEST FRIEND INDIGO SHE TALKS THE INCOHERENT TEEN TALK.

EASTMAN:
A VERY ELDERLY MAN, AN OLD TIME FARMER, PLEASANT WITH GOOD MANNERS, DRESSED TO THE TEE BUT FIFTY YEARS OUT OF STYLE, HE IS A LITTLE BIT HARD OF HEARING AND HIS EYE SIGHT IS ALSO A BIT OUT OF FOCUS. HE IS WILLING TO AGREE WITH HIS WIFE GERTRUDE PROVIDING HE HEARS WHAT SHE IS SAYING.

GERTRUDE:
A VERY ELDERLY WOMAN, PLEASANT, DRESSED NICELY BUT ALSO FIFTY YEARS OUT OF STYLE. A WELL-BUILT FARM WOMAN WHO IS ALSO A BIT HARD OF HEARING, SHE IS CONSTANTLY CHANGING HER GLASSES, A VERY LIKABLE AND BUBBLY PERSON, SHE KIND OF OVER DO'S WHAT SHE SAYS AND DOES.

KISCALL:
A THEATRE CRITIC, SEEMINGLY GAY WITH EMPHASIS ON THE FEMININE SIDE, THE ONE TO BREAK DOWN EMOTIONALLY, HE IS DRESSED VERY CASUALLY WITH TELL TALE SIGNS OF A GAY PERSON, HIS MATE IS ALLBURT AND IS ALSO HIS RIVAL CRITIC AT ANOTHER NEWSPAPER.

ALLBURT:

A THEATRE CRITIC, SEEMINGLY GAY WITH EMPHASIS ON THE MASCULINE SIDE, HE IS THE ONE TO ANTAGONIZE THEN TO COMFORT. HE IS DRESSED VERY FORMAL WITH ONLY SLIGHT MANNERISMS OF BEING GAY, BUT NOT AS NOTICEABLE AS HIS MATE KISCALL. HE IS ALSO A CRITIC FOR A RIVAL NEWSPAPER.

BILL:
A YOUNG TEEN IN HIS AWKWARD YEARS WORKING AS A THEATRE USHER. HE IS DRESSED IN AN USHERS UNIFORM WITH MATCHING HAT AND A THEATRE FLASHLIGHT, ACTS SOMEWHAT LIKE AN ADULT BUT HIS YOUTH GETS IN THE WAY.

SIR TREVOR:
A FADED HAS-BEEN BRITISH THEATRE ACTOR, HE IS WELL MANNERED IN HIS PRESENTATION OF WHO HE IS, HE TENDS TO OVER DO NORMAL TALK AS HIS PROFESSION INTERMINGLES IN REAL LIFE. HE FEELS HE IS THE GREATEST ACTOR ALIVE. HIS ATTIRE IS FORMAL EVENING WEAR, TAILS AND TOP HAT, SILK SCARF. HIS WIFE IS DAME EDNA.

DAME EDNA:
AN OLD TIME VAUDEVILLE ACTRESS OF THE CHORUS LINE AND ONCE A COMIC SIDE KICK, SHE IS NOW FLAMBOYANT TO THE EXTREME, SHE DRESSES IN A FLAMBOYANT STYLE WITH EVERYTHING LARGER THAN LIFE, EVERYTHING IS A HOOT TO HER. SHE IS SCEPTICAL OF HER HUSBAND SIR TREVOR BUT ADORES HIM TO THE FULLEST.

BASIC STORY LINE:
IT IS OPENING NIGHT OF A THEATRE PRODUCTION IN AN OLD THEATRE IN AN OUT OF THE WAY AREA OF A TOWN, VARIOUS PEOPLE WITH VERY DIFFERENT BACKGROUNDS ATTEND THIS PRODUCTION AND JUST HAPPEN TO SIT IN THE SAME SECTION OF SEATS, THEIR LIVES ARE REVEALED TO EACH OTHER, OVERHEAD BY OTHERS, COMMENTED ON BY OTHERS, NO SECRETS ARE LEFT UNREVEALED, THE THEATRE ACTORS STEAL THE SHOW, INTERESTING CHARACTERS, CHARACTERS THAT ARE WITHIN OURSELVES THAT WE TEND TO KEEP HIDDEN, ATTEND THE PRODUCTION AND LAUGH AT YOURSELF.

SET AND PROPS:
INCLINED FLOOR.
THEATRE SEATS.
TWO RUNWAYS.

FLASHLIGHT.
POPCORN.
VEGETABLES.
STUFFED DOG.
KNITTING.
PROGRAMS.
FOOD CONTAINERS (TAKE OUT STYLE).
ASSORTED SANDWICHES.
SUNGLASSES.
TRENCH COATS.
USHERS UNIFORM AND HAT.
VARIOUS ACTORS' ATTIRE.

PART ONE

THE STAGE IS DIM, THE EMPTY SEATS CAN BE SEEN, THE MUSIC
OF A FULL ORCHESTRA TUNING UP IS HEARD ECHOING
THROUGHOUT THE THEATRE. A PAUSE, THEN THE MUSIC
BEGINS. ENTERING FROM THE RIGHT EXIT, BILL THE THEATRE
USHER BEGINS TO SLOWLY WALK THE AISLES AS HE REPEATS
SEVERAL TAPS ON THE FLASHLIGHT UNTIL IT SUDDENLY
COMES ON BRIGHTLY INTO HIS EYES, NOT TO MISS THE
OPPORTUNITY, BILL BEGINS TO MAKE GHOULISH FACES IN THE
LIGHT. THE STAGE LIGHTS COME UP VERY SLIGHTLY, BILL
SHINES THE FLASHLIGHT AT HIS FEET AND BEGINS A SOFT SHOE
DANCE AS IF HE WAS IN THE SPOT LIGHT. WITH AGGRESSION,
BILL DANCES FASTER AND FASTER UNTIL HE LAPS INTO A FAST
TAP DANCE. SUDDENLY HIS SHOE FLIPS OFF, BILL HOBBLES
ABOUT WITH HIS FLASHLIGHT SEARCHING THE FLOOR FOR HIS
SHOE. THE STAGE LIGHTS GAIN A BIT MORE, RETRIEVING HIS
SHOE. BILL SITS IN THE FRONT ROW SEAT AND BEGINS PUTTING
IT ON, WIGGLING IN HIS SEAT, BILL REACHES BETWEEN HIS LEGS
AND PULLS GUM FROM UNDER HIM. AFTER TRYING TO DISCARD
THE GUM UNDER HIS SHOE, BILL BEGINS TO CHECK ALL THE
ROWS OF SEATS.

FROM EXIT RIGHT JACK ENTERS DRESSED IN HIS TRENCH COAT
WITH COLLAR UP AND HANDS IN HIS POCKETS AND DARK
SUNGLASSES ON HIS NOSE, SLOWLY INCHING ALONG THE AISLE,
JACK STRAINS TO SEE WHERE HE IS GOING. JACK THEN SITS IN
THE FRONT ROW. ENTERING EXIT LEFT KISCALL WAITS AT THE
TOP OF THE AISLE PREENING AND PAMPERING HIMSELF IN A
VERY DAINTY MANNER, KISCALL WAVES GENTLY TRYING TO
GAIN BILL THE USHER'S ATTENTION. STAGE LIGHTS BUILD

SLIGHTLY MORE, THE MUSIC BEGINS TO FADE INTO THE BACKGROUND BUT IS TO CONSTANTLY BE PLAYING IN THE BACKGROUND THROUGHOUT THE PERFORMANCE.

KISCALL:
Yu-who, yu-who, Mr. Usher.

(Bill looks questionably around)

KISCALL:
Yu-who, up here, Mr. Usher...would you be a dear and assist me.

BILL:
Yeah all right. (move the beam of light up and down Kiscall as you examine him, with an uncaring voice) What can I do for you?

KISCALL:
Well you do not have to be so rude...you should say… in a pleasant voice...may I have the privilege of assisting you...and you should always smile.

BILL:
(in a somewhat sarcastic voice) May I have the privilege of finding your seat for you... (pause then give a forced grin)

KISCALL:
(place your hand on Bill's shoulder, with the other hand present ticket) Trust me dear boy you need to work quite a lot on your mannerisms and professional conduct.

BILL:
(with flashlight look at ticket) Row C, seat two...this way your Highness. (lead Kiscall to his seat)

(from stage exit right enters Indigo and Cista, as they talk they walk the length of the aisle then head to back row to sit)

INDIGO:
Like totally radical.

CISTA:
Not.

INDIGO:

188

For sure.

CISTA:
Billy...are you sure...I can't.

INDIGO:
Believe.

CISTA:
Not.

INDIGO:
TOTALLY RADICAL!

CISTA:
Tonight...totally embarrassed.

INDIGO:
Hey Billy boy!

BILL:
(look around to see who called your name) Here is your seat sir...enjoy the show.

KISCALL:
Thank you, dear boy...I will.

INDIGO:
Like you wanted to meet Bill.

CISTA:
Like embarrass me.

(entering from stage left Sandra is wearing dark glasses and a long winter type coat with something large under the coat in the stomach area, Bill stops by her)

BILL:
May I help you?

SANDRA:
(try to hide face in the collar of your coat) Oh no... No thank you, I am fine...I know where my seat is.

(Bill exits as Sandra walks to her seat all the while trying to hide her identity)

INDIGO:
Duh...you wanted to come to this dumb play...like you knew I had better things to do.

CISTA:
Right...like what...read a book... religious prayer...clean the house...do the dishes?

INDIGO:
Get real...I bought this real nice black nail polish...I was going to do my nails and my toenails.

KISCALL:
Yes yes...black does suit you...pale colours are not you...blue black would go with your eyes.

INDIGO:
I know...I've searched everywhere for the right black.

CISTA:
Right...you're some kind of makeup critic.

INDIGO:
Like rude Cista.

KISCALL:
Excuse me...and yes, I am a critic...a theatre critic. (turn away and fluff up your shirt sleeves)

CISTA:
A theatre critic who knows about make up...right...he's what...thirty...and he knows about the right make up for us.

INDIGO:
Like well... (look at Kiscall) ...he just might.

(from exit right Eastman and Gertrude enter and bump into Bill)

BILL:
Sir...Madam...please follow me this way.

EASTMAN:

I haven't hayed in years...how long has it been Gerty, ...the summer of sixty-nine.

GERTRUDE:
No...no it can't be...I think it was...yes, yes, our son John was born in nineteen fifty-eight... and...

BILL:
(raise voice) Your seats are this way...down near the front.

EASTMAN:
John was a wee baby...but he was no runt.

BILL:
Front...front.

GERTRUDE:
Eastman...the nice boy said our seats are near the front.

EASTMAN:
It's about time he shows us to our seats...youngins think us old folks have all the time in the world to chit-chat about haying...don't they know our old bones get tired and we need to sit down...in our seats.

BILL:
This way.

EASTMAN:
Don't rush me...I've got all the time in the world...I'm retired...retired from farming...been retired for nearly forty years.

GERTRUDE:
Eastman...he doesn't think you are retarded.

EASTMAN:
Who are you calling retarded...I said retired?

GERTRUDE:
Yes, yes dear...I am tired too...my bunion is killing me...are these are seats?

BILL:
Yes madam...row B, seats two and three.

(Eastman enters the row followed by Gertrude. Jack and Sandra are secretly making gestures and eye contact. Kiscall is fluffing his clothes and is constantly looking at his watch. Indigo and Cista are checking their makeup)

EASTMAN:
Quit rushing me Gerty.

GERTRUDE:
I am not rushing you...I am pushing you to hurry up...I need to sit down…my bunion is killing me.

EASTMAN:
Women...always in a hurry...hurry here...hurry there...we got to get there early...I was dressed and ready two hours ago...I was waiting for you.

KISCALL:
I was dressed and ready over an hour ago...my man wasn't ready...so I left without him... now look at me...I am here waiting for him.

INDIGO:
Like here he comes...do something to get his attention.

CISTA:
What...yell out his name...like you did.

INDIGO:
Make eye contact...stick out your chest.

CISTA:
I ain't got that much weaponry.

INDIGO:
Use your tongue.

CISTA:
GROSS!

INDIGO:
It's a turn on...wet the outside of your lips with your tongue...like your licking ice cream.

CISTA:
Ripple vanilla fudge.

INDIGO:
Whatever...here he comes...hey Billy...what's up?

BILL:
(shine light into the girls eyes) Hey... (pause, look at Cista) Hey Indigo...ah...your friend is spacing out.

CISTA:
(shrink into your seat) AH...!

INDIGO:
She's not always nerdy like this... (turn to Cista) ...like what's with you.

KISCALL:
Usher...usher. (wave daintily) Would you please help me.

BILL:
(turn towards Kiscall...shine light onto his face) Yes, your Queeness.

KISCALL:
Oh, the spot light is on me... (ham it up a little) ...I am a star.

BILL:
How may I help you?

(Sandra moves one seat closer to Jack, both continue to make eye contact through dark glasses)

KISCALL:
My date is late, and I wait not knowing his fate...oh...a rhyme.

BILL:
Impressive...dah...please I don't have all night.

KISCALL:
Oh, hang on dear boy...puberty is just around the corner.

(Indigo and Cista giggle)

BILL:
(turn back on girls) Please sir get to the point.

KISCALL:
I am looking for a man.

(Bill steps back quickly and with his hands closes his coat at the waist)

KISCALL:
I said a man not...a boy.

BILL:
(brag) I'm a man...but... I'm straight.

KISCALL:
Don't worry fluff..., I am not interested in you.

INDIGO:
Ooh...he's a man.

CISTA:
(sarcastic) I'm impressed.

KISCALL:
Would you please go into the lobby and page a Mr. Allburt...a tall...rugged...good looking fellow...oh just thinking of him gives me goosebumps.

BILL:
Yuch...two fellows...together.

KISCALL:
When was the last time you got lucky?

(Indigo and Cista lean forward)

BILL:
Ah...ah.

KISCALL:
Love is a wonderful thing...when two people share love...and yes sex...it is fulfilling...I can say I get my share of action...how about you?

BILL:
I get my share.

INDIGO:
In your dreams.

CISTA:

Quiet...quiet... you are making a scene.

KISCALL:
Allburt... the man I am looking for... is probably talking to every Tom...Dick and Harry...you tell him to get his tight little ass in here.

BILL:
Yes, Sir I'll tell him. (walk with a wiggle out the right exit)

(Indigo and Cista giggle)

KISCALL:
(talk towards the girls) Ooo... yes... he does have potential.

EASTMAN:
What time does this... this...whatever it is get started?

GERTRUDE:
I haven't started anything...I have been just sitting here minding my own business.

EASTMAN:
It is my business...I paid for these tickets...I have a right to know what we are here to see...I hate opera.

KISCALL:
(stand and bellow out a line of music) Figarow...Figarow...Figarow.

EASTMAN:
I hate that stuff...with people prancing around in tights... Shakespeare stuff.

INDIGO:
(stand and hold hands to heart) Romeo...Romeo...like where art thou Romeo.

CISTA:
(extend arm towards Indigo) Juliet...Juliet...you are totally radical.

EASTMAN:
I am not going to sit here for two damn hours listening to some damn musical.

INDIGO:
CISTA:
KISCALL:

(stand, give individual actions and renditions) Hello Dolly...Well hello Dolly...well hello Dolly... (do several lines if need be for proper feeling) ...it's good to see you back where you belong.

EASTMAN:
And I can't stand it when there are would-be actors in the audience.

GERTRUDE:
What's that Dear?

EASTMAN:
What's what?

GERTRUDE:
What?

EASTMAN:
What?

JACK:
(turn and gaze at the group)

EASTMAN:
(look at Jack) What's your performance going to be?

JACK:
(quickly turn back, hide behind collar)

SANDRA:
(move bundle under your coat)

EASTMAN:
They remind me of gangsters...or spies...maybe they are spies from another theatre group...come to get the lowdown on this production...Gertrude...what in heaven are we going to see?

GERTRUDE:
Nothing right now...the show has not started yet...there is plenty of time before the show starts...why don't you go...have something to drink.

EASTMAN:
Think...why would I come here to think?

GERTRUDE:

Drink!

EASTMAN:
Gerty you could drive a man to drink. (get up and exit left)

(Gertrude with exasperation on her face pulls out her knitting. Jack reaches slowly for Sandra's hand. They play finger tag, they eventually hold hands and drag out antics while dialogue continues)

SANDRA:
(be nervous as you talk to Jack) This is the first time I have ever done anything like this...it is strange.

KISCALL:
I remember my first time...my first real date...the high school prom...that night I came out of the closet.

GERTRUDE:
Why were you in the closet?

INDIGO:
That's where guys like him live.

GERTRUDE:
You lived in a closet.

KISCALL:
No... no... not living in the physical sense.

CISTA:
My dad says it is all in the head...in the mind...something to do with the water.

KISCALL:
Water...what...I drank bad water at puberty.

GERTRUDE:
Oh...that must have been just awful...were you sick for very long?

SANDRA:
I am sick of sneaking around like this...I feel like hiding all my emotions in my closet and never coming out.

KISCALL:

I know how you feel...I have been there...but you have to come out...break free.

GERTRUDE:
How did you break out?

INDIGO:
Like soaring...his emotions were free of the confines of humanities chains of inhibitions.

GERTRUDE:
I tell you...any parent that kept a child in a closet...chained...and fed bad water should be...be...be...

CISTA:
Hanged.

GERTRUDE:
Be...be...

INDIGO:
Flogged.

GERTRUDE:
No...be...be

KISCALL:
Incarcerated.

GERTRUDE:
Given a good talking to...I have a mind to do it...that's it…a good talking to.

SANDRA:
Jack, we have to talk this out.

(Jack begins kissing Sandra's hand. Allburt enters from the right exit and stands there a moment looking Macho)

INDIGO:
Look at that prime rib.

CISTA:
I am a vegetarian.

198

INDIGO:
Look at that prime brussels sprouts...like that kind of puts a damper on the description of a good hunk of meat.

KISCALL:
Sorry girls...that is my hunk of meat.

INDIGO:
Totally unfair.

CISTA:
Unfair...look at the way you are dressed...How can you attract someone with...with.

INDIGO:
At least I don't look like Goldy-Locks.

CISTA:
With that kind of outfit, you'll attract bikers…punkers...sleaze-balls...like not a lawyer or a doctor.

(Eastman enters from left exit and wanders down one aisle then up the other looking for his seat then exits right)

INDIGO:
Baker man...corporate tycoon...I am expressing myself...it is what's inside of me that counts.

KISCALL:
I had the same problem...Allburt wouldn't even look at me...until I started wearing pink shirts.

INDIGO:
Pink shirts!

KISCALL:
Allburt over here... (wave to Allburt who is still posing as if hoping someone will notice) ...Down here.

GERTRUDE:
Eastman...you walked right by your seat...Eastman where are you going...A blind bat has more sense of direction than that old coot.

ALLBURT:

Kiscall...are these our seats...you know I prefer the side section...middle aisle seat.

KISCALL:
Well...nice to see you too.

ALLBURT:
How am I going to critique this production from this...this inferior location?

KISCALL:
If you would have been ready when I was...

ALLBURT:
I have an improper focal point.

KISCALL:
The seats were taken... (give a slow-motion breakdown)

ALLBURT:
My whole mood will be...totally compromised.

KISCALL:
I...I... paid for these tickets myself...you always do this to me...now look at me...my eyes are going to start leaking...I have to critique this theatre production also...like you I work for a big-name newspaper...

...and I have to give a true account of what is presented on that stage...but now...you are making me emotionally drained...your paper...your column... they always come before...me.

CISTA:
Look what you've done...men...they are all the same...even the ones in the closet.

GERTRUDE:
Oh, my dear you were locked in a closet too...did you drink that bad water...give me your parents' names...I will have a stern talk with them.

ALLBURT:
I beg your pardon...Kiscall...what's with her?

KISCALL:
(take hanky from Cista) Thank you sweetie...at least someone cares.

ALLBURT:
I am sorry...I know I am at fault... here...I brought you some mint coated chocolate kisses...I know you cannot refuse them.

KISCALL:
(give a big sigh, show some forgiveness, place one mint in your mouth and savour it then pass one to Indigo and Cista and Gertrude) Oh you're so sweet and thoughtful...you always think of me at the right time.

ALLBURT:
(open program) A play in three acts...a cast of twenty...Kiscall do you have any idea what this play is about?

KISCALL:
Well of course...I did read the play book...it was right here on the night table...you had plenty of time to read it...but no....you had other things on your mind.

(Jack has his hand in Sandra's coat in the belly area)

SANDRA:
Sex...is that all you think about Jack?... We meet... in out of the way places...in the dark...sunglasses...trench coat...I do all the talking...and you want to kiss...pet and make out.

JACK:
(pause, think, then nod head in an agreeable manner)

ALLBURT:
A pretty straight forward question.

INDIGO:
I would say so.

CISTA:
No other way to answer.

KISCALL:
Allburt would answer exactly the same way.

GERTRUDE:
Eastman on the other hand...thinks about sex...then forgets what he was thinking about...the past twenty years there was no action at either end.

SANDRA:
I need more...more...

KISCALL:
SEX!

SANDRA:
...more then the basic animal grunts and desires.

JACK:
(rub Sandra's stomach then kiss her hand)

ALLBURT:
What else is there?

CISTA:
Men...like totally out of it... you are all like have a one-track mind.

KISCALL:
Dinner...small talk...flowers...

INDIGO:
Like forget the flowers...after a couple of days they are dead...wilted...that's a good indication of a man's affection...as long as he gets to first base...after that he leaves out the effort...but expects the rewards.

KISCALL:
Uh...hu...that's right.

ALLBURT:
We cannot be expected to know what to do all of the time.

INDIGO:
Some of the time would be nice.

(Eastman enters exit right and walks down the aisle and up the other, eating popcorn)

CISTA:
Women should be treated like Queens...all of the time.

ALLBURT:
What about the men...you don't show us all that much respect...we do deserve a bit of it once in awhile?

202

GERTRUDE:
(raised whisper) Eastman...over here...Eastman... (speak to others) ...he spends half of his time dreaming...the other half dreaming about dreaming...no sense at all...(to Eastman)...Eastman turn your hearing aid up...damn fool forgot it at home..(raise voice as Eastman exits left) EASTMAN....!

KISCALL:
They all listen about the same... (look at Allburt) ...right Allburt...Allburt!

ALLBURT:
Yes what?

KISCALL:
Exactly...you have confirmed our suspicions of men.

ALLBURT:
What!

(Jack is busy kissing Sandra's hand, Sandra begins to wiggle and with one hand adjusts her stomach, Bill is entering right exit and surveys the theatre then notices a commotion at the front row)

INDIGO
:(to Cista) There you go Cista...a man in the making...now take Bill and mold him into the kind of man you want.

CISTA:
Like...hopeless.

KISCALL:
I would love the challenge...but I have my hands full trying to teach this one.

ALLBURT:
What! ...What did I do now?

KISCALL:
Now...yesterday...two weeks ago...one year and four months ago.

ALLBURT:
Another one of your...special anniversary things.

KISCALL:
Thing...it is a thing!

BILL:
(point light on Jack and Sandra, clear throat) ...Ech...um...is there something wrong...can I... can...should I get a doctor... or call 911?

SANDRA:
(a loud voice) NO... THERE IS NOTHING WRONG...NOTHING AT ALL.

JACK:
(with a wave of your hand shoo Bill away)

BILL:
But...I... think you are pregnant.

KISCALL:
Oh, how sweet.

INDIGO:
Bright...Cista that Bill of yours...he's bright.

CISTA:
Like he is not my Bill.

INDIGO:
Dah...he is all you talk about.

BILL:
Is the baby due anytime now?

SANDRA:
AH...AH...JACK.

JACK
:(shrug shoulders)

BILL:
I know first aid.

SANDRA:
No... no ...that won't be necessary.

GERTRUDE:
Drugs are necessary.

INDIGO:

204

I have some.

GERTRUDE:
Believe me...I've wrestled with ten births...Eastman was prolific in his time...I'll tell you...there was all total about twenty minutes of excitement and pleasure and affection when we were creating those beings...(become a little excited and angry)...but a total of twenty-two hours of excruciating pain to deliver those beautiful brats of mine...we as women deserve drugs.

KISCALL:
I can just imagine going through all of that pain.

ALLBURT:
Thanks to male gender...you won't.

SANDRA:
Oh...I'm not expecting...ah not expecting at any moment soon...indigestion...that's all...a mild case of indigestion.

BILL:
Well if...if things change...you just holler...I'll come running.

INDIGO:
Bill just wants to look up her dress.

SANDRA:
Believe me...if I am expecting everyone will hear... the whole theatre will hear.

JACK:
(with your hand wave Bill away)

(Bill backs his way-out right exit)

INDIGO
:(speak about Bill as he passes) Pig...look up a lady's dress...a male pig.

SANDRA:
(speak to Jack) This was a bad idea...I should not have come here tonight...I can't go on...it is bloody hard to come up with excuses to see you...right now I am supposed to be walking the dog...

JACK:

(begin kissing the back of Sandra's hand, and with the back of your hand caress her cheek)

SANDRA:
...And the dog doesn't like walking...I had to carry it the last two blocks to get here.

EASTMAN:
(enter right exit and look about as you put popcorn in your mouth as you begin to call out Gertrude's name) Gertrude...Gertrude...where the hell are you?

GERTRUDE:
Down here... (begin to wave) ...over here...you are the most useless man... (pass a thread of yarn to Kiscall who hands it to Allburt who hands it to Indigo who hands it to Eastman) ...please pass this line to my so-called husband.

(entering exit left Sir Trevor and Dame Edna enter and stand displaying their exaggerated theatre garb)

TREVOR:
My dear Edna... have you ever in your whole theatrical life seen such a theatre of shambles.

GERTRUDE:
Follow the line Eastman.

EASTMAN:
You treat me like a child...do you think I can't find my way to our seats.

(Indigo, Cista, Kiscall, Allburt shake their heads no)

EASTMAN:
Well I can.

GERTRUDE:
Cannot.

EASTMAN
:(mumble and grumble) Can too.

EDNA:
The patrons are a sure give away to the class of a theatre.

TREVOR:

Truly peasants.

GERTRUDE:
Eastman...you have been wandering around for...

EASTMAN:
I was… trying to find some folks I know...strike up a conversation.

GERTRUDE:
This ain't no barber shop...now sit down.

(Eastman sits as Gertrude rolls up the yarn)

TREVOR:
Riff raft...not a single mind of intelligence.

EDNA:
Sir Trevor do you think anyone shall recognize us as true actors of the stage...
(hold head high and strike a pose)

TREVOR:
My arm Dame Edna... (begin to walk to front centre)

EDNA:
Thank you, Sir Trevor.

TREVOR:
I doubt very much these... (gesture to stage audience) if one of them knows
of such talent as ours.

EDNA:
London....Prince Albert Hall...the Queen Mother was in attendance.

TREVOR:
Yes...and that bitch of a director should have given you the part. (exaggerate
all moves dramatically)

EDNA:
I offered to sleep with him...but no... he would have no such encounter. (be
always flamboyant)

TREVOR:
His eyes were on that young stage hand...his features were quite feminine.

INDIGO:
Hey...who are those two fashion models from the sixteenth century.

KISCALL:
Can't say that I know them...Allburt do you?

ALLBURT:
At the moment I don't recall their names... I do remember reviewing a stage production they were in... some years ago.

KISCALL:
Yes yes... (place a hand on Allburt's arm) ...I remember...that night I was reviewing the show...the night we first met...we had dinner late...

CISTA:
What about the old fogies?

ALLBURT:
They somehow came to Canada on a whirlwind promotion from the British Theatre...the show bombed.

KISCALL:
That was the only review we both agreed on.

ALLBURT:
I've seen them around...but not in any major production.

INDIGO:
Like total has-beens.

ALLBURT:
Quite right.

EASTMAN:
(throw popcorn at Sir Trevor and Dame Edna) Get out of the way...I can't see the show.

GERTRUDE:
Eastman...the show hasn't started yet...but they look like theatre people...maybe they are part of the cast...don't throw your popcorn around...what about the poor people that have to clean this place.

EDNA:
I don't recall that you had all that impressive a part.

TREVOR:
Not visually...the lines...oh the profound integrity of the lines... (become the actor of the past) ...Be it not...that I have not...not what thou my Lord has saken me to bring forth...this night through wind and rain and sleet I have failed in my quest to deliver...what my master has quested of me...(pause)...I am shamed...for sanctuary in a hovel of maid and drink this night of sleet and rain and wind...yet the night sky be of dishevel...and cast a wintry layer of snow upon the cobblestones that thou has named pathways that leads a man of my stature from home to castle to merchant building...come this night I have failed in my Lord's eyes...(pause)....drink, drink, liquor of sweetness savoured on my lips as did the keeper's daughter of large bone...hence in a stupor I did awake a throbbing in my skull as it lay in her ample bosom...I gasp for breath...light of morning next greeted a man of no pride...as a dog with tail between legs...cowering and begging for forgiveness from a Master...my former employer...disgraced through the slums of Londonary I am scorned by my new peers...quivering I wish to hide from the slurs...(gesture and point as if to scorn yourself)...whom disregarded his oath did not through sleet, rain, wind and snow deliver the King's mail...(drop head, lower hands to side, a pose of disgrace)

EDNA:
(lift hands and slightly clap almost inaudible) Bravo...bravo...you did steal the scene.

EASTMAN:
All of that just to say he didn't deliver the mail...he was a bit long winded about the whole story.

GERTRUDE:
Hush up Eastman...they may hear you.

EASTMAN:
If a mail man ever gave me that excuse...I'd...I'd...

GERTRUDE:
You'd what?

KISCALL:
Bring back the use of the stage hook.

ALLBURT:
Yet another thing we agree about Kiscall...yank his carcass right off of the stage.

INDIGO:
How about tomatoes and fruit...like rotten vegetables.

KISCALL:
Oh no never...never do that.

ALLBURT:
Out of work actors...bad actors like him just love to do a scene like that.

KISCALL:
If they are on stage like that and the audience boos them and begins to throw vegetables and fruit the actors are under contract to clean the stage and are allowed to keep the take...they eat like Kings and Queens.

ALLBURT:
So never give them the satisfaction.

TREVOR:
That was my finest hour...adulations from the patrons.

EDNA:
We did eat good that week. (walk with Trevor to your seats)

CISTA:
(get up to leave) Like excuse me.

INDIGO:
Where are you going?

CISTA:
Mother...do you need...like need to know everything?

INDIGO:
Sure.

CISTA:
To pee...okay (exit right)

INDIGO:
Enjoy yourself.

JACK:
(move your hand to Sandra's knee, kiss her about the neck)

ALLBURT:
It would be a better presentation then what Sir Trevor did...we gave his performance two thumbs down. (with Kiscall give thumbs downs)

GERTRUDE:
See that Eastman...they are in love...tenderness...affection...why were you not ever like that?

EASTMAN:
I never did like that smooching stuff...it got in the way of the sex.

EDNA:
Try doing a love scene with his Lordship here...after he has devoured a bunch of little green onions.

TREVOR:
Onions were all they threw onto the stage that day...I was hungry.

SANDRA:
Ooh... (hold stomach and move about as Jack puts his hand into your coat and stops the movement) Ooh...

GERTRUDE:
Ooh..did the little one kick?

SANDRA:
Oh no... ah yes...just a little.

(Cista enters exit left and walks to the front and sits beside Sandra as the coat begins to move about again)

SANDRA:
She must be a little restless...all cooped up in there.

CISTA:
Like totally amazing how a baby that big just...just... (with hands gesture a baby being delivered) ...plop out just like that.

JACK:
(hesitate and make a face as you cares Sandra's hand)

GERTRUDE:
Deary...it seldom just happens like that.

CISTA:
I don't really think I'm going to have kids.

SANDRA:
At a certain time in your life you will get that special urge...your body will say it is time...it's time.

GERTRUDE:
Men are ready all of the time...any time...I should know... (elbow Eastman) ...after ten kids.

EASTMAN:
Mighty fine brood... if I say so myself.

GERTRUDE:
You would.

EASTMAN:
Would what?

GERTRUDE:
What?

(Bill enters exit right and walks towards the front as he checks the seats)

CISTA:
I absolutely...definitely say one is plenty.

SANDRA:
What about the man in your life... what if he would like more than one?

CISTA:
Then he can have them.

KISCALL:
I would...I think I really would... (look questionably at Allburt)....Allburt...

ALLBURT:
Not in my life time.

SANDRA:
What about your boyfriend Cista... (point to Bill) ...what does he think?

CISTA:

Him... (point to Bill)

KISCALL:
Usher dear boy...when the time in your life comes...how many children would you like to have?

BILL:
Excuse me!

ALLBURT:
Your girlfriend was wondering about how many children you would like to father.

CISTA:
He's not my...

EASTMAN:
The fathering part is the fun part...after that it's all up to the woman.

GERTRUDE:
Yes, you have been of great help.

EASTMAN:
Just doing my duty.

BILL:
I... I... never... never...

INDIGO:
Like, you are still a virgin.

BILL:
I... I'm not...not a ...

INDIGO:
Virgin.

BILL:
I've done it plenty of times.

CISTA:
(be upset) With who?

BILL:

No one...I've stopped...I'm saving myself for the right person.

INDIGO:
Still a virgin.

CISTA:
Who was it...Betty-Lynn Ohanlin?

EASTMAN:
I was...oh...it was behind my pa's farm...I was twelve...she had deep blue eyes...

GERTRUDE:
Don't go telling that sheep story again.

BILL:
No...no one... (put a hand to cup the side of your mouth) ...I didn't want Indigo to think I was...you know.

KISCALL:
My first...before I met Allburt...the spring formal...the captain of the football team.

ALLBURT:
His date freaked when she saw the two of them...if I recall she is now a nun.

BILL:
I am kind of interested in... you.

CISTA:
Like cool.

KISCALL:
So, Bill...how many kids do you want?

BILL:
Five or six...all a year apart...enough for a hockey team.

CISTA:
No way...my body will be totally totalled...stretch marks...extra wrinkles...and flab...a sagging butt...boobs hanging down to here.

(all the men grimace and blurt out ugh)

TREVOR:
Devastating...quite devastating that a young firm...lush nymph shall simply fall apart when their child birthing years have ended.... devastating.

(all women are dejected and respond with thanks a lot)

EDNA:
Trevor do you always have to make a big production out of everything?

TREVOR:
I tell it the way I see it.

GERTRUDE:
How would you like me to close your eyes for you... (hold up a fist)

TREVOR:
My dear lady.

EDNA:
I'll help.

BILL:
Fine...fine...I won't father any children...I'll become a Monk... (look at Cista) ...are you satisfied now? (stop by Indigo before you exit right) ...get your feet off the seats.

KISCALL:
Their first lovers quarrel.

CISTA:
And it's all Indigo's fault.

INDIGO:
Mine.

CISTA:
You called him a virgin... (return to your seat, upset)

SANDRA:
Jack...I would like to have a child with you...would you do that for me?

JACK:
(nod yes then begin to kiss her neck)

GERTRUDE:
Eastman...how many times are you going to embarrass me...with that old sheep story.

EASTMAN:
Why are you so upset...it was way before I met you?

TREVOR:
Edna, I am sure glad you got fixed before we pursued our romantic rendezvous.

EDNA:
Fixed...what am I to you...some stray dog?

TREVOR:
Edna dear...you know me...if those big medical words are not in the script...I cannot say them.

ALLBURT:
Opposite sexes...always bickering...Kiscall...aren't you glad we are of the same gender?

KISCALL:
A child of our own would be nice... if there was an operation for men...I would gladly have it...I would do that for you.

ALLBURT:
Don't do me favours.

EDNA:
I would like to fix a few men.

GERTRUDE:
If I knew then what I know now...I would have had Eastman fixed years and years and years ago.

INDIGO:
Total castration...the only way to go.

JACK:
(cross legs and frown)

KISCALL:
ALLBURT:

TREVOR:
OUCH!

EASTMAN:
We did that to an old plough horse...pitiful...just pitiful...he kept checking out the mares...but nothing happened...no levitation...pitiful...just pitiful.

CISTA:
Like get real...a bit drastic don't you think?

INDIGO:
Drastic...like do men really use their heads to think.

SANDRA:
To have a baby with the true love of your life...is wonderful...an accumulation of two people...their combined emotions...thoughts... features...they are the future...our hopes and dreams that they will accomplish everything in life that we haven't.

JACK:
(pick at your teeth with a toothpick)

TREVOR:
(place finger in your ear and wiggle it)

EASTMAN:
(wipe nose on your coat sleeve)

KISCALL:
(with a wet finger brush your eyebrows)

ALLBURT:
(make a face in an attempt to sneeze)

SANDRA:
To grow old and look back with pride at the way your children have turned out.

EDNA:
(glance at the men) Well look at these descendants.

GERTRUDE:
Their parents must be turning in their graves.

BILL:
(enter exit left and with your hand scratch your butt)

SANDRA:
It takes a mother and a woman to make a man to be proud of.

EDNA:
And there is no end to it...look at these men...like a bunch of monkeys on display.

BILL:
May I have your attention.

EASTMAN:
(stand to attention and salute as if you were in the army)

EDNA:
I can never take you anywhere in public.

TREVOR:
What dear lady are you on about now?

EDNA:
Can you not do your grooming at home before we go out?

GERTRUDE:
And what are you doing Eastman?

SANDRA:
Jack...that is annoying.

JACK:
(without your hands chew on a toothpick, in a cartoon manner move it all about the mouth)

GERTRUDE:
Sit down Eastman.

BILL:
Excuse me.

INDIGO:
Cista...Bill...he's trying to get your attention.

KISCALL:
Allburt...do you like children?

ALLBURT:
They are all right...I guess.

GERTRUDE:
The usher said give me your attention...not to stand at attention.

CISTA:
He's scratching his butt...he's attracting enough attention...he doesn't need mine.

BILL:
Ladies and gentlemen.

INDIGO:
Oh...Bill has manners.

GERTRUDE:
Ask any one around what the usher said...will you sit down Eastman.

EDNA:
What are you digging for...is there gold in the recesses of your ear?

KISCALL:
Little ones' pitter pattering around the house.

TREVOR:
I need to itch now...not yesterday...or a week ago...but now.

ALLBURT:
Kiscall...if you want to hear the pitter patter of tiny feet on the floor...get a guinea pig.

BILL:
(raise voice) Excuse me.

CISTA:
I'm not interested in Bill.

INDIGO:
Dah...

SANDRA:
Jack you're disgusting sometimes.

GERTRUDE:
Sit down you ole fool.

EASTMAN:
I used to love to play pool...back in the army I...

GERTRUDE:
Sit... (pull Eastman into his seat)

BILL:
(yell) Quiet!

(all turn quickly to look at Bill standing at the left exit. All freeze in position, there is a long pause. Bill puts his hand over his brow and looks out over the real audience and slowly points the flashlight from person to person. Bill strains to see something, one by one other cast members begin to turn and stare out at the audience, each in their own way with expressions and mannerisms attempt to gain laughter from the audience with their silence. Milk the audience until the sufficient giggles, comments and laughter are gained then fall back into the flow of the play as if nothing interrupted it in the first place)

BILL:
(yell) Quiet!... thank you....(straighten hat and then walk to the middle of aisle)... thank you...I...I...I

EASTMAN:
You have our attention...spit it out boy.

BILL:
The management regrets to inform you that there will be a slight delay of tonight's performance.

JACK:
(shrug shoulder then take Sandra's hand and begin to kiss it)

ALLBURT:
What's up?

BILL:
Oh...ah...one...of the man actors is...is a little bit hung...a little sick.

220

ALLBURT:
I know a few actors... (look at Trevor) ...that should be hung.

TREVOR:
I should have shot the critic that critiqued my performance.

EDNA:
Trevor...mind your blood pressure...do not let those understudies for tinker-bell rile you.

KISCALL:
Tinker-bells...Allburt she called us tinker-bells.

ALLBURT:
Well...we are.

KISCALL:
Quite right.

ALLBURT:
After all they are the has-been want-to-be actors.

BILL:
(clear throat loudly, point flashlight on Allburt)

KISCALL:
Sorry dear boy...go ahead.

BILL:
As I was...

KISCALL:
Continue on...you were about to mention.

BILL:
Yes I...

KISCALL:
That some poor actor was fed up with acting...and was about to hang himself.

BILL:
I did not.

ALLBURT:

I truly feel that I would like to string up one particular so-called actor.

BILL:
DO YOU MIND!

KISCALL:
Allburt...you are interrupting this dear boy.

ALLBURT:
Yes...yes...by all means continue.

KISCALL:
You said someone hung themselves back stage.

BILL:
I...

GERTRUDE:
That is just dreadful...a shame...will the play go on?

INDIGO:
What is that saying...you know...people say it at funerals about the dead guy.

CISTA:
(with a tissue to an eye give a fake tear) He would have wanted it that way.

SANDRA:
(with one hand in Jack's hand the other stretched out) The show must go on without me...do it for me.

KISCALL:
(stand and put a hand to brow and turn head) I am not worthy...carry on without me.

ALLBURT:
She was twenty...he was eighty...he died a happy man...he would want you to spend his money on a gigolo.

GERTRUDE:
Marry any woman you want when I'm gone...but don't give her my clothes...hairbrush or my shoes.

EASTMAN:

I'm telling you right now all those sayings are bull...dead people...are dead people...they don't say or mean anything...people just say things like that so they can carry on with a clear conscience...when I go...I'm going to make sure everyone feels guilty.

BILL:
He did not hang himself...the show is going on with him...as soon as he sobers up.

TREVOR:
(stand) I...with great sacrifice do offer my eminent talent...I will...for the sake of the audience stand in for my fallen fellow actor...boy hurry...get me a script...one quick glance through it then I will be ready...a performance of superior grandeur...not a tearless eye shall be seen as accolades of applause fill this theatre from wall to wall to balcony on high...

EDNA:
Bravo...bravo... a true trouper...bravo Sir Trevor.

ALLBURT:
That's bull...but the best acting I've ever seen you do.

KISCALL:
I for one would like to see Sir Trevor glance through a script then give a faultless performance.

ALLBURT:
It is ludicrous...there is no way he can do it...I would stake my reputation on it.

EDNA:
Willing to wager a small note on it, Mr. Newspaper Critic?

ALLBURT:
A bet...you are willing to put up money on this.

EDNA:
I'll give you two to one odd's...that Sir Trevor...at the end of his performance will have mothers...fathers...and children weeping in the aisles.

TREVOR:
Thank you, my dear lady.

KISCALL:

Weeping from an over exertion of laughter.

INDIGO:
I've got like five bucks that say Sir Trevor can do it.

EASTMAN:
A hundred says the fancy man can't.

GERTRUDE:
Where in blazes did you get one hundred dollars?

EASTMAN:
It was just laying in a dresser drawer.

GERTRUDE:
Stuffed in a sock...rolled up in my underwear and covered by my bras.

EASTMAN:
Right there in plain view.

CISTA:
I say he totally can't...like do it in one try...what is two to one odds?

INDIGO:
Like just say you pretend to bet with me...I say he can...you say he can't...I give for pretend two to one odds...you bet one dollar and if he can act...

TREVOR:
I assure you I am an artist.

INDIGO:
Yeah...yeah...whatever...if he can act, I win, and I take your dollar...now if he can't act...then you win....and I'll pay you two dollars.

CISTA:
Oh, that's easy...okay I'll bet...fifty cents.

INDIGO:
Fifty cents...like get out of town sister.

BILL:
You can't bet on him...the management won't let him act in this play anyway.

EDNA:

What? ...do they know who this man is?

BILL:
(attempt to speak then shrug shoulders)

EDNA:
This is none other than Sir Trevor Hargove esquire of Devonshire...knighted by her majesty in a gala ceremony at the Royal Theatre...London...England.

BILL:
(again shrug shoulders)

EDNA:
Don't you realize you are in the midst of a great actor.

ALLBURT:
He does now...everybody does.

KISCALL:
All of that happened in the past...the dark ages of theatre.

EASTMAN:
What have you done lately... have you been on the Love Boat show...or Murder She Wrote?

GERTRUDE:
All of the old actors are on those shows...I don't recall ever seeing you.

TREVOR:
My dear lady...I am a master of the live theatre...not a second-rate exhibitionist of trivial drivel of domesticated television.

GERTRUDE:
Trivial...On 'Nowonder the World Turns' lives are happy...tragic... emotional...(dab eye)

JACK:
(place a hand on Sandra's inner thigh)

SANDRA:
I've never missed an episode...Brent's girlfriend from a year ago murdered Brent's second wife so she could get back into his arms before...

EDNA:

...before Brent's brother Byron buys her off so she doesn't get her hands on the family fortune.

TREVOR:
Edna!

EDNA:
It is soap opera...real people in real life situations...it is not trivial.

EASTMAN:
Trevor old man...if you can't get onto television...did you ever think of changing careers...you ever think about farming?

ALLBURT:
Pig farming...you could really ham it up on a farm... a captive audience.

KISCALL:
Pig and ham...I get it...a ham actor.

CISTA:
Like you're saying 9926910 is like drivel too.

INDIGO:
No way man...real problems of real kids in an adult dominated world.

CISTA:
That is heavy...real heavy...I can relate to their retaliation against the establishment.

INDIGO:
Adults...like totally buggered up totally everything.

TREVOR:
Fine...if you all wish...I will not offer my services to this play...though it may need to be save.

EASTMAN:
Pig farming...that is the future...they call it the other white meat...bacon is brown...ham is red... anyway it's called the other white meat.

TREVOR:
(sarcastic tone) Oh really.

EASTMAN:

226

Do you want to know something?

TREVOR:
Not really.

GERTRUDE:
Have a seat...he is going to tell you anyway.

EASTMAN:
There are too many pencil pushers...computer tapers and too many actors.

ALLBURT:
Intriguing...how do you figure that?

EASTMAN:
Logic...plain simple logic...everyone wants to have a fancy clean office job...ninety per cent of children can't function in their daily lives without a computer only a finger tip away...and damn too many want-to-be actors wishing for stardom with an income larger than a small country's wealth.

KISCALL:
Your point sir.

EASTMAN:
In another couple of years there ain't going to be no farmers… no one growing food...no one herding cattle.

TREVOR:
If they can't make a living farming or ranching, they should find another line of employment.

INDIGO:
Acting.

CISTA:
A computer programmer.

EASTMAN:
If there ain't no farmers… then there ain't no food...no farmer...no food...no farmer...no food...

TREVOR:
Yes?

EASTMAN:
All those pencil pushers...computer whizzes and actors ain't going to eat.

TREVOR:
I trust that you have a solution?

EASTMAN:
Darn tooting, I do.

TREVOR:
By all means enlighten us with all of your peasant intelligence.

GERTRUDE:
Them are high flouting words...spoken with elegances...but I get this gut feeling that you've been insulting my Eastman.

EDNA:
Hell, Trevor is just good at it...years of theatre.

EASTMAN:
I figure a quota system... them that ain't good actors...ones that ain't been on the Love Boat or Fantasy Island...they have to become farmers.

TREVOR:
Absurd!

EDNA:
I think it would be kind of nice to grow fruits and vegetables instead of heaving it thrown at us on stage.

KISCALL:
It has been some time since you have been on stage.

TREVOR:
Good acting parts are few and far between.

KISCALL:
So are good actors.

EASTMAN:
Plenty of room for hog farmers.

JACK:
(begin kissing Sandra about the neck)

SANDRA:
(become infatuated, begin to accept Jack's advances, put a hand on Jack's leg and caress his knee)

TREVOR:
Do you know Edna...I have suddenly achieved a craving for a ham on rye with mayo...a dill pickle...usher... usher...

BILL:
(flash a light onto Trevor) You bellowed.

TREVOR:
Edna look...I am in the spotlight again.

BILL:
(turn flashlight off) Now you're not.

TREVOR:
You must be a union man.

BILL:
What?

TREVOR:
Oh, never mind...there is a deli just across the street...I would like a ham on rye with mayo...and a dill pickle...Edna...anything for you?

EASTMAN:
Sounds good...make mine the same...except I'll have it on whole wheat...none of that Chinese Mayo guy...no pickle...fresh green onions.

GERTRUDE:
Eastman...onions give you gas.

JACK:
SANDRA:
(begin to indulge in heavy passion)

EASTMAN:
It's still early...it won't affect me for at least another six hours.

GERTRUDE:
It will affect me...unless you've decided to sleep with the hogs...hold the green onions.

EDNA:
A ham and cucumber sandwich on whole wheat...no crust.

GERTRUDE:
Oh, I haven't had that in ages...make mine the same.

INDIGO:
KISCALL:
ALLBURT:
(all at the same time) Fries, lots of French fries, Oh, yes, a cucumber sandwich, Italian sausage on a bun.

(pause)

CISTA:
A medium rare steak sandwich, lettuce, pickles, onions on a sesame seek bun...and Canadian spring water.

BILL:
I am an usher...not a waiter...or a gopher...I don't take food orders.

JACK:
(pull a ten-dollar bill from your pocket and wave it in the air, do not stop intimacy with Sandra)

BILL:
(snatch the money slowly) ...Unless there is an incentive... (pull out note pad and a pen, place flashlight under an arm) ...okay...who wanted what.

ALL:
(begin to place orders at the same time, a free ad-lib method, do not be too confusing, do not let the pace slow)

INDIGO:
French fries...lots of fries with ketchup.

KISCALL:
A cucumber sandwich with ham on watercress.

EDNA:
Ham and cucumber...thinly sliced.

GERTRUDE:
Yes...yes...decisions...the same please.

230

TREVOR:
Ham on rye with mayo...a dill pickle.

ALLBURT:
Italian sausage on a bun with sauerkraut.

EASTMAN:
Ham on whole wheat...no Chinese mayo.

GERTRUDE:
EDNA:
Whole wheat for ours.

EASTMAN:
Ham on whole wheat...no mayo guy...little green onions.

INDIGO:
A coke.

CISTA:
Canadian spring water.

ALL:
Yeah Canadian spring water.

CISTA:
Medium rare steak sandwich...lettuce...

BILL:
(begin to sing in a jingle fashion) ...pickles, onions on a sesame-seed bun.

KISCALL:
(hand a wad of money to Bill) That should just about cover it.

BILL:
And.

KISCALL:
A handsome gratitude for your assistance.

BILL:
That's... (read from order list) a steak sandwich with the works...two ham and cucumbers one without ham...one piggy on rye...one piggy without emperor

Mayo...a piggy in a bun...a coke and fries and a round of Canadian spring water.

(pause)

JACK:
SANDRA:
(your passion has increased, pay no attention to the others)

(all slowly cast eyes on Sandra and Jack, retain mannerisms of characters as you watch)

BILL:
Excuse me...what can I get for you...a ham sandwich...cold cuts...sausage...a Canadian spring water shower...a bed...

JACK:
(wave a no committal to Bill)

SANDRA:
(in a voice void of strength) Anything!

BILL:
(dot the pad with pen and begin to exit left) Two ham on rye...mayo...pickles...etc...etc.

(all begin to chat among themselves as Jack and Sandra begin to entangle themselves with moans of passion. As Jack and Sandra really get intimate in a slap stick comic way, the others slowly one by one begin to watch, little whispers to each other, all should at different times react to what Jack and Sandra are doing, stretch out antics as long as possible for as long as audience is reacting favourably. Jack and Sandra build as much as possible to a climax, others should be wide eyed, mouths open, snickers, panting with as much variance as possible, when the feel is right Bill enters right exit)

BILL:
I've got ham on ham...ham and mayo...ham without ham...cucumbers as substitutes...fresh fried French fries...a mouth-watering steak sandwich and Canadian spring water.

(Jack and Sandra break apart panting then stretch out in their seats physically drained)

KISCALL:

Oh, just in time... (fan face) ...I was ready to go home.

GERTRUDE:
I had some heavy thoughts of my own.

SANDRA:
Boy am I hungry.

JACK:
(nod with agreement, raise a hand and Bill will slap a sandwich into it)

(Bill begins to hand out the food orders to everyone, they all accept their orders but hesitate to eat them)

EASTMAN:
Those two must have been going at it for over fifteen minutes.

EDNA:
And that was just the warm up round.

CISTA:
Like they are old people.

INDIGO:
You would totally figure that at their age all that sex stuff would...like...have worn off.

GERTRUDE:
Eastman once attempted foreplay...he managed to make it last a good five minutes.

ALLBURT:
Once...and you have how many children?

EASTMAN:
That beginning stuff is a waste of time...I like to get a good night's sleep.

TREVOR:
Once...

GERTRUDE:
Once...it was winter.

EASTMAN:

Damn cold...I was milking the cows...milk froze before it hit the pail...clink...clink...clink, clink.

GERTRUDE:
Eastman had three layers of clothes on...a one-piece long john with a trap door...a belt and suspenders sewn right onto his pants.

EASTMAN:
Confounded woman.

GERTRUDE:
You took off your shirt first then tried to pull off your long johns before taking off your suspenders...I lay in bed in my new Christmas nightgown waiting patiently...I could not stop giggling...it was the best strip tease I ever saw....it got me so excited.

EASTMAN:
Confounded woman.

GERTRUDE:
The next morning when I tried to untangle his clothes...I couldn't get them undone....

(Jack and Sandra are munching away on their sandwiches as they listen, Bill is slurping his spring water through a straw)

GERTRUDE:
I had to use my scissors...all I was left with was patches...they made a nice fine quilt for my youngest daughter...conceived that night...ain't that right Eastman? (giggle)

EASTMAN:
Confounded woman... (open coat and with thumb pull on your big red suspenders) ...Gertrude did manage to save my suspenders.

KISCALL:
I could just cry...now that is love.

(all begin to take a look at their sandwiches, pause then begin to call out what they have in their hands)

TREVOR:
Greasy steak sandwich...(hand it to Cista)

CISTA:
Ham without Mayo Ce Tung... (hand it to Eastman)

EASTMAN:
Ham with cucumber. (hand it to Edna)

EDNA:
Ham with cucumber. (hand it to Gertrude

GERTRUDE:
Plain cucumber. (hand it to Kiscall)

KISCALL:
Italian sausage. (hand it to Allburt)

ALLBURT:
Ham on rye. (hand it to Trevor)

INDIGO:
No problemo...I've got my French fries.

(Jack and Sandra look at their sandwiches, shrug their shoulders and continue to eat)

INDIGO:
(get up and walk to Bill and eye him up and down)...In a geeky sort of way...you're not all that bad to look at...like you're no jock or anything...I mean like you're not a total geek.

BILL:
Thanks...I guess...and you're... you're plain weird.

INDIGO:
Yeah...like really thanks.

(Cista exits right and Bill watches her every move)

INDIGO:
Put your eyes back in your head.

BILL:
I was not staring or anything.

INDIGO:

I like know...that you like her...you've been gawking at her since grade nine...peeping around corners...hiding behind lockers...pretending to tie your shoe laces...you tied…(begin to laugh) your shoes together in gym class...one step and splat on your face...totally awesome.

BILL:
Total embarrassment...(put a hand over your eyes)

INDIGO:
No totally cool...it got Cista's attention...she giggled then said 'I hope he's not hurt'...she was serious...she had feelings for you.

BILL:
She did.

INDIGO:
I know about stuff like that...she really digs you...but she's waiting for you to make the first move.

BILL:
I...I can't....I wouldn't know how...she may turn me down...I may be scarred for life...total rejection.

INDIGO:
So what if she says no...it's no big deal...you like just go and ask someone else.

BILL:
I couldn't...Cista is the only girl for me...if she turns me down...I'll become a monk.

EASTMAN:
Monks are good hog farmers...they make excellent smoked hams.

TREVOR:
Act boy...pretend you are someone else...then get into character...think like that character.

EDNA:
The same way Trevor proposed to me...on stage in the middle of a fight scene.

KISCALL:
Recreate the scene...it may give Bill some idea.

TREVOR:
Here...now?

ALLBURT:
Are you not able to create the scene?

TREVOR:
Preposterous...I'll give you an unforgettable performance any place any time.

EDNA:
Picture this...the lights are low and there are shadows on a chair...there sitting on the chair crying is me...(start to act a new character, hunch over some and moan and cry)

TREVOR:
I enter and slam the door.

(the sound of a door closing is heard, all look out to the audience)

TREVOR:
So I am a little late...I cannot be on time all of the time...some time I am not going to be on time..you will just have to get used to it.

EDNA:
You promised...you promised this time you would be on time...did you not say to me you wanted to meet my parents?

TREVOR:
I did...did I not?

EDNA:
Yes.

TREVOR:
Well...too bad.

EDNA:
Too bad...that is all you have to say...too bad...I've been sitting here alone...too bad the dinner reservations were cancelled...too bad my parents chastised me for putting up with you...too bad my feelings are hurt.

TREVOR:
A man cannot be hemmed in by a woman...and not by just one woman...(change character)...I need to ask you something Edna...(change

back)...I need my space...an ability to come and go when I please...(change character)...but I'd like to be with you every moment...(change back)...and I feel like leaving at this very moment.

EDNA:
Then go...I hate you, hate you, hate you.

TREVOR:
(grab Edna in your arms)...I despise you...utterly despise you...(change character)...will you marry me...(change back)...I discard you with no remorse.

EDNA:
I hate you...(pound on Trevor's chest with your fists, change character)...yes I will marry you...(change back)...you conceited arrogant...man.

(Both look scornfully at each other than with force, embrace and kiss)

(pause)

TREVOR:
The audience was totally confused.

EDNA:
We got married that night...and fired the next morning when the reviews came out.

ALLBURT:
(with one hand turn thumb down)...I give it one thumbs down.

KISCALL:
(with one hand turn thumb up)...I give it a thumbs up...it was passion in a subtext of bitter attraction.

ALLBURT:
The acting was too common...no distinction between the feelings of the characters...droll...the premise is always the same...boy meets girl...and his anatomy says he's in love...girl plays hard to get...they have a bittersweet romance... another woman and his best friend come between the two lovers...both turn to hating each other...an underlying love is born in the anger...it's been done a zillion times.

INDIGO:

238

You got all that information from Trevor and Edna's lines...like did you write the play or something?

KISCALL:
Yeah...where did you get all that information Allburt? love in a pure form is not a complicated matter as you make it out to be...Trevor and Edna were in love and just acting out life's ugly side...but they triumphed with an act of true love.

BILL:
I don't get it.

TREVOR:
If you listen to those two...you will never get it.

SANDRA:
The point is...they took a chance and committed themselves to each other...(sarcastic look to Jack as Jack caresses your knee)...not like some guy I know....(raise voice)...like someone I am acquainted with.

GERTRUDE:
Romance has nothing to do with it...some people are just meant to be together...love grows as two people get to know each other.

EASTMAN:
Take Gerty and me...we didn't do all that much courting stuff....it was a waste of time.

GERTRUDE:
Maybe from your point of view.

EDNA:
Men...Eastman got you into a fix and your Pa said you had to get married.

GERTRUDE:
Heavens no...I had never been on a date in my whole single life...I was just turning seventeen when I married Eastman.

EDNA:
Seventeen...what did he do...kidnap you from your home?

GERTRUDE:
Almost...I was picking yellow beans from the garden beside our farm house...A distance down the road a stranger was heading my way...it was

Eastman...but I didn't know it was Eastman at the time...this stranger walked close by the fence...my eye caught him looking at me.

EASTMAN:
One look...that's all I needed...I walked back to the front door...tidied up my tie...polished my shoes on the back of my pant legs and knocked on the door.

GERTRUDE:
I peeked around the corner of the house.

EASTMAN:
A good firm knock to let them know that I was a determined man.

GERTRUDE:
Pa opened the door...a big old turkey hung limply in Pa's big burly hands.

EASTMAN:
I wasn't scared...and I said my peace without a flinch or a tremble in my voice.

GERTRUDE:
Pa looked Eastman up and down and finished wringing the turkey's neck...then with his booming voice called me over.

TREVOR:(in the character of Gertrude's father)...Gertrude look at this fellow...does he look good to you?

GERTRUDE:(shy tone) Yes.

TREVOR:
(in the character of Gertrude's father) Well speak your mind son...if it's okay with Gertrude then I'll agree to your proposal of...let's say...one full year of free labour on this farm.

EASTMAN:
I noticed you in the garden...you seemed to come from good farm stock...will you take my hand in marriage?

GERTRUDE:
I...I should.

TREVOR:
(in character of Gertrude's father) Think girl...I have six daughters...I could use a good man on the farm.

240

GERTRUDE:
He's pretty good looking Pa...I think I will...and we did the next day when the preacher came for dinner.

EASTMAN:
Ole girl...I would have worked two free years for you.

GERTRUDE:
Fiftieth anniversary next July...I have grown to love him...it took forty-five years...but I kind of fell in love with the old goat.

KISCALL:
(sigh) Two thumbs up (lift both thumbs up)

(Indigo, Sandra and Edna all give thumbs up)

ALLBURT:
Touching...but unrealistic in today's society.

KISCALL:
It is romantic...a true love story that touches the heart strings...did you not get a slight knot in the back of your throat.

ALLBURT:
Okay...okay...one thumb up for sappiness.

KISCALL:
Allburt has a heart...he is just trying to be macho...afraid to show his feminine side.

ALLBURT:
I don't need to show my feelings in a public place.

KISCALL:
Allburt is lying...when we first met, he was romantic...his eyes caught mine through the mist rising on the ice-skating pond...there was a slight smile on his lips as he watched me skate awkwardly across the frozen ice surface.

ALLBURT:
I was watching everybody...not just you Kiscall.

KISCALL:
Right...you were watching me...when I stumbled and sprawled like a squashed spider you rushed to me filled with all the concern of an old mother hen.

ALLBURT:
I was worried about all the other people you might have mangled...you were like a spinning airplane propeller taking the feet out from under panic-stricken skaters.

KISCALL:
Allburt cradled me in his arms...with his own hanky he tenderly brushed snow and ice from my cheeks.

ALLBURT:
I was checking for abrasions.

KISCALL:
Our eyes met...there was a feeling...something special...and don't you deny that it happened.

ALLBURT:
Alright...it was romantic.

GERTRUDE:
(show a sniffle and tap your hanky to your heart) That gets me right here...every time.

KISCALL:
Men...they are all the same.

BILL:
How does that help me...I thought you were going to show me how to ask Cista out.

SANDRA:
It is easy...just ask Jack here.

JACK:
(turn to Bill, point to Indigo, attempt to speak)

INDIGO:
I'll like be, Cista...okay you ask me.

BILL:
Ah...ah...ah...

JACK:
(slap forehead then shake head from side to side)

SANDRA:
No...no...all wrong...Jack tell them how you would do it.

JACK:
(nod head and point to Bill)

SANDRA:
Jack and I were sitting in a bagel shop late at night...I was sitting at the end of the counter...I was feeling bad...I had walked out on my husband.

(all look at Sandra with surprise)

SANDRA:
Yes, my husband...yes, I am having an affair.

(all eyes look at Jack who slouches in his seat)

SANDRA:
Jack is good to me...we just have to sneak around a bit...until my divorce.

(all nod their heads yes)

SANDRA:
Jack sat at the far corner of the counter...his eyes sparkled...he looked deep into my eyes...as if looking deep into my soul...his mouth quivered...then Jack walked towards me...his hand touched my cheek...a tingling touch...I shivered with a sense of evil delight...without a word Jack clasped my hand and quickly walked me out of the door...ooh a night like no other...I didn't feel guilty waking up the next morning beside Jack...his arms around me.

BILL:
(quickly place an arm around Indigo and pull her close to you) You and me babe...my place...now...

INDIGO:
(quickly grab Bill's belt and lift hard until Bill is on his tip toes) What sleaze ball?

BILL:
(in high voice) nothing...I just lost my mind for a moment.

INDIGO:
Don't let it happen again.

BILL:
No problem...(tug down on your pants)

SANDRA:
Pretend Indigo is Cista...look deep into her eyes...take her hand in yours...lightly caress the top.

KISCALL:
Don't slouch...stand tall.

EASTMAN:
Whatever you do, don't scratch.

GERTRUDE:
I just hate it when baseball players do that.

EDNA:
Dirty dogs.

TREVOR:
It is a man's thing...women just don't understand.

SANDRA:
Now with a firm voice...not harsh...say...Cista...with your permission I would like to escort you out on an evening of fine dining and heartfelt conversation.

BILL:
I can't afford no fine dining.

ALLBURT:
If you have good conversation and you talk about her and make her feel like the centre of your thoughts...then any old greasy hamburger joint will be a formal dining room in her eyes.

EDNA:
Go ahead Bill...give it a test drive with Indigo.

BILL:
(clear your throat, stretch tall and stick out chest, in a bold deep voice speak) Cista...I would wish very much if you would allow me to be your escort on a night of stimulation of conversation at a fine establishment of renown reputation.

INDIGO:

(with a squeaky voice) Oh...like I totally would.

KISCALL:
Excellent...you had it in you all the time...now just say it exactly that way to Cista and you will have her swooning.

BILL:
Swooning?

KISCALL:
Swooning.

INDIGO:
Swooning?

EDNA:
GERTRUDE:
Swooning.

INDIGO:
BILL:
Swooning?

ALLBURT:
TREVOR:
(acting) swooning.

EASTMAN:
Salivating in a frenzied ritual that all creatures of domestication tend to do when the act of mating is weighing heavy on the mind...and the only relief is copulation...preferably with the other half of the pair intending to complete the act.

GERTRUDE:
Heavens no...Eastman don't fill the poor boy's mind with sophisticated barn yard jargon.

EDNA:
Swooning...a romantic feeling a girl feels inside when the man of her dreams expresses his true feelings about her and says it directly to her heart.

BILL:
Swooning!

INDIGO:
Like she will be drooling all over you...stuck to you like a lovesick puppy.

BILL:
FOR SURE!

INDIGO:
Duh.

SANDRA:
Here she comes.

(all quickly turn away, Indigo rushes to her seat, others stare skyward, pick their teeth, hum, only Jack watches intently on Bill and Cista's encounter, Cista enters exit left and stops, looks about over the group then focuses on Bill who is fidgeting)

CISTA:
What happened...did I miss something?

BILL:
No...no...we were just talking...about the weather.

CISTA:
It is awfully quiet...like not much conversation about the weather going on.

BILL:
Ah...well...the weather has been pretty good lately...no need to complain about it.

(Indigo gestures to Bill to get on with asking Cista)

BILL:
What?

(as Cista begins to turn towards Indigo, Bill quickly gains her attention)

BILL:
Nice weather we are having...ain't it!

CISTA:
It's been okay...like not too hot or too cool.

BILL:

Just right for going for a moonlight walk.

CISTA:
Yeah...I guess if you are into that kind of thing.

BILL:
Ah...would...

(Indigo again gestures to Bill, all the others are leaning and listening with an ear towards the conversation)

BILL:
What?

(Cista begins to turn, Bill again gains her attention)

BILL:
I am!

CISTA:
You are...like what?

BILL:
I am glad we could have this time to talk.

CISTA:
O...kay...(slowly back up)

BILL:
(reach a hand out to Cista) would you like to go for a walk with me...tonight...together...on a kind of first date.

CISTA:
Like not...you and me...never.

(Indigo slaps her head with a hand, Cista returns to her seat. Allburt and Kiscall shake their heads to each other, Trevor puts the back of his hand to his forehead in a dramatic tragic manner. Edna puts a hand to her lips also in a dramatic fashion. Gertrude takes Eastman's hand and pats it softly in a grieving manner. Sandra questionably looks at Jack who raises his hands as if to say too bad. Bill's mouth is hanging to the floor with his shoulders slumped, his arms hang limply) (over the PA system is heard. 'Your Attention please...will Bill the usher please report to the manager's office...oh never mind Bill...there is a slight delay in the start of our production...so at this time we will extend our pre show intermission...as soon as we dry out our lead actor...(begin a fading dialogue)...get that drunk sobered up...I don't care if it takes all night...this show will go on...Throw some water on the two bit actor....never mind I will do it myself...get me some water...where is Bill...Bill come to the manager's office...Bill...Bill)

(lights fade as the orchestra music builds then fades, intermission music builds)

END OF PARTONE

PART TWO

THE SOUNDS OF THE INTERMISSION MUSIC FADES, THE ORCHESTRA MUSIC BEGINS TO BUILD AS THE LIGHTS SLOWLY COME UP. SANDRA AND JACK ARE BUSY IN PRE-MATING RITUALS, THEIR HANDS FONDLE THE OTHER'S HANDS. THEY EXCHANGE LIGHT KISSES ON THE CHEEKS AND FINGERS, THEIR FACES ARE NOSE TO NOSE LIKE LOVESICK BIRDS. GERTRUDE IS BUSY KNITTING. EASTMAN IS HOLDING A DIFFERENT COLOURED BALL OF WOOL IN EACH HAND, AT THE SAME TIME HIS HEAD IS BOBBING BACK AS HE ENTERS THE PRE-SLEEP MODE. TREVOR IS BUSY MAKING FACES INTO A HAND-HELD MIRROR, HE IS ADMIRING DIFFERENT PROFILES. EDNA IS ALSO LOOKING INTO A HAND-HELD MIRROR AS SHE APPLIES ALL KNOWN APPLICATIONS OF MAKEUP TO HER FACE. KISCALL AND ALLBURT ARE LEANING CLOSE TOGETHER READING THE PLAY PROGRAM. KISCALL HAS A HAPPY SMILE TO ALLBURT'S FROWN THAT IS REMINISCENT OF THE THEATRE MASKS. INDIGO IS LOOKING DISAPPOINTINGLY DOWN ON CISTA. CISTA IS TURNED AWAY BUT GLANCES AT TIMES TOWARDS INDIGO)

INDIGO:
(stand and glare down on Cista) Girl..what is wrong with you...like you devastated his ego...you shattered his machoism...you reduced him to a shell of a man.

CISTA:
Boy.

INDIGO:

248

A potential man...but now it may take him years and years...maybe three years to climb out of the pits of his doldrums.

CISTA:
So.

INDIGO:
So?

CISTA:
(raise voice) So.

INDIGO:
(raise voice) So...so.

GERTRUDE:
I use to sew but now I find knitting more creative and relaxing...it gives me time to sort out the complexities of life...and on this subject of boys and girls dating I have come to a conclusion...(raise voice)..you Cista have devastated Bill...a poor boy heartbroken.

CISTA:
A child.

GERTRUDE:
You are acting like the child...you are not too old for me to put across my knees...Eastman give me your belt.

CISTA:
You wouldn't dare...you are not my mother.

INDIGO:
Maybe I should tell your mother.

SANDRA:
(push Jack away slightly as you swallow well needed air) One day you may be the one dumped by someone you are deeply in love with.

EDNA:
Shame, shame, shame...on you.

KISCALL:
You will be sorry.

(all disgustedly glare at Cista, Cista quickly and somewhat annoyed stares back with tension and shakes her head. Bill enters exit left with his arms full of play scripts)

TREVOR:
Here he comes...Bill the usher.

(all quickly try to resume a casual position except Jack who strains to watch Bill...Cista refuses to look at Bill but her eyes are watching)

BILL:
(in a hurt cracked voice attempt to speak)...May I have your attention...your attention...(your voice begins to crack)...your attention please...the management wishes to express their regrets with the slight delay with the start of this play.

TREVOR:
Heaven forbid...is the actor taking sips of a mickey between cups of coffee...I paid good money to see this production...I want to see this production...up with the curtain...up with the curtain...(stand and with your arms try to rally the others to join with the chant)...up with the curtain...up with the curtain.

(sparse words come from the others, Edna gives one round and stops, Jack rises half way out of his seat and raises his arms slightly)

TREVOR:
Up with the curtain...give me a script...I will do the part myself.

(Bill places a script into Trevor's hand)

TREVOR:
What pray tell is this?

BILL:
(begin to hand our scrips to everyone)...The management does not want anyone to be ripped off by the slight...I stress slight intoxication of our physically challenged actor.

ALLBURT:
There is no challenge for him to drink...he is a pro...at being drunk.

BILL:
We are not allowed to say drunk.

250

TREVOR:
But is he not?

BILL:
I am not a doctor...I can't truly say.

EDNA:
Is he heaving over the porcelain bowl...(show with gestures)

BILL:
Well...yes.

ALL:
Drunk.

BILL:
OKAY...we all know he's drunk...but the management says the show will go on.

GERTRUDE:
And what do we do with these play scripts?

BILL:
So, you can follow along with the play.

TREVOR:
Preposterous.

EASTMAN:
Gerty...do you have my glasses ole girl.

GERTRUDE:
If you have the gases...then excuse yourself and go to the lavatory.

EASTMAN:
Laboratory?

GERTRUDE:
The indoor plumbing place.

EASTMAN:
What do I need with an indoor outhouse?

TREVOR:

I will not watch a play and at the same time read the lines of a mumbling...drooling...incoherent lush of an actor.

(everyone begins to open their play books)

ALLBURT:
(with old English accent)...What hast brought us to meet in plain sight of those wishing to look upon us as mire mortals.

TREVOR:
(flip through your play book)...What page is that on?

KISCALL:
Page twenty-two.

TREVOR:
(point to each person starting with Indigo and ending with Jack)...Each one of you take a part in order of the next character...one, two, three, four, five, six, seven, nine, ten and eleven.

(everyone tries different accents, emotions and gestures randomly inconsistently to what is actually being said)

TREVOR:
Let us bring forth this play with artistry and I shall show you a master of his craft...(pause, then gesture a hand to Allburt)...please continue.

ALLBURT:
Behind a blinding light cast upon our naked bodies...beings so slight of masculinity wish to touch...fondle...caress...fondle as they wish.

JACK:
(take Sandra's hand and with passion rub her hand over your face, neck, chest, and belly, make satisfied facial expressions)

SANDRA:
(pull your hand away and make a fist thrusted into the air)...I would rather...squeeze the last drip of life from you external appendages.

EDNA:
Food for thought oh great master...please may I be the one...I would relish the honour to devour this mire mortal.

JACK:

252

(quickly cross your legs and put up a hand to stop any attack)

TREVOR:
No...no...no...I can not let my second in command risk such pleasures...who shall know what evil...deadly organisms may be unleashed... devastation of our species may occur.

INDIGO:
CISTA:
Ah...ugh...they got me...I can't...like move...ugh…the pain...totally...

BILL:
It is not my desire to inflict pain...my orders are clear...from the most powerful ruler of all universities.

TREVOR:
Universes!

BILL:
Universes...I am under Vadar's intellectual sub...standard.

TREVOR:
Sub station...my boy.

BILL:
Sub station...my boy.

TREVOR:
Not my boy...just sub station.

BILL:
Just sub station mind waves.

INDIGO:
CISTA:
Ugh...it is okay...like I am getting use to thou master's power.

EASTMAN:
Over there...over there...over there...and over there...you guys bring all the ammunitions needed...we can't let those...strange...beings…from a distant universities fill our minds with...hog wash.

GERTRUDE:
They came from far distant universities.

TREVOR:
Universes!

GERTRUDE:
Universes...to abduct our intelligent children.

(pause, all look questionably to Indigo and Cista)

INDIGO:
CISTA:
Ah...ugh...(notice everyone looking at you)...like what?

ALLBURT:
As the president of the confederation of divided but united provinces of this fragmented continent I promise I will not let...these...these...strange beings take our children.

EDNA:
What good are they to you...we have the power to put their minds to a more useful fulfilment.

(pause, all look at Indigo, Cista and Bill, in return all three give a like what look)

BILL:
What...what?

KISCALL:
What more usefulness can beings of your weak physical...somewhat pathetically looking anatomy do with the children of our world?

GERTRUDE:
We can't even get them to do our housework...not even a few little chores.

SANDRA:
You tell them Gertrude.

GERTRUDE:
Lazy...just plain lazy.

INDIGO:
I cleaned my room...yesterday.

CISTA:

That's right...I know...it was a week after I cleaned my room.

INDIGO:
So there.

TREVOR:
The script...follow the script.

EDNA:
Brain food...slowly sucked from the base of the neck.

INDIGO:
CISTA:
Ugh...ugh...they are taking us... help...help...help!

BILL:
I am sorry...I cannot resist my master's mental powers...I must ravish you.

CISTA:
Like you wish.

TREVOR:
I am great...the most powerful ruler of all the universities.

KISCALL:
ALLBURT:
Universes.

TREVOR:
What?

KISCALL:
ALLBURT:
Universes...you said universities.

TREVOR:
Preposterous...an actor of my ability does not make mistakes.

GERTRUDE:
You did...I heard you.

EDNA:
He did not...Trevor said universes...and I heard him.

TREVOR:
Thank you dear.

KISCALL:
Typical!

TREVOR:
And what does that mean?

ALLBURT:
Kiscall...never mind...you know how pre-Madonna's are when they are over the hill.

TREVOR:
Who are you calling over the hill...you third rate has-been ten cent paper critics?

EASTMAN:
Gerty...what page are they on?

GERTRUDE:
Yes dear...I think Trevor is in a rage.

EASTMAN:
Cage...I don't see nothing about a cage.

JACK:
(take Sandra's hand to your chest and belly, slowly rub it in a circular motion)

SANDRA:
With a mighty force your appendages will burst.

JACK:
(nod head in quick yes motions)

(Bill is acting like teenage Frankenstein with his arms and hands hovering over Indigo and Cista's head, the girls pretend to cower)

INDIGO:
CISTA:
Ugh...ugh...ohh....ehh... ah...

TREVOR:

Pray tell...what kind of acting is this...this is suppose to be a classical drama...you are acting...(pause, puff up face as if it is ready to explode)...like imbeciles...am I the only one here able to act?

KISCALL:
You can't act.

EDNA:
Sir Trevor is a great actor.

TREVOR:
Thank you my dear.

ALLBURT:
The both of you put together can't act.

(Indigo, Cista and Bill are frozen in a climatic horror scene)

GERTRUDE:
I thought the acting would be on stage up there....I wasn't expecting to pay for a show then be expected to act the play out myself.

KISCALL:
You were just fine Gertrude...much better than some seasoned actors.

TREVOR:
(turn to Edna and in a loud voice to be directed at Allburt and Kiscall) Critics are too far beneath us Dear Edna...even the lowly peasant cast rubbish onto critics.

EASTMAN:
When is the real show expected to start?

GERTRUDE:
Sandra's expecting...maybe she will deliver before this theatre's production ever does.

(Eastman leans over Sandra's shoulder and in a loud voice scares her, Sandra grabs her belly as she lets out a scream, Jack jumps from his seat and backs away in a nervous fit)

EASTMAN:
(speak in a very loud voice) Is your baby expected any time soon?

SANDRA:
(let out a scream)...AHH...

(Allburt and Kiscall stand, Kiscall romantically holds onto Allburt's arm. Trevor stands stiffly with his face sternly askew with his eyes peering at Sandra. Eastman stands and staggers as he holds a hand to his heart as his eyes blink and his mouth gasps for air. Edna and Gertrude rush to Sandra's left side, Indigo and Cista rush past Bill and hurry to Sandra's right side, when Bill realizes what is happening, he flies down the aisle to a stop then makes a turn and slides to his knees in front of Sandra's spread legs. Bill holds his hands at Sandra's knees)

BILL:
Okay...okay...everybody be calm...I've got everything under control...lift your dress please...I'm ready...lift your dress.

SANDRA:
(fight with coat around the belly area) That is not necessary...uh...

BILL:
It's okay...I've seen the 911 Rescue show.

CISTA:
Like totally informed are you...you just want to look up Sandra's dress...you pervert.

INDIGO:
Cista...like maybe he knows what he is doing.

GERTRUDE:
Fourteen hours of pain...there was no one there to console me...my second born...oh he gave me pain...my husband Eastman...gone...fishing.

SANDRA:
Ouch...ouch.

INDIGO:
Did the baby kick you?

SANDRA:
No...no...I am fine.

GERTRUDE:
That's what they all say before the big pain comes.

BILL:
Hot water...blankets...a clothes pin... a pocket knife.

EDNA:
Maybe Bill does know what he is doing.

CISTA:
He's guessing.

BILL:
Lift your dress please....I need to see.

(all the other men are pacing the rows as if they are the expectant fathers)

SANDRA:
Not in my life time.

(from off stage a loud growl and a bark is heard. Cista, Indigo, Edna and Gertrude quickly step back, all the men stop their pacing. Bill stays in position and lifts his head slightly)

BILL:
Excuse me!

SANDRA:
What?

BILL:
What was that sound?

SANDRA:
I have no idea.

BILL:
A dog's bark...There is a dog in here.

(from off stage a bark, Sandra moves about agitated and tries to hold the bundle in her coat still)

BILL:
You have a dog in your coat...a dog... house rules say no cats, mice, ferrets, birds, snakes, etc...etc...and no dogs...(stand and turn half way away from Sandra, hold out hands in a manner to grab the dog by the back of the neck)...Madam the dog please...the dog please.

(Sandra hands the dog to Bill then she looks at the others who are talking among themselves. Indigo and Cista are happily cooing over the dog. Jack wipes a worried look from his face. Gertrude and Edna wave off Sandra as if she were an unfit mother and then return to their seats, the men sit in bewilderment)

SANDRA:
I needed an excuse...to get out of the house...the dog needed to go for a walk...I couldn't leave him tied outside the theatre...he would have been frightened.

(no one is paying attention to Sandra. Indigo and Cista follow Bill as he exits, right then the girls sit in their seats, Jack returns to his seat with a blank deadpan face)

SANDRA:
What?...Jack you really thought that I was pregnant?

JACK:
(pause, think a slow look to Sandra then attempt to speak)

KISCALL:
So far, this little bit of theatrics has shown more drama, black comedy and more intrigue then this production that is not on stage.

ALLBURT:
I give Sandra two thumbs up...for a fine performance.

KISCALL:
The cute little dog gets my thumbs up for just being himself.

ALLBURT:
Kiscall...what are you going to write about this production?

KISCALL:
I have not seen the presentation.

TREVOR:
And you may never.

ALLBURT:
I hate to agree with Trevor...but he just may be right.

KISCALL:

260

It is not right to pre-judge.

ALLBURT:
Why not...your paper has done it before...what's her name...Robin...you know that woman who thinks she is a theatrical critic.

KISCALL:
Please!....do not even consider her a justifiable critic.

TREVOR:
She has given me rave reviews.

KISCALL:
My point exactly...Allburt you cannot put me in the same class as Robin...she has glorified Sir Trevor...and we have never given him even one thumbs up.

EDNA:
Trevor...you do not need a critic's review to tell you if you are untalented or talented...you can build up your own ego all by yourself...and if you forget I will remind you.

TREVOR:
Thank you dear...you do know who has talent...and you are a fine actor also.

EDNA:
Thank you dear.

(Allburt and Kiscall both turn their thumbs down. Eastman and Gertrude begin to nod off with slight snores that wake the other, both look questionably at each other)

ALLBURT:
We cannot wait all night for this performance to get started...let alone endure until it's conclusion.

KISCALL:
You are right...I was planning to cook up some appetizers for us after the show...you could open that bottle of wine you gave me...the one you picked up in the north of France.

ALLBURT:
We still can...if we write our reviews now.

(Jack and Sandra are ignoring each other but with their fingers they playfully play. Indigo and Cista are busily discussing the other's clothes. Trevor and Edna are eves-dropping on Kiscall and Allburt)

KISCALL:
Okay...(pull out a pad and pen)...okay...lets get started.

ALLBURT:
(Quickly pull out a pen and pad)...Go ahead.

KISCALL:
(pause, put pen to lips)...Tonights...performance..the name of the production...featuring...the actors' names.

ALLBURT:
Great...(quickly jot down what Kiscall dictated)...Great...go on.

(pause)

KISCALL:
It...was....blank...blank...blank..

ALLBURT:
Great...(jot words down then hesitate)...great....that is not much to go on.

KISCALL:
I am sorry...but I have no idea what this play is about...like what is the motivation...the curve of potential intrigue...the insight to each character's being.

ALLBURT:
I am not sure...I cannot really say.

TREVOR:
Edna...I do think theatre should have a fail-safe system.

EDNA:
For old time actors.

TREVOR:
No Edna...critics...to critique critics...they should be under the same immoral scrutiny as everyone else.

(Kiscall, Allburt, Edna and Trevor glare at each other, silence befalls, only the slight snoring of Gertrude and Eastman are heard, they both wake and stare at the other as if the other's snoring caused the interruption of their sleep. Pause. Bill makes a flash entrance at right exit and quickly flashes the light onto each person as he walks down the aisle then across the front and up the aisle and out through left exit. Bill pops head back through the exit curtain)

BILL:
Is there a problem I should know about...(pause)...there is no problem?...(slowly pull head back)

(a long quiet pause, all begin a sequence of theatrical sound effects, continued randomly building and fading, milk this section over if possible)

ALLBURT:
(a long drawn out boo, staring low and building)...Boo...booo...boo...

EDNA:
(low short boos)...Bo...bo...bo...

SANDRA:
(lightly clap)...Bravo...bravo...

KISCALL:
(be happy and giddy)...Take a bow...again...another bow.

EASTMAN:
(with agitation)...Shoot the bum...put him out of his misery.

INDIGO:
CISTA:
(begin to do the wave)...Hurray... hurray...hurray...

TREVOR:
(be dignified with a light palm clap)...Encore...encore...

KISCALL:
Author...author...

JACK:
(give a closed fist hurray, pump arm into the air)

GERTRUDE:
That was beautiful...delightful...just beautiful...

BILL:
(Enter quickly from left exit and flash flashlight beam over the actors and out towards the real audience)...What's the problem...has the show started...is the curtain going up?

KISCALL:
Heavens no dear boy...we are just practising.

INDIGO:
CISTA:
(do a faster wave)...Hurray... ...hurray...hurray.

EASTMAN:
(angrier)...put him out of his misery...feed him to the dogs.

TREVOR:
(louder)...Encore...encore... encore...(look to Edna)

EDNA:
(short quick boos)...Bo...bo...bo.

SANDRA:
Bravo...bravo...bravo

KISCALL:
Author...author...author...bring out the author.

EASTMAN:
Kill the bum.

GERTRUDE:
Beautiful...delightful...just beautiful...a pleasure to watch.

ALLBURT:
(loud strong boos)...Boo...boo...boo..

BILL:
(back slowly through the left exit, lower flashlight in a state of bewilderment)...Great job...you are doing a great job...keep up the good work.

ALLBURT:
Boo...boo...boo...

(as quickly as Bill has left all except Jack quickly begin to throw vegetables towards the audience, preferably loose lettuce leaves, little green onions, celery leaves, loose or broken up cauliflower. Jack dodges the onslaught and scampers to the side in a Buster Keaton fashion)

EASTMAN:
Take that, you, lousy two-bit actor.

TREVOR:
Forget the encore...we will give you our encore.

EDNA:
(louder and longer boos) Boo...boo...boo.

KISCALL:
The author is a lousy writer...lousy... lousy...lousy.

GERTRUDE:
Look at all the beautiful colours in the light...delightful.

CISTA:
What a great shot.

INDIGO:
Like you too.

SANDRA:
Bramisivo...bramisivo...

(suddenly all stop and sit quickly and silently down. Bill enters with a quick draw of the flashlight and points it directly at Jack who is standing to right front. Jack shrugs shoulders then lifts his hands as if he was being arrested. Bill straightens up and in a John Wayne walk slowly backs out through the curtain. Jack moves towards his seat, as he is almost sitting all give a final flurry and bombardment of vegetables towards the audience. Jack rushes away then sneaks back to his seat on his hands and knees. Everyone begins to settle down. Eastman and Gertrude begin to nod off, everyone becomes fascinated at the way the two are carrying on their snoring. Stretch snoring as far as possible with a variety of different sounds and different facial expressions from all)

BILL:
(enter exit left and begin searching for the strange sounds)...Excuse... me...(tap harder and raise voice)...Madam...excuse me.

GERTRUDE:
(wake up startled and give Eastman a good elbow)...A fire.

BILL:
No...but you...

GERTRUDE:
The show is cancelled.

BILL:
No madam...you...

GERTRUDE:
The show is about to begin.

BILL:
No...it is not about...

GERTRUDE:
That little dog is loose.

BILL:
No madam.

GERTRUDE:
Then why did you scare the living daylights out of me?

EASTMAN:
Your snoring Gertrude...it is loud enough to wake the dead.

GERTRUDE:
(elbow Eastman) You should talk...a sonic jack-hammer...it was not me...was it Dear boy?

BILL:
I...am...afraid that the manager in his office down the hall and up three flights of stairs and behind two inch thick doors was a little concerned about a strange sound...he mistakenly thought it was the plumbing...so he asked me to ask...politely...if everyone would hold the noise down...so he can hear if the pipes are groaning.

EASTMAN:
A cup of Draino should clean up her old plumbing quite well.

GERTRUDE:
I don't snore...(give an elbow then hit Eastman with your knitting)

(Bill begins to back up the aisle to the exit and waits at the opening)

EASTMAN:
The building's plumbing...the old plumbing in this building...give it some Draino.

GERTRUDE:
Anybody that has delivered a truck load of children is bound to have a few plumbing problems...but you shouldn't call me old.

EDNA:
That is right Gertrude...men are the first ones to blame something on us women....oh they never do anything wrong.

GERTRUDE:
And cry about it if you blame them.

KISCALL:
Allburt does that all the time...it always has to be his way...his way.

ALLBURT:
Are you comparing me with other men?

EASTMAN:
I did not say anything about you getting old.

JACK:
(begin to try to get close to Sandra)

SANDRA:
(push off Jack's advances)... Men are childish.

GERTRUDE:
From the time they are babies until they are wrinkled and old...women have to baby them.

EDNA:
And they cry and whine.

TREVOR:
Never...have I ever whined.

EDNA:
No...what about that time we were up for the same award...you said if I won you would be proud of me.

TREVOR:I am proud of you.

KISCALL:
Oh sure...for one moment.

ALLBURT:
Trevor...I must say deserved it more then Edna.

KISCALL:
Typical male logic.

INDIGO:
This should be a good fight...men against women.

CISTA:
Like whose side are you going to root for...the men or us women?

INDIGO:
Us women...girl I am a woman...more woman than you.

EDNA:
Oh you smiled for the camera... and congratulated me...then for the rest of the evening you pouted and sulked.

KISCALL:
I was surprised he didn't lay on his back and have a tantrum.

TREVOR:
I was coming down with the flu...I wasn't healthy enough to be in a party mood.

INDIGO:
I am just woman enough to show you how good a woman I am.

CISTA:
Like, what is that supposed to mean?

INDIGO:
Bill.

CISTA:
Bill...the usher...a boy.

INDIGO:H
e likes you...he is nice to you...but like you're on some woman's lib thing.

GERTRUDE:
Women should have unionized years ago...and curtailed this baby breeding thing...and fought for equal rights.

EASTMAN:
Equal rights...I was out slopping the hogs at six-thirty...you never showed up until after eight.

SANDRA:
The poor woman was taking care of your children...(slap Jack's hand away from your leg)

GERTRUDE:
Men enjoy the sex...then get off scot free...women maybe get to enjoy sex...but then have to endure carrying around a belly full of a growing baby for nine months...then labour pains...early morning feedings...then out of the door and down to the barn and help you slop the hogs.

KISCALL:
I agree and feel for my sisters and I am glad to be spared all of that pain...(look at Allburt with disgust)...men.

INDIGO:
I could make Bill change his mind about you...(snap fingers)...just like that..he would fall for me...I would make him glad that he's a man.

CISTA:
Is that all you think about is sex...you are as bad as men.

SANDRA:
That is all they think about...morning, noon and night...and when it is convenient for them...I couldn't take it any more..I couldn't take it.

EDNA:
For a week he pouted...then finally I was fed up...I had to tell Sir Trevor here...that if it were not for him I would not be deserving of this award.

KISCALL:

That did it...Sir Trevor's ego was back in place.

TREVOR:
Edna was a struggling understudy...until I nurtured her under my wing.

EDNA:
Blow hard.

INDIGO:
I believe in equal opportunities...why should men be the only ones to crave and enjoy sex...I am going to take my share of life's pleasures...I am not going to be like you.

SANDRA:
I wanted to be wanted...someone to spoil me...to think of only me...to be put up on a pedestal...adored...(turn to Jack with a loving and forgiving expression)...Jack has done that for me...taken all that hum drum home life of being a wife, cook, housemaid...Jack has helped me escape all that.

JACK:
(begin to kiss Sandra's hand, become close and intimate with Sandra)

KISCALL:
I feel like a kept woman...I clean...cook...do your laundry...and half the time I write your critic's column.

ALLBURT:
You write my columns...I give you all of the ideas.

KISCALL:
When was the last time you ever thanked me?

TREVOR:
That is the thanks I get...you call me a blow hard...such common street dialogue...years of coaching and voice training.

EDNA:
Oh...blow it out your ear.

GERTRUDE:
The same goes for you Eastman.

EASTMAN:
What goes?

270

GERTRUDE:
The same thing Edna said.

EASTMAN:
What did she say?

TREVOR:
Nothing of importance.

EASTMAN:
They never do.

GERTRUDE:
EDNA:
(build up of anger, look at each other then look at your man) We are on strike.
TREVOR:On strike!

ALLBURT:
Typical..if you can't get your own way...you go on strike...lack of pay ...go on strike...don't like the work...go on strike.

TREVOR:
What pray tell are you on strike about?

EDNA:
(look at Gertrude for confirmation)... Whatever you expect of us...that is what we will strike against.

TREVOR:
Even...you know...you know...

EDNA:
Yes even sex.

EASTMAN:
How long is this strike going to last?

GERTRUDE:
As long as it takes.

INDIGO:
Like I'm totally not joining that strike.

KISCALL:

(look at Allburt)...What they say is good for me.

ALLBURT:
You are going to side with...I thought our lifestyle was beyond this male female...hang up.

CISTA:
Their strike is legitimate...and I am going to back them up...and do what they do.

INDIGO:
Withhold having sex...like with who...you haven't and don't have sex...I'm your best friend...I know.

CISTA:
It is the principle of the cause I am backing.

INDIGO:
Oh right...if you haven't participated ...how can you make a conclusion about good or bad.

CISTA:
And like it's good for you.

INDIGO:
Well if you're not interested in finding out for yourself then Bill is wasting his time...I think I might...(look towards Bill)

(Cista becomes confused, Jack and Sandra are having a good time hugging, touching and smiling to each other)

EASTMAN:
Gertrude...are you still going to...I mean...will you still...You know...in the morning help me slop the hogs.

EDNA:
Gertrude don't you dare.

GERTRUDE:
On strike.

TREVOR:
Edna...you are taking this too far...we should talk about this.

EDNA:
Sorry...we are on strike...no talking to the strikers...(turn away)

EASTMAN:
Balderdash...now listen here Gerty.

GERTRUDE:
Do not talk to the strikers.

KISCALL:
We don't have to negotiate without proper representation.

ALLBURT:
This is gone far enough.

KISCALL:
GERTRUDE:
EDNA:
(pull up small signs that read on strike) On strike.

(Eastman, Trevor and Allburt show different expression as they slump in their seats, Jack and Sandra are having a good ole time, Sandra pulls her coat around Jack, they are hidden from sight, they build up playful sounds, Eastman, Trevor and Allburt show some resentment to Jack's good fortune)

CISTA:
I thought Bill was interested in me...but you would take him away...seduce him...just for your own pleasure.

INDIGO:
Why not.

CISTA:
Like we have an understanding.

INDIGO:
An understanding about what?

CISTA:
He shows his intentions...I play hard to get...that's the way it's done...and like years from now we get married and everything's cool.

INDIGO:

I don't think Bill was totally informed about the rules...and if you don't tell him...then he's fair game.

CISTA:
(become prissy) Then you want him...go ahead...I know him...he won't be interested in you.

INDIGO:
(push past Cista and head for Bill)... we'll see.

(Cista clinches her fists and stamps a foot. Indigo in a rough manner parleys her interests to Bill by caressing his usher's coat)

INDIGO:
What's up Bill?

BILL:
(awkwardly look Indigo over)...Oh...not much...the show should start...pretty soon..the star is almost sobered up.

INDIGO:
No...no...I mean with you?

BILL:
Me...You're interested in me?...(glance towards Cista, she turns away)...what about Cista...I thought she was interested in me?

INDIGO:
No such luck...she is on some kind of cause....a woman's movement about sex.

BILL:
(embarrassed move eyes and head a bit upward, your voice should crack in volume)...Oh...yeah...what those women were talking about.

INDIGO:
(take Bill's arm and walk forward down the aisle and stop at the first row)...I think that maybe you and me...should get together and explore our adolescence.

BILL:
Explore!

INDIGO:

You know...kissing...touching.

BILL:
Touching!

INDIGO:
How else are we going to get to know each other.

BILL:
Should I ask you out on a date?

INDIGO:
We could have our date right now.

BILL:N
OW?

INDIGO:
Show me your...little office.

BILL:
Now,

INDIGO:
Now.

(Indigo leads Bill by the hand across the front, Bill's flashlight is going on and off, Eastman and Gertrude are beginning to snore, Indigo and Bill exit right, Cista ignores Bill and Indigo as they pass. Cista is fuming inside then with her hands and legs she performs a tantrum. Eastman and Gertrude are sound asleep and snoring on and off, Trevor and Edna are ignoring each other, Jack and Sandra are still moving about under her coat)

KISCALL:
Oh to be young and in love.

ALLBURT:
He ran off with the wrong girl.

KISCALL:
That doesn't matter...it's love...maybe she is the right girl for him.

TREVOR:
That director...what's his name...he had the hots for you.

EDNA:
The hots?

TREVOR:
He convinced the judges to vote for you...that's how you won that award.

EDNA:
The hots?

KISCALL:
Bill...I would say about now he has the hots for Indigo.

ALLBURT:
What's gotten into you?

KISCALL:
We were on strike for a reason.

ALLBURT:
What has that got to do with Cista sitting alone and Bill playing Randy-Andy with Indigo?

CISTA:
(stand and yell)...Ahh...(stomp down row towards the left exit, look at each man when speaking)... Men...men...men...men.. like totally useless...(exit)

ALLBURT:
Now see what you have done.

KISCALL:
Me...she was condemning men.

ALLBURT:
You are a man.

KISCALL:
Well if you are going to talk physically.

TREVOR:
Edna...you cannot deny…he worked extra long and intimately on your love scene.

EDNA:

And Sir Trevor the flamboyant... cocky man about town has not had the hots...as you say...the hots for every floozy two bit chorus girl from London to New York and this second rate amateur town you willingly brought us to dwell in...or should I say rot in.

ALLBURT:
Let's not start to be like every other man and woman and their relationship...I thought we were different.

KISCALL:
We are different.

SANDRA:
(pull coat down until head is showing, Jack is still covered up)...Jack...stop... (giggle then try to be serious)...that's enough Jack...(giggle and pull away and stand, leave coat open to display clothes in a dishevelled array)...Jack...oh...wee...

JACK:
(slump in chair exhausted, pant for air then express a dry mouth)

SANDRA:
Jack...it is getting late...Fred is going to be wondering why it is taking so long to walk the dog...(straighten up clothes, hesitate then straddle Jack quickly and ravish him then just as quickly stand and close coat and calmly speak)....I have to go home to my dull but caring..sexually inept husband.

JACK:
(show total exhaustion, stare up at Sandra with wanting lust)

SANDRA:
Tomorrow...the city park...behind the old oak tree...I'll tie a yellow ribbon on a branch...three o'clock...be there...(exit aisle right)

(Jack very, very slowly begins to straighten himself up, it takes a very long time, Gertrude and Eastman are joyfully enjoying their sleep)

KISCALL:
(become overwhelmed with emotion)...I do have certain feelings you know...certain needs...I need you to need me.

ALLBURT:
I do understand what you are saying...and I will act on that very need.

KISCALL:
You will?

ALLBURT:
Of course,...now about this review...I need you to write my copy for me.

KISCALL:Write it for you!

ALLBURT:
Yes...I need your talent...and you are good at it.

KISCALL:
(stand) Men...you are all alike...(gather all of your belongings, Allburt tries to help you but you slap his intentions away with your frilly scarf)...You men will never change...(turn and exit on aisle left)

ALLBURT:
(quickly follow)...You said you needed me to need you...I do need you...okay...okay...need me to need you for something different...give me a chance...I know I can do it...I will get this one right... (exit aisle left)

TREVOR:
(slowly and calmly speak)... Edna... you were once a second rate chorus girl floozy I picked up in Stratford...together we struggled to overcome the obstacles of theatre...our names together on the marquees...we were the toast of the town...guests of royalty...we received the Order of Canada... there we were with the eyes of Canada upon us...a team every theatre house and director wanted...and it is all because of me...I am the inspiration...(stand and begin to gesture dramatically)...that has inspired the youth of Canada to pursue this noble dramatic art.....yes art in the visual and in the spoken words of the great playwrights of the centuries...no other than I and you my Dear are most worthy of

such acclaim and worship that has been bestowed upon us in the limelight of our years...fools are those that do not...will not...because of their own pettiness refuse to believe that we are living legends and only out of our own humble humility do we lower ourselves to live in semi retirement in a hovel of a dwelling in this city that has a deficiency of intelligence as to whom so great lives among them.

EDNA:
(all in awe of Trevor clap royaly and rise slowly)...Sir Trevor..my Sir Trevor...forever my tormentor and guiding light...if only a stage for you in this world.

278

TREVOR:
Come...Dame Edna...let us depart this...excuse for a theatre.

(Trevor and Edna dramatically depart with all the finesse of a performance made possible by two great actors full of themselves as if the world was watching, they exit from row to aisle and parade across the front and exit up aisle right, Jack ignores them as he finishes tucking in his shirt as he attempts to read the program, Gertrude and Eastman begin to snore louder building until the sound echos, Gertrude snorts awake and elbows Eastman)

GERTRUDE:
(yawn)...Eastman...it is getting late...almost time to slop the hogs.

EASTMAN:
Yup...yup...give me a hand old girl.
(Gertrude and Eastman with sleepy eyes and slow movements exit up aisle left, by this time everyone has left the stage, Jack is sitting alone twiddling his thumbs as he looks around, Jack eventually stands with various movements, adjusts his pants by putting hands in his pockets and arranging his shorts in the crotch area, Jack cannot decide to stay or leave, he makes several steps to and fro)

JACK:
(exasperated)...On with the show!... On with the show! ...Look...Look... (turn to the seats behind you, the orchestra builds in volume)...the show is starting.

(lights go to instant black, the orchestra music builds)

THE END

CURTAIN CALL
LIGHTS COME UP, JACK BOWS AND THEN SITS, IN TURN EACH ACTOR ENTERS AT EXIT IN ORDER OF ENTRANCE OF BEGINNING OF PLAY, EACH TAKES A BOW THEN SITS, ONCE ALL ARE SEATED, ALL STAND TOGETHER AND BOW, LIGHTS GO TO INSTANT BLACK.

THREE PLAYS BY ME
Copyright March 1, 1996
BY
Richard Mousseau
1
THE CRABTREES ON BUTTERNUT CORNERS
2
TWO POETS IN BELLEVUE PARK
3
WOJO AND YOUNG`IN

1
THE CRABTREES ON BUTTERNUT CORNERS

STAGE:
AT CENTRE OF STAGE IS A DOUBLE BED SET. AT A SLIGHT
ANGLE.   BESIDE THE BED IS AN OLD RADIO CABINET WITH A
LAMP ON TOP. AN OLD-STYLE BIG BEN CLOCK SITS ON RADIO.
WINDOW FRAME HANGS IN FRONT AND TO SIDE.

LIGHTING:
LIGHTS SHOULD BE FOCUSSED ON BED AREA AND SHOULD
HAVE THE FEELING OF LATE NIGHT.

ACTING PARTS:
LEAD WOMAN: MILDRED CRABTREE
LEAD MAN: WILBUR CRABTREE

SOUND:
BIG BAND MUSIC COMING FROM OLD RADIO. SOUND EFFECTS OF
MAN GARGLING AND SPITTING. THE SOUND OF HEAVY FOOT
STEPS. THE SOUND OF A TOILET FLUSHING AND THE
SOUND OF A DOOR CLOSING.

CHARACTERS:
MILDRED CRABTREE; A WOMAN BETWEEN THIRTY-FIVE AND
FORTY-FIVE YEARS OF AGE. HAIR IS UP WITH THE ODD HAIR
CURLER. SHE WEARS A NIGHT GOWN PINK IN COLOUR WITH A
FUR TYPE COLLAR.

WILBUR CRABTREE: A MAN BETWEEN THIRTY-FIVE AND
FORTY-FIVE. HE WEARS LIGHT RED PAJAMAS WITH RED WOOL
SOCKS, ONE IS PULLED UP AND ONE IS FLOPPY ON HIS FOOT.

280

BASIC STORY LINE:
WILBUR HAS WORKED HARD ALL DAY AND JUST WANTS TO
SLEEP WHEN HE GETS HOME. MILDRED HAS FOUND THE NEED
TO KEEP WILBUR AWAKE TO DISCUSS THEIR LIFE TOGETHER.
WILBUR IS A PROCRASTINATOR AND HAS LOST INTEREST IN
LIFE'S GOINGS ON. MILDRED IS A BUBBLY BLONDE WHO
CRAVES AFFECTION AND CONVERSATION. THE ONLY TIME SHE
FINDS TIME FOR BOTH, IS IN THE MIDDLE OF THE NIGHT. THE
FEELING OF THE PLAY SHOULD BE DATED TO THE NINETEEN
THIRTIES OR FORTIES.

SET AND PROPS:
BED AND ACCESSORIES.
LARGE OLD TIME RADIO CABINET.
BIG BEN CLOCK.
LAMP.
WINDOW FRAME.
NIGHT SHADES.
PINK NIGHT GOWN.
FUR COLLAR.
DYED GREY RABBIT SCARF.
LIGHT RED PAJAMAS.
RED WOOL SOCKS.

THE STAGE IS BLACK. AS THE BIG BAND SOUND OF GLENN
MILLERS' 'IN THE MOOD' BUILDS, THE LIGHTS SLOWLY BUILD TO
GIVE THE FEELING OF A BEDROOM LATE AT NIGHT. MILDRED IS
DANCING TO THE MUSIC AT THE SAME TIME SHE TRIES ON AND
ADMIRES HER DYED GREY RABBIT SCARF. WHEN SHE HEARS
THE SOUND OF A CLOSING DOOR MILDRED THROWS SCARF
UNDER BED. AS THE SOUND OF A MAN GARGLING AND
SPITTING, SHE LOOKS AT THE LATE HOUR ON THE CLOCK.
MILDRED QUICKLY GETS INTO BED, PUTS ON HER NIGHT SHADE
AND COVERS UP, WHILE THE SOUND OF A TOILET IS HEARD
FLUSHING AND A DOOR SLAMS SHUT. QUICKLY MILDRED
REMEMBERS TO TURN THE RADIO OFF, THE MUSIC ENDS.
HEAVY FOOT STEPS ARE HEARD, BUILDING.
WILBUR ENTERS SCRATCHING AND YAWNING, HIS FOOT
KICKING AT HIS FLOPPY SOCK. AFTER SEVERAL GLANCES AT
MILDRED HE HEADS TO THE WINDOW, HIS EYES GET BIG AS HE
NOTICES SOMETHING, WITH HIS HANDS, HE MAKES THE SHAPE
OF A WOMAN'S FIGURE. MILDRED IS TAKING PEEKS AT WILBUR
FROM UNDER HER NIGHT SHADE.

HE:
(a big sigh) Betty BOOBS Ohanlin.

WILBUR RUBS HIS HAND OVER HIS CHIN, AS HE PRETENDS TO
SLOWLY PULL THE WINDOW SHADE DOWN. WHILE THE SHADE
IS BEING PULLED DOWN, WILBUR PEEKS OUT UNTIL THE VERY
LAST. AS IF TRYING TO SHAKE OFF HIS FLOPPY SOCK WILBUR
HEADS TOWARDS THE BED AND SLOWLY CRAWLS IN SOCKS
AND ALL. AFTER PUTTING ON HIS NIGHT SHADE WILBUR GIVES
A BIG SIGH, CROSSES HIS ARMS ON HIS CHEST AND LAYS BACK
IN BED. WITHIN A SECOND WILBUR IS SNORING, ONE LONG DEEP
THEN A KIND OF DESCENDING WHISTLE, BOTH ARE REPEATED
THREE TIMES. MILDRED IS DISGUSTED AND QUICKLY SITS UP,
TAKING HER NIGHT SHADE OFF SHE LEANS OVER WILBUR, A
POUTING FROWN ON HER FACE.

SHE:
Wilbur...Wilbur...where have you been all night...for heaven's sake why do
you snore and whistle like that? Who are you dreaming of...I bet it's that Betty
BOOBS Ohanlin over in the next apartment...Wilbur wake up...wake up? I
can't sleep...you're snoring too loud.

HE:
(snoring stops) Mildred I'm tired...I worked all day...let me sleep...I'm tired.
(Lifts up night shade.)

SHE:
You...never talk to me...you're gone all day and I don't see enough of
you...You come home late at night and...and you never, never kiss me or hug
me...you never...we never do...you know what.

HE:
We do too...I fulfilled my husbandly obligations on a Saturday...six weeks
ago.

SHE:
It was a Monday six weeks ago and you... you fell asleep...You don't care
about me. (sob sound)

HE:
I care...I care...but I work hard Mildred... I need my rest...I slave all day so I
can give you nice things...and Tuesday was another work day...I need my rest.
(a somewhat sexy voice) We'll play love birds in the morning.

282

SHE:
You say it...but you won't...If you meant it you'd do it now...If Betty BOOBS
Ohanlin offered you'd do it and you wouldn't holler.

HE:
I holler all the time and she still offers. (raised voice) We never do it... leave
Betty BOOBS out of this.

SHE:
Tell me you love me.

HE:
I do.

SHE:
How much do you love me?

HE:
How much do you need?

SHE:
Say you love me...tell me you'll love me until the end of time.

HE:
I love you. (build in volume) I love you...I'll love you until I die.

SHE:
You say it but you won't, if you meant it, you'd do it right now.

HE:
(sit up saddened) You want me to die?

SHE:
No, I don't...I'm sorry...but it would be nice if you thought of me occasionally
instead of yourself...Only two weeks ago you had your life insured for fifty
thousand dollars.

HE:
What about it.

SHE:
You're only thinking of yourself.

HE:

What kind of fool talk is that...if I kick the bucket you get the money?

SHE:
You know perfectly well you have no intention of dying...you only got your life insured to tantalize me.

HE:
(angry and raised voice) I'll drop dead in the morning.

SHE:
You say it...but you won't do it.

HE:
(pleading) Do you know what you are saying?

SHE:
I'm sorry...I didn't mean it that way.

HE:
For heaven's sake.

SHE:
I don't think you love me any more...When we first met...you use to kiss me every time I turned around.

HE:
I never kissed you when you turned around.

SHE:
If you really loved me, you'd make out a will.

HE:
(raised voice) A will, you get my life insurance...and you want more.

SHE:
You don't want me at the mercy of your relatives...the minute you drop dead.

HE:
Don't talk like that...can't you say passed on...or something like that.

SHE:
You always say that.

HE:

Only when I'm talking about your no-good mooching brother. You should be more delicate when discussing a will...especially mine...You make it sound like I could go any minute.

SHE:
Well Saint Peter doesn't deliver you two weeks notice you know...Every man should make out his will for the loved ones he leaves behind.

HE:
(lays back) Okay, I'll make one out tomorrow.

SHE:
You say it, but you won't, get up and do it right now.

HE:
You're out of your mind, in the first place you need two witnesses and in the second place I have nothing in the first place to leave you.

SHE:
You're a stubborn man Wilbur Crabtree.

HE:
Why...why am I stubborn?

SHE:
It is the hardest thing in the world to make you admit I'm right when you know I'm wrong.

HE:
(pause) There's woman's logic for you...You get my life insurance...everything in my will and the first thing you do (start to speak faster and louder) is find a new no good bum...and he takes all my hard earned money...drives by my grave in my brand new car...loafs around like a prince...never amounts to anything...make him get a job Mildred.

SHE:
I will...I mean I won't...I won't Wilbur I promise.

HE:
(relaxing with mumbled speech) I worked eight hard years...struggled, did without...and what do I have to show for it...a wife.

SHE:
I just need you...I never sleep until you are in bed with me.

HE:
(lay back) You were sleeping when I came home.

SHE:
You said you'd be home at ten after one drink.

HE:
Well I had ten drinks and got home at one.

SHE:
What other woman would put up with your antic's night after night...you snore and whistle like a bag of old bones...and you keep me up all night...Wilbur what do you think I'm made of?

HE:
Old bones.

SHE:
(sarcastic) Thank you...You'd rather stay out all night tom-catting around with your old cronies...It kills you to stay home with me.

HE:
It doesn't kill me.

SHE:
I don't need anybody, (turn away) I'm just satisfied to be with you.

HE:
You're in better company than I am.

SHE:
(pouting) I'm sick.

HE:
(concerned) What's the matter? (lean over)

SHE:
 It's my head...the doctor said there is something wrong...I've had it on and off for the past three weeks.

HE:
Then take it off and let's get some sleep. (lay back)

SHE:

How would you like to go through life with a pain in the neck?

HE:
I married you for better or worse...yet to come.

SHE:
You took advantage of my innocence and youth.

HE:
You were no spring chicken.

SHE:
I must have been to pick up a worm like you ...I wish I had known you better before we got married.

HE:
You knew me plenty.

SHE:
(begins to poke at his stomach) What about that tattoo on your stomach? Oh, that's a real indication of a man's character...I wish I had known.

HE:
I had that tattoo long before I met you...I was just a silly kid. (softer voice, embarrassed) It was foolish.

SHE:
You ought to be ashamed of yourself. A hula girl with a dimple in her chin.

HE:
That dimple was there before she was.

SHE:
Why don't you have that ugly picture removed?

HE:
I'll have it removed in the morning.

SHE:
You say it, but you won't...do it now.

HE:
IT'S TWO O'CLOCK IN THE MORNING.

SHE:
You'd get rid of it right away if you were married to Betty BOOBS Ohanlin.

HE:
(fed up) Don't mention Betty BOOBS.

SHE:
She'd holler plenty if you didn't do what she liked.

HE:
I do what she likes, and she never hollers...I mean (sit up) don't mention her name in this house or else.

SHE:
(turn away) Mother was so upset that we eloped and got married by the Justice of the Peace.

HE:
(lay back) It should have been the Secretary of War.

SHE:
I want a real wedding...If you loved me, we'd get married in a church.

HE:
I'll arrange it in the morning.

SHE:
You say it but you won't...get up and do it right now.

HE:
It's too late...the preacher is sleeping...he's dead tired too.

SHE:
You don't love me...you even hate the cat and the canary.

HE:
I love the cat...I love the canary (raise voice) and I love you...I don't know which one I love the most.

SHE:
(with affection) Am I the only wife for you?

HE:
I swear you are the only wife in the world for me.

SHE:
Do you swear Wilbur?

HE:
I swear I wouldn't have another wife like you as long as I live.

SHE:
Am I the last person you dream about when you go to sleep?

HE:
You're the last person I ever think about.

SHE:
You wouldn't say that to Betty BOOBS Ohanlin...You would be a gentleman if you had her in your dreams.

HE:
She's been in my dreams plenty of times and I've never been a gentleman. (sit up and become angry) I hate Betty BOOBS...don't get her and me involved. (lay back)

SHE:
(pleading) I cook...I clean...I sew...I do everything for you...Do I get any thanks.

HE:
Thanks.

SHE:
Thanks...that's all the thanks I get...You're so cheap...we can't afford it...leave it there...you're always looking for a bargain...When you married me you didn't get no bargain.

HE:
(elated) How well I know.

SHE:
You're lucky you've got a cheap wife like me...If you were married to Betty BOOBS Ohanlin you'd have to pay her for kisses.

HE:
I'm not married to her and I get them for nothing. (louder) Don't mention Betty BOOBS in my presence.

SHE:
(not caring, not really listening) I got a bargain last week...a dyed grey rabbit's scarf...for only ninety-nine dollars. (reaches for scarf under bed) Do you want to see it?

HE:
(wide eyed and in hysterics, sit up) Ninety-nine dollars for a dead rabbit...bring it back...we can't afford it...You spend our money foolishly and I do without...I had my teeth pulled to save on eating...I sewed collars on your old bloomers and wear them as shirts...I have no new pants...Last week I put a whisk broom on your old plaid skirt and went to work dressed as a Scotsman...and you spend ninety-nine dollars on a dead rabbit...Take it back.

SHE:
 Okay...okay...I will. (shee sound) (pause) If my granddad were alive, he wouldn't let you treat me like that...I always took his advice...and if he were here, he'd say keep that scarf... When I get to heaven, I'll ask him.

HE:
(lay back) What if he's not in heaven?

SHE:
Then you can ask him. (turn away then turn back excited) It's my birthday next week...so is it too much to ask for a little close affection.

HE:
Nobody gives you as little affection as I do.

SHE:
And when you bring the car around...you could open the door for me...No, I must fling the door open and jump in by myself.

HE:
I slow down, don't I.

SHE:
How could you?

HE:
How could I what?

SHE:
How could you forget it's my birthday next week?

290

HE:
This is really getting silly...You'd better see a shrink.

SHE:
That kind of talk won't help you...you're just trying to make me forget you forgot to remember not to forget my birthday.

HE:
(shaking head) What? Coming from you that must make some-kind of sense.

SHE:
(excited) What did you get me?

HE:
A genuine imitation fake fur alligator travelling bag.

SHE:
A travelling bag...Last year you gave me a large print dictionary...and the year before that a beauty kit...You think I'm ugly...stupid and you want to get rid of me.

HE:
I don't want to get rid of you.

SHE:
You think I'm ugly and stupid?

HE:
I didn't say that.

SHE:
You think it of me.

HE:
I never think of you.

SHE:
(turn head upward) Never a kind word or a compliment...just work me until I'm skin and bones...You hate my meals and you complain about my cooking.

HE:
I never complain about your cooking.

SHE:

Then why didn't you eat that pie I made for you last night.

HE:
(looking directly at her) I did eat it...I ate every bit of it.

SHE:
You didn't like it.

HE:
I couldn't chew it...the crust was as hard as cardboard.

SHE:
Crust...There was no crust...I served it on a paper plate.

HE:
The plate tested better than the pie.

SHE:
On our eighth anniversary you gave me an eight-dollar bathrobe.

HE:
(Lay back) We had no money then...we were just getting on our feet...we were poor.

SHE:
I figure that's a dollar a year for cooking...cleaning...sewing...and bringing up your children.

HE:
(confused) Children...we don't have children.

SHE:
What do you expect for a dollar a year?

HE:
(dreaming state) She spends every dime I earn...I have nothing...what's a man to do? If I had the guts, I'd climb a building or a bridge...she'd be better off without me...she'd get the will and my insurance...There's only one thing to do. (attempt to get out of bed but then put head down and begin to snore and whistle, repeat twice)

SHE:
WILBUR. (shake Wilbur) Wilbur I heard you in the kitchen when you came home...did you put the dishes away and clean the counter?

HE:
(moaning yes as Mildred talks) I was fixing the toaster and your curling iron like you asked.

SHE:
Do they work?

HE:
(excited) Do they work...they work fine...only...the toast popped up with a permanent curl.

SHE:
Did you make sure the cat was in, he got out three times last week.

HE:
He won't get out.

SHE:
Where did you put him?

HE:
In the bird cage.

SHE:
(concerned) Where's the canary?

HE:
IN THE CAT.

SHE:
Wilbur, how could you?

HE:
Don't worry...the canary's fine and the cat is asleep in the oven...I set it on low.

SHE:
Don't scare me like that...Are you sure all the animals are alright.

HE:
I'm sure.

SHE:
How about the fish...did you heat up the water for the new baby gold fish?

HE:
(build to a yell) I heated his water...gave him his pablum...burped him twice and changed his diapers...Please let me get some sleep Mildred...I'm tired.

SHE:
Wilbur...you may need all the practice you can get.

HE:
(sleepy) Practice for what? I'm too tired to practice tonight.

SHE:
Call your girlfriend...Betty BOOBS Ohanlin.

HE:
Don't start with Betty BOOBS.

SHE:
You'd play mommy and daddy if Betty BOOBS Ohanlin was willing.

HE:
(soft) She's always willing and we never play mommy and daddy (loud) how in the heck do you play mommy and daddy?

SHE:
Wilbur...I forgot to tell you that a letter came for you today...It was marked private and personal...I forgot to give it to you.

HE:
What did it say?

SHE:
You don't have to be so snide about it...I accidentally steamed it open when I was pouring a cup of tea.

HE:
Tell me what it said...for Pete's sake.

SHE:
IT...is from Doctor Hiron...he said...Mr. Crabtree...our tests confirm that there is nothing physically wrong with you as your wife insists there is...there is plenty of action in your test tube sample in order to have children...I suggest more intimacy...(slowly get closer to Wilbur with more expression on each word).. love...affection...romance...cuddling ...kissing...hugging...and SE..

294

HE:
I get the idea. (shakes off Mildred's advances) The Doctor said that did he...well...

SHE: Wilbur take me...ravish me, I'm all yours.

HE:
All right Mildred...I should be ready in the morning.

SHE:
You say it but you won't do it...do it right now.

HE:
All right...I give up...have it your way.

AS LIGHTS FADE MILDRED THROWS HER ARMS AROUND WILBUR. LIGHTS GO BLACK.

SHE:
(with a sexy voice) Wilbur...Wilbur...OH WILBUR.

HE:
(snoring and whistling)

SHE:
(speaks through Wilbur's snoring) (voice becomes angry then whines on last Wilbur dragging word out) WILBUR...WILBUR...WIL...BUR...

SNORING FADES AS THE BIG BAND SOUND OF GLEN MILLER'S 'IN THE MOOD' BEGINS TO BUILD.

THE END

2
Two Poets In Bellevue Park
By
Richard Mousseau

STAGE:
CENTRE STAGE THERE IS A LONG PARK BENCH WITH A BUS SIGN AT ONE END, AT THE OTHER END IS A GARBAGE CAN. A LONE BARE TREE IS BEHIND BENCH. ON BACK DROP IS A CITY SKY LINE FRONTED BY AN ASSORTMENT OF TREES. A DOG IS SLEEPING UNDER CENTRE OF BENCH.

LIGHTING:
A DIM LIT BACKGROUND. FOCUS OF LIGHTS IS ON THE PARK
BENCH.

ACTING PARTS:
LEAD WOMAN: MISS PENELOPE
LEAD MAN: MR. MILLFORD

SOUND:
BACKGROUND SOUND SHOULD CONTAIN CITY SOUNDS WITH
FAINT ZOO SOUNDS.

CHARACTERS:
MISS PENELOPE: AN OLD MAID LIBRARIAN-TYPE. A HIGH BUN
OF HAIR. BUSINESS-TYPE CLOTHES. VERY BUXOM. HALF MOON
GLASSES ON END OF NOSE. CARRIES A PAIR OF WOMEN'WHITE
SKATES.

MR. MILLFORD: A NERD TYPE, TYPICALLY UPTIGHT.
UNCOORDINATED CLOTHES. SHIRT BUTTONED TO TOP. HORN
RIM GLASSES. HAIR GREASED BACK.   GOATEE TYPE BEARD.
PENS IN POCKET WITH PROTECTOR. PANTS A BIT SHORT WITH
TURNED UP CUFFS. SCARF OVER SHOULDER.   CARRIES A PAIR
OF BLACK MEN'S SKATES.

BASIC STORY LINE:
TWO POETS MEET ON A PARK BENCH. THEY RELATE THEIR
LIVES, PAST, PRESENT AND FUTURE TO THE AUDIENCE WITHOUT
REALLY INTERACTING WITH EACH OTHER. THEIR POETRY DOES
RELATE TO EACH OTHER AND THEY SHOULD REACT BUT
AUDIENCE SHOULD SENSE THEY ARE ONLY COMMUNICATING
WITH THEM. ACTORS SHOULD BE ACTING OUT LINES OF EACH
POEM.

SET AND PROPS
LONG PARK BENCH
BUS STOP SIGN
GARBAGE CAN
TREE
PARK AND CITY SKY LINE ON BACK DROP
NOTE PADS
HALF MOON GLASSES
HORN RIM GLASSES

STUFFED DOG
WOMEN'S WHITE SKATES
MENS' BLACK SKATES
TWO COVERED DOLLS TO RESEMBLE BABIES

THE STAGE IS BLACK, THE SOUNDS OF TRAFFIC AND ZOO SOUNDS BUILD. LIGHTS COME UP WITH AN EARLY MORNING FEELING.
MILLFORD IS SITTING AT ONE END OF THE BENCH READING AND MAKING NOTES ON HIS NOTE PAD. A DOG IS LYING UNDER THE CENTRE OF THE BENCH. A PAIR OF MENS' SKATES IS AT THE END OF THE BENCH.

MILLFORD NOTICES PENELOPE ENTER AND WALK BY AS HE JOTS SOMETHING ON HIS NOTE PAD.
PENELOPE LOOKS AT BUS SIGN THEN LOOKS RIGHT THEN LEFT THEN TOWARDS THE BENCH. MILLFORD BEGINS TO FIDGET AS PENELOPE BEGINS TO SIT ON THE OTHER END OF THE BENCH. PENELOPE PUTS HER SKATES DOWN AT THE CORNER OF BENCH. SEVERAL TIMES THEY GLANCE TOWARDS EACH OTHER THEN LOOK AWAY NONCHALANT. PENELOPE TURNS AWAY AND TAKES OUT A NOTE PAD AND BEGINS TO WRITE.

THE TRAFFIC AND ZOO SOUNDS FADE A BIT BUT CONTINUE THROUGHOUT PLAY BUILDING AND FADING AS REQUIRED.
LIGHTS COME UP FULL.

MILLFORD: (clears his throat and attempts to speak but cannot, he jots something on a notepad. He then takes the posture of the thinking statue.)
Here I sit to think.I would rather be on a rink.

Other couples skating arm in arm.
Dreaming that dream does no harm.

Love of my life do you think.
You and me just once around that rink.

(shyly looks hopefully at Penelope then turns away)

PENELOPE: (is writing on her note pad then looks towards audience)

It is amazing the way men think.
Everything pertains to a hockey rink.

Just let him place a hand on my arm.
I'll show him I mean him some harm.

Just one good check into the boards.
And he'll rest up good in a hospital ward.

(a glance at Millford then with nose in air turns and holds stance then frowns
as Millford speaks)

MILLFORD: (jerks thumb at Penelope then looks towards audience)

I once saw a lovesick moose.
He was wild and on the loose.

His mate stood with nose in the air.
Lovelorn he could only sit and stare.

She played hard to get that female moose.
(put hands around own neck pretending to gag)
But she reeled him in and tightened the noose.

PENELOPE: (with hand on hip she looks down on Millford over her glasses)

A man is like a mule.
A stubborn little fool.

They are always wrong, never right.
And are always in a deplorable sight.

A man like that, I would surely pass.
For he is absolutely an ass.

MILLFORD: (Jumping in on last word)

Ask my Mother she'll say I am sweet.
For any girl a worthy treat.

My Dad says I am not a mouse.
A handy man to keep around the house.

(sitting up proud)

PENELOPE: (looks left to right as if looking down a road then notices the
dog and points at it)

298

A dog is a dog.
He sleeps like a log.
If you ever lounge around.
(shake finger at Millford)
I surely will be bound.

To send you packing to the street.
The end alas of me and my sweet.

MILLFORD: (depressed lowers head and slouches on bench then slowly perks up)

May I ask you out on a date.
I promise not to be late.

Flowers for you I will bring.
Songs from my heart I will sing.
(stands up straight up)

I dreamt about you one night.
Oh, you were a lovely site.

Yes, you I would love to meet.
I rushed down to the street.

Face to face we did stare.
Such a meeting so rare.

Not asking your name is strange.
Somehow this poem must change.

I heard a strange sound.
In my room, noise all around.

Through my window shines the moon.
The clock-radio say's wake up soon.

Visions of you fade from sight.
Along with the fading of the night.

(sit in a praying pose)

Where is the girl of my dreams?
Unlucky am I it truly seems.

I roll over in bed to see.
A dog lying there next to me.

It was my dog I named chip.
(point to dog)
Awe dog slobber on my lips.
(frantically wiping lips)

PENELOPE: (pause...looks at dog then at Millford and makes a grimacing
face then looks to audience)

He is kind of a cute guy.
I think he is a bit shy.
(gets up dreaming)

Each night I sit by the phone.
Hoping for a call I am all alone.

I am just like any other girl.
I need someone to give me a whirl.
 (move behind bench)

A blue-eyed Mr. Muscle, please don't flaunt.
Those guys for me I don't want.
(put hands on back of bench and with a girlish flare)

Is there such a thing as love so true.
To heck with this, this guy I will pursue.

MILLFORD: (Looks around then checks out Penelope's ring finger)

I looked at her tender hand.
There was no wedding band.

My body begin to tingle.
By chance could she be single.

I tend to beat around the bush.
And I am not one to push.

But I will be so bold.
Her I would like to hold.

She is quite impressive.

I hope I'm not too aggressive.

All I must be assertive.
At courting I am primitive.
(begin to sulk)

PENELOPE: (Turns towards tree and in a reminiscing mood begins to pluck leaves from tree)

It is almost spring.
I have no, no ring.

For lasting love to linger.
A wedding band on my finger.

For too many years.
Several unwanted tears.

I have missed love's call.
Spring now becomes fall.

Though I am a bit past prime.
To be alone is no crime.

I am not too bitter.
Park benches I litter.
(moves to front and sits)

Hoping to catch someone's eye.
Maybe I will pretend to cry.

A wanting man may happen by.
There is always hope says I.
(a big build up of emotion then a lingering sigh)

MILLFORD: (being cocky fold leg and lean back on bench)

That's life.
No wife.
No strife.
What a life.

No money.
No honey.

No company.
It's agony.

In a flurry.
I do worry.
It is a drudgery.
Life is a quandary.

No love.
Hey above.
Why the strife.
Boy ain`t that life.

(do not make physical or eye contact but make audience feel you are)

PENELOPE:

I would love to be someone's wife.
Years to share one another's life.

MILLFORD:

Through all the ups and downs.
Through all the sad and happy frowns.

PENELOPE:

Yes, yes, yes, I will say I do.
I'll stick to my love like glue.
(inch closer to Millford)

MILLFORD:

It is for love I am looking.
It helps if she does good cooking.
(inch closer to Penelope)

PENELOPE:

It is true my first love will be my last.
It shall be written in the history of the past.
Our love will surely be a blast.
I can't wait, let's get married fast.
MILLFORD:

It is not that I feel I am getting older.
It is not my hormones making me bolder.
At night I will love to hold her.
It's because the nights are getting colder.

PENELOPE: (moves away with slow depression)

Will this happen on our honeymoon.
Will he act somewhat like a baboon?

Will he not make my heart swoon?
Will he sleep all night and wake at noon?

MILLFORD: (moves away with slow depression)

I will make it up to you soon.
I will never act like a goon.
With love I will shower her like a monsoon.
Just as soon as we move to Saskatoon.

PENELOPE: (looks at dog then Millford, slowly gets up and moves up front
and to side)

Yes, he is a man a male.
He's used but is for sale.

For the right woman a treasure.
For your standards come and measure.

He comes with all sorts of attachments.
Fishing gear, car parts, all those implements.

Sunday, yard sale, one loveable honey.
Don't forget, final sale, bring money.

MILLFORD: (gets up slowly, puts hands in pocket and moves up front to
side)

Of course, I remember our wedding day.
All those words to you I truly did say.

Every year on that day I'll make you swoon.
Tell me dear is our anniversary any day soon.

To the bone I've worked my fingers honey.
To bring to you all my hard-earned money.

What in heaven do I get in exchange.
is very little of the money change?
(pull hands out of pocket turning pockets inside out)

PENELOPE: (Move to centre stage with back to Millford)

He bought me an ironing board.
I'd rather have a surf board.

I do the ironing, I don't surf.
By the T.V. all day I watch the smurfs.

MILLFORD: (moves to centre stage with back to Penelope)

At night she craves mustard and pickles.
I must say she is one to be fickle.

She is constantly rubbing her belly so round.
Is she saying that soon fatherhood I'm bound?

(attendants bring out babies one each for Millford and Penelope)

PENELOPE: (with mixed feelings and a womanly glow)

Do you remember that one night?
We had a big good old fight.

We stayed up way past two.
No one in the house but me and you.

We fell asleep in each other's arms.
Nine months later kids with charm.
(Penelope goes to bench and sits and smiles motherly. Millford at the same
time fans the air over his baby.)

MILLFORD: (looking around as if there is no one around)

Dear isn't it so quiet.
Earlier it was quite a riot.
With children no need to diet.
(move to bench and sit)

It is now two a.m. a moments rest.
In four hours, we will be put to the test.
No rest, no sex, shattered nerves, do not jest.
Like birds I soon hope they leave the nest.

And when we are old and grey.
Their little ones will come to stay.
With old bones I am unable to play.
Dear, send them home, let's call it a day.
(plead and show exasperation with legs stretched out and arm limp over side of bench)

PENELOPE: (happily cooing baby)

Darling daughter blow your nose.
Love hurts like a thorn of a rose.

Someone did not raise that boy right.
Put him out of your mind and your sight.

There are many a fish in the sea.
Your dad fished a long time to land me.

If not for the love on that hook.
Pictures of you would not be in our scrapbook.
(continue to coo baby)

MILLFORD: (fidgets with baby awkwardly)

Baby, now open wide.
Don't run and hide.

This is your favourite food.
Don't pout, that is rude.

I will taste this stuff first.
This is good, this liverwurst.

Baby, you get the phone book.
For baby pizza we will look.

(Both get up and give babies to the attendants. Millford puts hands in pockets and wanders a bit and pretends to kick a pop can. Penelope at same time puts hand to lips and gives blow away kisses as baby leaves, pulling hands to chest expresses happy and sad moods)

MILLFORD: (continues to kick at ground and as he speaks his voice is raised to the audience.)

Sex...Sex...SEX...SEX.
This word ends with an X.

When said out loud we blush.
(hide head between shoulders)
In shadows we say with a hush.

We love that little word with an X.
Sex...Sex...SEX...SEX.
(move to centre as voice builds)

PENELOPE: (with stern voice as if teaching students move to centre stage)

SEX...SEX...SEX...SEX.
It is a curse, a witch's hex.

We fall for men with a crush.
But they are always in a rush.

Men are always ready to flex.
When you mention the word SEX.

(Millford and Penelope exchange saying sex with different connotations as if competing to say the word last then wither to their own side of the bench and sit there silently for a moment)

MILLFORD: (acting old without teeth and can hardly see)

I gazed across the bingo table.
I could not read her name label.

To me she looked pretty-fine.
If only I could make her mine.

All the other guys over ninety-four.
Sit around and don't do anything more.

My grand kids would say, 'what a foxy lady'.
I think her name tag says Saidi.

Just when I want to say something sweet.
The bingo caller says next game take a seat.

The game lingers on way past eight.
Not much time left to ask for a date.

Fifteen minutes says the warden, out go the lights.
The young battle axe sure knows how to spoil the night.

It's a race to the door, she's out in front.
A blur of silver hair, for her I'll have to hunt.

Hobbling behind are the old guys over ninety-four.
I'll have no problems, I'll beat them to the door.

My wheelchair's stuck, I'm losing that beauty tall and lanky.
Not tonight say's the warden, for you gramps no hanky-panky.
(shake head in disappointment fade into bench)

PENELOPE: (as an elderly lady reminiscing)

To be young and in love, to visit old Rome.
Me, I'll be an old maid in an old folk's home.

Old men with bad eye sight, me they will ogle.
While giddy busy-bodies play a game of Scrabble.

To find a true love at ninety-eight is hard.
Even after sending out a hundred want-add cards.

For a seat on this park bench every day I tussle.
For a single man to find, with a smile, I will hustle.

Back in sixty-three I had a great old plan.
I puffed up my bosom and cooled them with a fan.

With extra long eye lashes, I winked at a good-looking man.
He did not take a second look, he just took off and ran.

I was sad to find out that he was a man of the cloth.
From above God brought down upon me a lingering wrath.

A loveless life over endless years is a hindrance.
No kissing, no dating, no love, no sex is my penance.

(become young and in the present)

He is alive, breathing, should I take a chance?
Before life passes by and we both miss the dance.

A smile, a wink, a little cleavage, did he look my way?
Maybe he's not my type, what else is there to say?

(both attempt to glance at each other with hope and despair)

PENELOPE AND MILLFORD:

Two lonely people on a park bench.
Longing for our love to quench.

How can two lonely hearts meet.
If each other we do not greet.

I think it will do no harm.
To skate together arm in arm.
(both pick up skates)

In life you must take a chance, I think.
You and me just once around that rink.

(both turn to each other slowly as lights fade. Sounds of traffic and zoo sounds build and then slowly fade)

THE END

3
WOJO AND YOUNGIN
BY
RICHARD MOUSSEAU

STAGE:
A BIG ARM CHAIR IS IN THE CENTRE OF STAGE. SLIGHTLY AT BACK CORNER OF CHAIR IS A STANDING LAMP. BESIDE CHAIR IS AN END TABLE WITH A PHONE. ON THE OTHER SIDE OF THE CHAIR IS A BIG HOOK RUG FOR THE DOG. TO THE FRONT AND RIGHT OF STAGE IS A DOOR FRAME FACING THE AUDIENCE. ON

THE OTHER SIDE OF STAGE AND TO THE FRONT IS AN OPEN WINDOW FRAME. BEHIND CHAIR IS A HANGING PICTURE. TO THE SIDE OF STAGE AND WITHIN WINDOW AREA IS A KITCHEN TABLE.

LIGHTING:
NATURAL BRIGHT LIGHTING AS WOULD BE IN THE MORNING AS THE SUN SHONE INTO THE DEN OF A HOUSE.

ACTING PARTS:
FIRST LEAD: YOUNGIN
SECOND LEAD: WOJO
THIRD LEAD: MA

OFF STAGE VOICE: DOC GOOD.

SOUND:
VARIOUS BARN YARD SOUNDS.
HOUSE SOUNDS, MAN WALKING DOWN STAIRS, TOILET FLUSHING.

CHARACTERS:
YOUNGIN: A CONFIRMED BACHELOR IN HIS MID FORTIES, WEARS TYPICAL OVERALLS WITH RED CANADIAN PLAID SHIRT, FARM WORK BOOTS. A POCKET FULL OF STRAW TO CHEW ON. A SLOW LAID-BACK FARM BOY, NEVER IN A HURRY AND THIS IS HIS DOWNFALL IN LIFE.

WOJO: MAN'S BEST FRIEND, BUT OLD AND LAZY, A CROSS BETWEEN A BLOOD HOUND AND A ST. BERNARD. TENDS TO BE A BIT SARCASTIC AND SOMEWHAT WORLDLY AND MORE INTELLIGENT THAN HIS MASTER. FLOPPY EARS, BLACK NOSE, HAIR COVERING HANDS AND FEET, WEARS OVERALLS, PLAID SHIRT. TENDS TO TALK IN A GRAVEL FILLED VOICE. AT TIMES MOVES ABOUT AS IF HUMAN AND DOG AS REQUIRED.

MA: GRANDMOTHERLY AND LIKE VOICE, TYPICAL FARM WOMAN IN KITCHEN GARB, APRON, HAIR IN BUN.

OFF STAGE VOICE OF DOC GOOD: A CONCERNED VETERINARY.

BASIC STORY LINE:

A DAY IN THE LIFE OF YOUNGIN AND HIS DOG WOJO. DAY LINGERS ON IN THE DEN OF THEIR HOMESTEAD HOME. MA IS IN THE KITCHEN BAKING.

SET AND PROPS:
ARM CHAIR
GUITAR
GUITAR STAND
LAMP
PHONE
END TABLE
FLOOR HOOK RUG
DOOR FRAME
WINDOW FRAME
PAINTING
WATER BUCKET
KITCHEN TABLE
BAKING DOUGH

SONG: 'OLD DOGS'
WORDS AND MUSIC BY RICHARD E. MOUSSEAU
COPYRIGHT MARCH 27, 1989

THE STAGE IS BLACK, THE SOUNDS OF A ROOSTER CROWING ECHOS AND OTHER FARM ANIMAL SOUNDS BEGIN TO BUILD. A YELLOW LIGHT AS IF THE SUN SHINES THROUGH THE WINDOW AND ONTO THE DOG LYING ON THE RUG. FARM SOUNDS FADE AS LIGHTS BUILD FILLING THE ROOM. WOJO MOVES ABOUT SCRATCHING THEN AGAIN SETTLES DOWN TO SLEEP.
THE SOUND OF A TOILET FLUSHING AND WALKING SOUNDS OF A HEAVY MAN IS COMING DOWN THE STAIRS.
YOUNG`IN ENTERS AND IS ATTEMPTING TO DO UP HIS SUSPENDERS ON HIS OVERALLS. BLINDLY HE WALKS TOWARDS THE ARM CHAIR AND AS IF ON PURPOSE HE EXAGGERATES LIFTING HIS FOOT THAN PLANTS IT HEAVILY ON WOJO'S TAIL.

WOJO:
(yelping in pain and rolling onto his back with paws in air) Yelp...ouch.

YOUNG`IN:
(somewhat concerned) Oh sorry Wojo I...

WOJO:
What...you did not see my tail wagging?

310

YOUNG`IN:
(begins to sit in his chair) I... I'm afraid not.

WOJO:
(sits up with paws up stretched in a questioning manner) For the past... twenty years I have waited on this rug every morning wagging my tail...and for one hundred and forty dog years you have stepped on my tail...(growl)...you are pushing this man's best friend thing a bit too far. (grumbles as he rubs his tail)

YOUNG`IN:
(pats top of Wojo's head) What can I say, you're a mighty fine bloodhound...St. Bernard...general all-around mutt (Wojo snaps at Youngin's hand, Youngin pulls back hand and counts his fingers)

MA:
(enters carrying baking dough) Is that you Young`in?

YOUNG`IN:
(talking to Wojo) I've lived here for the past forty some years...

WOJO:
Forty-five point six

YOUNG`IN:
Pa's out milking the cows, Uncle Clyde and Aunt Bonnie haven't been around since twenty-eight...who else would it be.

WOJO:
Humour her.

YOUNG`IN:
(nodding) Yea Ma it's me.

MA:
I know son...who else would it be? (Wojo shrugs his shoulders) You've been here for the pasty forty some years...when in tarnation are you going to leave home? I work my fingers to the bone.

YOUNG`IN:
(starts to untie boot) Mothers...when you're young they say go out...meet girls...have fun. (Wojo leans and puts arm on chair) You do what they say and what happens... (act like old woman) ...they say, you're always out late...you never stay home any more...we never see you...

WOJO:
You cannot please her.

YOUNG`IN:
I try to be a good son...stay home...don't stay out late...and for forty some years later...

WOJO:
Forty-five point six.

YOUNG`IN:
...she still wants me to leave home.

WOJO:
You just cannot please Mothers.

YOUNG`IN:
(start to stand) I'm moving out tomorrow morning. (sits back down when Ma speaks)

WOJO:
Right on.

MA:
Oh, you'll move out...meet a girl...then you'll never come around any more...we'll never see you...I'll have a couple hundred oatmeal cookies made and no Youngin to eat them. (crying and sobbing sound fades as Ma leaves stage with a hanky to her nose)

WOJO:
(growls) Man's best friend ha...you treat your Mother just like you treat me...We give you everything...do you appreciate it, no... you step on our tails.

YOUNG`IN:
Well if it makes you feel better...here bite my leg. (sticks bare leg out)

WOJO:
(grabs leg, growls, barks and makes slurping sounds)

YOUNG`IN:
Do you feel better now?

WOJO:

(wipes slobber from face) I would if I had teeth...do you think you could get me a store-bought pair.

YOUNG`IN:
Ah...I don't think so. (Wojo sighs) (Youngin looks at Wojo from different angles) You're looking a bit peeked...are you feeling ok?

WOJO:
I have a slight... bladder problem...it has been nagging at me at night.

YOUNG`IN:
(quickly stands and crosses over to corner of the door and looks up and down from top to bottom) That explains the puddles on the floor. (lifts the water bucket) I thought the roof was leaking, but it hasn't rained for near on ten weeks.

WOJO:
(crawl up onto the chair, claws at cushion) I think we should go see Doc Good.

YOUNG`IN:
(still looking at puddle) Ok Wojo...I think that's a good idea... (walks backwards shaking head at the bucket on the floor, attempts to sit)

WOJO:
(growls and barks)

YOUNG`IN:
(jump forward quickly placing his hands on his butt then points from Wojo to rug
several times)

WOJO:
(slowly crawls over arm of chair onto the rug, sits down with front paws crossed, a frown on face)

YOUNG`IN:
(after sitting dial the phone) Hello, Doc Good, this is Youngin...

DOC GOOD:
Well hello Youngin...you still living with Ma and Pa, you must be...oh what forty...(Youngin sneers at phone)

WOJO:
Forty-five point six. (Youngin stomps foot towards Wojo)

DOC GOOD:
I thought you were sweet on Gerty the hog farmer's daughter?

YOUNG`IN:
Listen Doc., I'm calling about Wojo...he says he has a slight bladder problem. (pulls phone away from ear and looks at Wojo) Slight is an understatement...he's leaking like a sieve.

DOC GOOD:
Well Young`in I think Wojo should have a simple operation to correct his problem.

YOUNG`IN:
A simple operation?

DOC GOOD:
I should be able to arrange an operation first thing tomorrow morning.

YOUNGIN:
(turns away from Wojo) How much will a quick simple operation cost? (Wojo leans closer)

DOC GOOD:
Oh...with operation cost... my fee...hospital stay for one night and one day...oh...I would say about two thousand dollars.

YOUNG`IN:
 (Wojo begins to scratch his fleas, Youngin pulls phone away from his ear and yells at the receiver as he stands) Two thousand dollars for a simple quick operation on a flea infested dog.

WOJO:
(slowly stops scratching his fleas and looks up to Youngin with a sad forlorn face)

YOUNG`IN:
(covers receiver with hand to hide from Wojo) Doc., that's as much as I had saved up for a vacation on a tropical beach with an exotic native girl. (saying in a dreamy fashion)

DOC GOOD:
What about Gerty the hog farmers daughter...I thought you were sweet on her?

WOJO:
(pretends to shoot himself then rolls onto back with legs up) Man's best friend...I was there for you.... ...but now when I am old and sickly... (lays on side with a pitiful look on face) ...you would rather get sand between your toes and nibble on the soft neck of a beach bimbo...when I am gone you will miss stepping on my tail each morning.

YOUNG`IN:
(with a hand extended to Wojo shake head from side to side) I haven't had a vacation or a girl in about...

WOJO:
Forty-five point six years.

DOC GOOD:
Well Young`in what will it be...Wojo...a vacation...or dumping sweet Gerty.

YOUNG`IN:
(stomps foot at Wojo as frustration builds) I ain`t sweet on Gerty...and never was.

WOJO:
(gives a big sigh as if his last breath)

YOUNG`IN:
(slowly giving in) Ok Doc., make all the arrangements for the operation. (sits exhausted) Good bye. (hangs up receiver)

WOJO:
(puts paw on knee of Young`in) Young`in, a hospital can be a cold...dark..strange...did I mention a lonely place. (Youngin nods head) Operations can be tricky...there is not always a guaranty... ...I... I, just might not make it...I...am starting to feel poorly...did I mention lonely. (Young`in nods) A strange place filled with irritating cats...birds..that talk too much...waiting behind turtles in the washroom line...rabbits all
over the place...pigs squealing on each other...did I mention a lonely place to be.

YOUNG`IN:
Yes, you mentioned lonely...you're a DOG...snap out of it.

WOJO:
It is just that I cannot sleep in a strange place...and... you will not be there to sing me to sleep... will you sing me a song Youngin.

YOUNG`IN:
You have no problem sleeping around here...you sleep twenty-three hours out of the day...with one hour to spend eating and watering the door. (points towards the door)

WOJO:
I am a one hundred and forty dog years old. I have no teeth...I am going under Doc Good's scalpel tomorrow...I... I do not know if I will make...it.

YOUNG`IN:
Ok..Ok...One song to calm your nerves down. (picks up guitar and begins to strum)

WOJO:
 (lies down at corner of chair and pantomimes the story line of song)

YOUNG`IN:

NOTE: insert poem of 'Old Dogs'

WOJO:
(howls as last three bars are played then sarcastically speaks) Now that's a real joyful song to sing to a toothless one hundred and forty-year-old dog with leaking utilities...and you call yourself a dog's best friend.

YOUNG`IN:
(puts guitar down and pats Wojo's head) I'm sorry Wojo I... I just wasn't thinking. (gets up and walks towards door) Just in case you think you might want to water the flowers outside.

WOJO:
(laboriously gets up and head towards door) Well I guess I could try. (Youngin pretends to open the door as Wojo steps three quarters of the way out then lifts leg against door frame. Youngin lifts hand, shakes head as he looks at puddle, Wojo heads back to rug shaking one leg, Youngin closes door with a slam, sound effects sound echo)

MA:
(Ma enters with more baking dough) Is that you Young`in?

YOUNG`IN:
No Ma...it's just one of the neighbours checking to see if our door works.

Ma:

316

Well invite them in... I have hot coffee and fresh peanut-butter cookies to dunk.

YOUNG`IN:
Great...now I have to run five miles to the neighbours to get them to come over for coffee and cookies before Ma thinks I'm making fun of her...In forty some odd years...

WOJO:
Forty-five point six to be exact.

YOUNG`IN:
...you'd think Ma and Pa would have had time to give me a little brother...so I could send him a-fetching
...hey Ma...did you and Pa ever think of having any more kids?

MA:
We're working on it Young`in... It takes patience and practice...we kind of rushed it when we had you...we want the next one to be perfect.

YOUNG`IN:
I'm forty some years old. (pause and a glance at Wojo who is ignoring him while he chews on his paw)
...don't you think you and Pa have been practising long enough?

MA:
Well Young`in... your Pa isn't as young as he used to be...so we kind of given up on having another child... we'd rather have fun instead.

YOUNG`IN:
Ma!! I don't want to know the details.

MA:
We got you the next best thing. (Wojo enters the kitchen area, Ma gives him a cookie, he takes it and heads back to the rug).

YOUNG`IN:
A toothless flea-bitten dog.

MA:
Young`in... you don't be calling him names.

YOUNG`IN:

No Ma...not me...you old leaking...toothless... flea-bitten dog. (WOJO cocks head and stares questionably)

MA:
Young`in behave yourself...you're not too old to be put over my knee.

WOJO:
Not too old... (rolls over holding his belly) Ha..Ha..Ha...

YOUNG`IN:
Hey I'm just on the sunny side of forty.

WOJO:
More like the dark ages of forty.

YOUNG`IN:
Listen dog...I know some cats that would like to meet you out behind the barn.

WOJO:
(growls and begins to lunge forward)

YOUNG`IN:
(stamps foot several times in self defence)

MA:
(enters den area) Youngin...Wojo.. sit. (points to chair and rug, both sulk into their areas until Ma exits stage)

WOJO:
Ain`t you kind of old to be living at home with Ma and Pa? (put leg on arm of chair) What...after forty-five point six years you cannot find a girl to get hitched to.

YOUNG`IN:
I'm being patient...I'm waiting for that perfect girl to fall into my arms.

WOJO:
Homely boy can't get a date eh, eh...eh.

YOUNGIN:
I ain`t homely...and I can get a date anytime I want.

WOJO:

You have not wanted to in a long... long time...You had better give Gerty the hog farmers daughter a call...she could be your last chance.

YOUNG`IN:
Naw... (shakes hand in a pushing away manner) ... she's a bit homely.

WOJO:
At your age you cannot be picky.

YOUNGIN:
 Age is only a state of mind.

WOJO:
At your age the mind is the second thing to become useless...when that happens you forget what to do
when you bring a date home.

YOUNG`IN:
That hasn't happened to me...yet.

WOJO:
When was the last time you had a date...a girl...the female species... ...soft...curves...Hubba...Hubba...

YOUNG`IN:
I know what a girl is...I was trying to remember if the date was on a Friday or a Saturday.

WOJO:
...Last week...longer...longer...nineteen seventy... (looks at audience) ...I think Gerty may be his last chance, she may trip and fall into his armsat the retirement home for old hog farmers... (to Youngin) ...hey old man.

YOUNG`IN:
Listen hair ball, you'd last a lot longer stuffed and mounted above the fire place.

WOJO:
(suddenly begins sniffing the air) Hey Young`in, Gerty is coming...(sniffs) She has been living with those hogs too...long.

YOUNG`IN:
She ain`t all that bad...Now you be nice to her. (begins to straighten up suspenders)

WOJO:
You really must be desperate...old age is fogging up your head...She is the hog farmers daughter.

YOUNG`IN:
Her Pa has some pure-bred blood hounds...good hunting dogs. (stands and begin to slick back hair) ...if you play your cards right, I could fix you up with one.

WOJO:
(begin to look from Youngin to window and back)

MA:
(enters, sniffs, heads to window) Young`in, I smell Gerty and her dog a-coming...She's the last old maid
around...invite her in....I have coffee and cookies for dunking.

WOJO:
Well Youngin, you are not getting any younger...remember you are forty-five point six years old.

YOUNG`IN:
(Sarcastically) WELL OLD BOY... you're a hundred and forty dog years old.

WOJO AND YOUNG`IN:
(begin to take glances at each other then slick back hair and straighten up clothes) At our age this
may be our last chance for RO--MANCE.

BLACK OUT.
FARM SOUNDS BUILD THEN FADE.

THE END

OTHER AVAILABLE TITLES
FROM MOOSE HIDE BOOKS
Imprint of
MOOSE ENTERPRISE Publishing
Visit our web site at www.moosehidebooks.com for complete title listings.

TITLES
Steeltown
Steeltown Blues
Roosevelt Street
Executor of Mercy
A Print of a Man
Sky Flyers
Assault of a Princess
Assault
Basement Bargain Price Leafs For Sale
Reflection
Guilt in Accession
Déjà vu
Fragmentation of Life
Dodger
My Pecker Ain`t Working
Cowboy Poetry for Sale
Badland Trails
Existence
Opening night (theatre plays)
Part The Curtain (theatre plays)

www.ingramcontent.com/pod-product-compliance
Lightning Source LLC
Chambersburg PA
CBHW031157020726
47499CB00002B/406